Lyn Hamilton's
Archaeological Mysteries

" . . . a successful mystery—and series: a smart, appealing, funny, brave and vulnerable protagonist and a complex, entertaining and rational plot."

—*London Free Press* (Ontario)

The Xibalba Murders

Lara is drawn to the lush jungles of Mexico to uncover the secrets of the Mayan underworld known as Xibalba . . .

The Maltese Goddess

Murder on the island of Malta as ancient legend and modern intrigue collide . . .

The MALTESE GODDESS

AN ARCHAEOLOGICAL MYSTERY

Lyn Hamilton

BERKLEY PRIME CRIME, NEW YORK

This is a work of fiction. Names, characters, places, and incidents are either the product of the author's imagination or are used fictitiously, and any resemblance to actual persons, living or dead, business establishments, events, or locales is entirely coincidental.

THE MALTESE GODDESS

A Berkley Prime Crime Book / published by arrangement with the author

PRINTING HISTORY
Berkley Prime Crime edition / March 1998

All rights reserved.
Copyright © 1998 by Lyn Hamilton.
This book may not be reproduced in whole or in part,
by mimeograph or any other means, without permission.
For information address: The Berkley Publishing Group,
a division of Penguin Putnam Inc.,
375 Hudson Street, New York, New York 10014.

The Penguin Putnam Inc. World Wide Web site address is
http://www.penguinputnam.com

ISBN: 0-425-16240-0

Berkley Prime Crime Books are published
by The Berkley Publishing Group,
a division of Penguin Putnam Inc.,
375 Hudson Street, New York, New York 10014.
The name BERKLEY PRIME CRIME and the BERKLEY PRIME
CRIME design are trademarks belonging to Penguin Putnam Inc.

PRINTED IN THE UNITED STATES OF AMERICA

10 9 8 7 6 5 4

For my sister

ACKNOWLEDGMENTS

In researching this book I am indebted to the scholarship and writings of many people, most particularly the Goddess lectures of Professor Johanna Stuckey, Dr. Marija Gimbutas' *The Civilization of the Goddess*, and Dr. Cristina Biaggi's *Habitations of the Great Goddess*. I would also like to thank friends and colleagues who assisted with the research and the manuscript, including Dr. John Marshall, Candis McDonnell, Jim Polk, Sharon Gray, Joe Coté, and Jane and Tim Marlatt.

The MALTESE GODDESS

☿ PROLOGUE

I AM AT THE BEGINNING as I am at the end. I am the sacred circle, spinner of the web of space and time. I am the Cosmic "And": life and death, order and chaos, eternal and finite. I am Earth and all things of it.

For periods of time you call millennia, we lived in harmony, you and I. I gave the bounty of the lands and seas to nourish you, and taught you to use them. I gave you artistic expression so that through your sculpture, painting, and weaving you might honor me, and through me, yourselves. And I taught you writing that you might remember me.

How is it that you wrenched apart that which is inseparable? Why did you make the Either/Or? Flesh or spirit, body or soul, thinking or feeling. Because when you did, when you replaced me with your despotic sky gods who rule from Without, you made me something to be mastered, something to be conquered, just as you then thought you had to conquer each other.

Neglected, devalued, insulted, and profaned I may be, but I remain. I wait in my sacred places. I live in your dreams. Nammu, Isis, Aphrodite. Inanna, Astarte, Anath. Call me whichever of my manifestations you will. I am the Great Goddess, and I will be avenged.

ADONIS

❦ ONE

I LIKE TO THINK OF myself as an honorable person, but once I've explained to someone slowly, in words of one syllable, why it would be cheaper for them to deal with someone else, then if they insist, I'm as happy as the next person to take their money.

At least that is what I thought when Martin Galea, the best of the best of the Toronto architectural scene, came into my shop, Greenhalgh and McClintoch by name, accompanied by his timid wife and his platinum credit card, and began to spend what seemed at the time to be almost breathtaking amounts of money. We—my business partner Sarah Greenhalgh and I— were suffering through the doldrums of an economic downturn, a seemingly chronic turn of events, and Galea's purchase looked almost too good to be true. Which it was—and had I been gifted with the ability to foretell the future, no amount of money would have enticed me to agree to his terms.

It all started innocuously enough, though. It was a clear winter day in Toronto, and if there were tremors in the cosmic fabric that should have warned me of what was to come, I didn't notice them. Diesel, aka The Deez, the official Shop Cat, was at his favorite post, curled up in the front window enjoying the sunshine, as usual ignoring the activity of the mere mortals around him.

Even Galea's visit followed its normal course. He'd been in the store several times before, and the routine was always the same. A Jaguar pulled up in front of the shop, facing the wrong way, half on the narrow street and half on the even narrower sidewalk. Galea leapt out and bounded up the few steps to the store, leaving Mrs. Galea—if she had a first name, I was not privy to it—to negotiate her way out of the car on the street side, painfully aware, it seemed to me, of the hostile looks and rude gestures of the motorists and pedestrians inconvenienced by this display of automotive bad manners.

It never seemed possible for Galea to simply walk into a room. His entrance was always a dramatic event of some kind, although I would be hard-pressed to tell you exactly what he did to make it seem that way.

It helped, of course, that he was, let's face it, extraordinarily good-looking. Not particularly tall, but well built, and obviously a man who worked at it, he had a very stylish look to him. On this particular occasion he wore some kind of collarless shirt—it was silk, I think, although nobody has ever called me an expert on clothes—black, nicely cut pants, and a black coat, in what I'm sure was cashmere, which he rather cavalierly tossed onto the front desk on arrival. The clothes went well with the perennial tan and the dark hair, cut just long enough to be artsy but not long enough to offend his wellheeled clients. His features were almost perfect, except perhaps for a certain softness about the mouth, which men, jealous no doubt, liked to call effeminate, but which women found charmingly boyish.

In any event, we all—Sarah and I; my neighbor and our right-hand man Alex Stewart; and our only other customer, a young woman in the shortest black skirt I have ever seen, black tights and boots, and leather jacket, and who was not, my instincts told me, planning to buy anything at all—looked in his direction as he entered the shop, his driving gloves in one hand, his sunglasses twirling nonchalantly in the other. Sarah, who was a whiz on the business side but who found dealing with difficult clients troublesome, disappeared quickly into the little office in the back. Alex moved to assist our other customer.

"Ms. McClintoch." Galea smiled in my general direction as he looked about him. "I'm very glad to see you are here. I'd appreciate your advice and assistance with my latest project." Galea had a way of making you think your opinion was important to him, although my experience with him to date would indicate that the only opinion that mattered was his own.

"I'm building a house in Malta. I was born there, you know. A bit of a return to my roots. Nice little piece of property, sea view of course. I'll be needing some furnishings for it, so let us see what you have," he said, taking me by the elbow and guiding me toward the back of the store. He smelled very nice, I noticed, some exotic aftershave or men's cologne I did not recognize. "A little more Mediterranean in feel than what I usually do. A little more relaxed. More like my place in the Caribbean, which you may recall."

I nodded. Of course I recalled it. The last time we had supplied some furniture for Galea, it had been for the home he was referring to, a luxurious retreat on an exclusive island in the Caribbean. The house had been featured in one of the upscale architectural magazines, and indeed had won an award for its design, and Galea had been good enough to give Greenhalgh and McClintoch a credit. It had moved us into an entirely different league, so to speak, and had brought us some very exclusive customers. The point was, I didn't need to be reminded. This was Galea's way of telling me that I owed him, and while it was true, it irritated me because I had a feeling that payback time was near.

"Now, what have we here? Very nice—Indonesian, I believe," he said, pausing in front of a very expensive antique teak armoire and chewing thoughtfully on the arm of his sunglasses in a way that I confess I found suggestive. "I think that will do quite nicely, don't you?

"And what about this, Lara?" he said, sliding easily to a

first-name basis while pointing to a large old teak dining table and eight slat chairs. "What do you think?" he asked, standing much too close for comfort.

"I, of course, think they're perfect," I replied, backing away slightly. "But I should point out to you that the price quoted covers the cost of their having been shipped from Jakarta to Toronto, and I'd have to charge you to ship it from here to Malta. Malta, if my knowledge of geography serves me correctly, is very close to Italy, a country whose design industry is among the best in the world, so it might be better for you to shop a little closer to your new home." I tried to sound crisp and professional.

This apparently was not the answer he wanted. "What do you think?" he asked, turning to our only other customer. "Miss . . . ?"

"Perez," she said, blushing from the attention. "Monica Perez. I think it's . . ." Her voice trailed off as she thought about it. I could tell she was thinking by the way she chewed her lip and wrinkled her brow prettily. "It's lovely," she concluded.

"What do you think would look nice on the patio?" he asked her, drawing away from me and leading her toward a set of wrought-iron patio furniture, leaving me feeling in some unfathomable way bereft. I found myself wondering how Galea managed to turn the act of buying furniture into a seduction. He had a way with women that went with the looks, and it was said at least some of his design commissions owed much to urging on the part of his clients' wives, several of whom he was rumored to have had affairs with. These affairs never seemed to last long. When I wasn't falling under his spell, I liked to think that it was his incessant use of the first person singular that caused even the most infatuated to lose interest. More likely, however, it was he who did the dumping.

I couldn't hear what he and Ms. Perez were saying; they were almost whispering to each other by this time, their heads almost touching, but I couldn't argue with the results: the armoire, an antique Indonesian cabinet, the teak table and chairs, two carved mirrors, the wrought-iron and glass patio set, two side tables, and a large, intricately carved coffee table. The bill would be satisfyingly well into five digits, and even The Deez sat up and took notice, surprised no doubt to find a kindred spirit, someone who viewed the world as his oyster in the same way he did.

Throughout the entire performance, ignored by her husband and almost forgotten by the rest of us, Mrs. Galea stood, back to the wall, near the front door. Not once in this whole process did Galea consult with, or even acknowledge, his wife, although presumably she too would spend time in the house in Malta. Her opinion, at least insofar as furniture was concerned, did not appear to be of any consequence.

Rumored to be considerably older than her husband, she certainly looked it. She was a rather plain woman, about her husband's height, her features too sharp—perhaps patrician would be a kinder way of describing them—to be attractive. Her hair was cut way too severely, a blunt cut that accentuated the sharpness of her features and the square of her jaw. Her clothes—of the powder-blue twin sweater set and pearls variety, matching pleated skirt unfashionably long, pleats sewn down over the hips—while no doubt expensive, could only be described as dull. To be fair, I suppose, I should say that it was possible that twin sweater sets were back in style—where clothes fashion is concerned, I'd be the last to know—but more than anything else Mrs. Galea gave the impression of a colorless creature intent on blending into the background as much as possible. The only feature that commanded attention were her eyes, intelligent and inquisitive. If her husband was the charmer of the pair, she was the born observer.

Monica Perez, on the other hand, whose opinion apparently did matter, was quite the opposite of Mrs. Galea, flashy and, in my opinion, definitely more style than substance. And there I was to complete the female triangle, not entirely immune to his charms but definitely wary. For a moment I had a vision of the three of us as three little planets revolving around his sun, held there by the strength of his personality and the brightness of his charm.

Then, the selections made, Galea, bored already with Ms. Perez, turned his attention back to me. His most charming smile on his face, teeth perfect, head cocked disarmingly to one side, he once again took my elbow and steered me toward the desk. I knew that I was about to learn the quid pro quo to all this money being spent: Galea's propensity to keep a mental tally of owe-me's aside, there almost always is one when somebody spends that much money in the shop, and I tried to steel myself for what was to come.

He was standing way too close again, and since he was only a little taller than I am, his eyes were disconcertingly focused directly on mine.

"I have a small favor to ask of you," he began.

Say no, I told myself. Out loud I said, "If I can help, I will," trying to keep my tone neutral as possible.

"I am going to be entertaining some very important people at my house in Malta very soon, in about ten days, actually, and I need the place to be arranged to my standard, which as you know is rather exacting, shall we say. Unfortunately I can't go there myself right away—I have to make a presentation to one of the banks here—so I can't supervise the work personally. I need all of these pieces consolidated with some furniture at my house and shipped to this address," he said, handing me a slip of paper with the address neatly typed on it. "But most importantly, I need you to go over there and see that the finishing is up to snuff and that all the furniture is placed correctly. I will, of course, cover your airfare and compensate you for your time."

"I'm not sure I could be away from the store right now," I said, "and furthermore . . ." My voice trailed off as I searched for an excuse not to go.

"You could stay in the house too, which is already partially furnished, and I will reimburse you for your meals and other expenses while you are there. You could look upon it as a bit of a holiday,'' he said in a wheedling tone and giving me the high voltage smile.

"This will be expensive, Mr. Galea,'' I said, but I could feel myself weakening. "First of all, the deadline means we'll have to ship by air, not sea. And why not have someone there see to the placement of the furniture?''

"There is no one over there I can trust to do this to my standards. In fact there are very few people anywhere I would trust with this task,'' he said smoothly. "The meeting is an important one for me,'' he added.

I would accept, of course. I knew it, and so did he, but I didn't want to look like a pushover to his charms.

"Here is a check for $2500 as an advance on expenses. You can have the shipping and insurance charges billed directly to me, as usual,'' he said. "Will you do it?''

I nodded. There was no question we needed the sale. I looked at the check and capitulated totally. I called Sarah to come and do the paperwork, and then feeling slightly guilty, turned my attention to Mrs. Galea. She was now intently examining a small wooden carving, only three or four inches high, one of several we had in a basket at the front desk, a conversation piece and an inexpensive purchase for those just browsing.

"I'm Lara, Lara McClintoch, Mrs. Galea. I don't think we have been officially introduced. That's an Indonesian Worryman you're looking at. If you look closely you can see it is a man all hunched over. The idea is that you rub all your troubles onto his back, and he takes them all on for you.''

She smiled tentatively. "You're the owner, then,'' she said.

"One of them,'' I replied. "Sarah Greenhalgh, who is with your husband now, is the other.''

"You have lovely things,'' she said, smiling rather shyly.

At this point, her husband, his business done, turned to me and said, as if my time was now his alone to command, "Come to the house at ten o'clock tomorrow morning to see the furniture I want shipped and to pick up a set of plans.''

''Is ten convenient for you too, Mrs Galea?'' I asked, turning to her. If he wasn't going to ask her, I was. She nodded, blushing at the attention.

Ignoring her, Galea headed down the steps to the car, leaving her to follow him out of the store. As she got to the door, I rushed after her and pressed the Worryman into her hands. If anyone needed it, she did.

''With our compliments, Mrs. Galea,'' I said.

She looked surprised. ''Thank you,'' she said. ''And it's Marilyn.''

With that they were gone, a screeching of brakes from another car as Galea pulled away without so much as a glance at the rest of the traffic, leaving all of us, particularly Monica Perez, slightly breathless.

''Dreadful man!'' Sarah sighed when Monica Perez had also left and we once again had the store to ourselves. ''Imagine having a husband who flirts with other women right in front of you. That poor woman!''

''He certainly thinks he's God's gift to women, that's for sure,'' I agreed.

''That expression, 'God's gift,' implies the existence of a Being of higher consequence than Martin Galea himself, and therefore not something Galea could bring himself to support, I suspect,'' Alex said dryly.

We all laughed. ''I have to say I like his work, though,'' Alex continued, naming several of Galea's better known commissions. Galea did work all over the world.

I had to agree with Alex. Galea, despite his less ennobling qualities, had enormous talent to match the ego.

''You also have to agree he's good for business, Sarah,'' I said. ''Monica Perez, who I'm sure was just browsing, was so entranced she bought a mirror similar to one Galea bought! With any luck, she'll be back for more—furniture, I mean.''

''Why do you figure a man like that married a woman like

that?'' Sarah mused, ignoring the compliments we'd given Galea and our rather jejune attempts at humor.

"Money," Alex replied. "McLean money to be precise," he said, naming a well-known Toronto family. "Married while he was still an architectural student. Got him off to a good start, I'd think. Money and connections."

"Do you think she actually had something to say, opinions and such, before she took up with him?" Sarah went on.

"We'll probably never know," I said. "Now, we'd better get started arranging all this. We don't have much time. Are you sure you don't want this one, Sarah? You wouldn't have to deal with him directly very much, and you might enjoy having a few days in an exotic locale."

Sarah had purchased the business from me but had asked me to come back in with her when she found she didn't like the incessant travel it required nearly as much as she thought she might. She disliked the haggling with suppliers, the frustrating dealings with import and export officials in various countries around the world, the loneliness of being so far from home for so long.

I, on the other hand, loved it. It was why I had started the business in the first place. But I still felt a little guilty that I got all the travel while she minded the shop.

"Oh, I think learning to communicate with teenagers is about as exotic as I want to get right now," she replied. Sarah had a new beau who came as a package deal with two teen-aged sons.

"I'll look after things at this end, while you're over there, and we'll ask Alex to do his usual wonders with our shippers," she said.

I was happy with this, I had to admit. My partner in life, Lucas May, a Mexican archaeologist, had agreed to supervise a dig in Belize. He'd be off at a site in the middle of nowhere, out of cellphone range, for several weeks, so our regular time together, usually in Mérida or Miami, had been postponed until he returned.

Unlike Galea, Lucas was self-effacing, equally attractive, I thought, but quietly so. A brilliant archaeologist, an ardent supporter of the indigenous peoples of Mexico, he had a way about him that I had come to find immensely reassuring. But we were both feeling the strains of a long-distance relationship, and I had a sense a bit of a break might help us sort out our feelings. I thought a few days in Malta, away from the distractions of daily life, might focus things a bit for me.

I called our shipper, Dave Thomson, and understood his expressions of dismay when I told him what needed to be done, by when.

"Money is no object here, Dave," I said. "You know Galea. Just tell me how you want to do it. I'll take measurements of the stuff at the house tomorrow and mark it for you."

"Well, this is a new one for me. Can't say I've ever shipped to Malta," he said. "Do they have a lot of falcons there, do you think?" he joked. "I'll have to check into routings and costs. My favorite old movie, by the way, *The Maltese Falcon*. Humphrey Bogart at his best, I'd say. Anyway, I'll make a few calls, find the best way to do this, and the best rate I can. It'll be expensive, though, at least $3000, probably. But as you say, money is no object for this guy."

After some discussion about insurance and logistics and so on, he rang off, and I relaxed a little knowing that if it could be done, Dave was the one to do it. He'd performed miracles for me more than once, starting a few years ago when he found a furniture shipment lost out of Singapore and got it to a fancy design show only hours before it opened.

I'd been the supplier to a young up-and-coming designer who'd been asked to decorate a room in the show house that was to raise money for charity. That was the event that launched his career and my business. The designer was a man by the name of Clive Swain, who after that show became my first employee and then my husband. But Dave could hardly be held accountable for that, and Thomson Shipping had been my shipper of choice ever since.

When I came out of the office, Alex had already started moving Galea's purchases into our storage area and replacing them with stuff from our stock. Then we all surveyed the shop floor. Even with some replacements, it looked a little bare. Galea had certainly cut a swath through the place.

"I'd better get on to Dave about that shipment Lucas sent us from Mexico before he went to Belize," Alex said. Lucas, in addition to our personal relationship, was Greenhalgh and McClintoch's agent in Mexico. "We can fill some of the holes with the Mexican pottery and leather chairs he said he sent us," Alex said.

THE NEXT MORNING I DROVE over to the Galea residence. It was located in a part of town which had once been thought to have charm. But now interspersed between the older, more gracious homes, were what are commonly called monster houses, those in which ostentation and sheer size have replaced aesthetics and good taste.

In such a neighborhood, Galea's home came as something of a relief and a bit of a surprise to me, something more to the taste of Marilyn Galea, née McLean, more old Toronto than the work of a noted modern architect. The face it showed to the street was refreshingly simple, a pleasant Georgian facade, a simple circular driveway of interlocking paving stones leading through iron gates to a European-style courtyard, and a very plain door surrounded by ivy.

The door was opened by a pleasant-faced young woman in a grey uniform. Filipina, I thought, and we were joined almost immediately by the unpretentious Marilyn Galea herself, dressed in the camel version of what she had worn the previous day. I stepped into an elegant octagonal-shaped entrance, all creamy marble. Even the flowers matched, a sumptuous bouquet of lilies arranged in a crystal vase on a table in the middle of the foyer.

Leading off the entrance toward the back of the house was a hallway, more art gallery than hall actually, with several

works of modern art, a couple of them signed by Galea himself, discreetly lit from above. When we got to the end of the
hall, I stepped into a large open area at the rear and the house's
secret revealed itself.

I think I actually gasped out the word "Wow!" then immediately regretted it, such an inarticulate expression certainly
not in keeping with the sophisticated veneer I liked to think I
projected. Neither did it do justice to what I saw.

All the houses on this side of the street back on one of the
many lovely ravines that crisscross Toronto. But no others,
I'm sure, made such exceptional use of the landscape. The
back of the Galea house was two storeys of clear glass—perhaps two and a half, since the house was built down into the
ravine at the back. The house seemed to float out over the
ravine with no visible means of support. The eye was drawn
into the trees, then above them, seemingly forever, to the office
towers of the downtown core. Here, for certain, was the Galea
touch.

I'm not certain how long I stood there, just gaping at the
sight. When I looked around I found Galea himself watching,
a look of amusement in his eyes. "Like it?" he said.

"It's magnificent!" I said.

"You should see it at night, actually," he went on. "From
where we are standing, all the lights in the ceiling of the living
room—there are 360 of them—light up like little stars, and
reflected in the glass, they stretch out as far as the lights from
the city towers." He seemed to take a boyish pleasure in his
own work and my evident admiration. "Come and have a
better look."

We descended a couple of steps into the living room, to a
very elegant off-white sofa flanked by cream leather Barcelona
chairs. At one side of the room was a huge marble fireplace
which soared to the ceiling. Behind was the outside wall of
the old house, its original red brick now whitewashed to suit
its new environs in the addition of glass and steel. Most of
the furnishings were antique white, and everything was done

on a grand scale. Despite the proportions, however, the feeling
was one of calm and contemplation, a kind of pure space.

"Would you like a tour of the house before we get down
to work?" he asked.

"Sure," I replied.

The rest of the house was also lovely, the main living spaces
complemented by a palette of honey, cream, and buttermilk.
Wooden floors were the color of pale straw, covered in some
places with antique carpets, their colors worn to the same
golden hues.

The dining room was spectacular. It also had a view of
the ravine. But in a departure from the colors in the rest of
the house, it featured a black lacquered table that reflected the
myriad lights from a chandelier, designed by Galea himself,
he assured me, which caught the light in hundreds of pieces
of crystal, then burnished it and threw it back in sparkling
starburst patterns on the wall, the table, and the floor.

The upstairs hallway was the upscale equivalent of a trophy
room, decorated with framed drawings of some of the buildings he had designed and was famous for. Galea had attained
a point in his career where he was always referred to as the
award-winning architect, never just the architect, and here it
was easy to see why. I recognized a town hall that had won
an international competition in Milan, a grand public space in
Riyadh, a concert hall in Australia. It was all very grand. Next
to these were photographs of Galea accepting various prizes
and hobnobbing with assorted famous people—politicians,
movie stars, and the like. He pointed each of them out to me
with obvious pleasure, like a little boy boasting about his ex-
ploits in the schoolyard.

After the tour was over and my genuine exclamations of
admiration expressed and accepted, Galea got down to business and showed me the plans for the house in Malta. His
drawings already incorporated the furniture he'd purchased the
day before. "There's one shipment of furniture already there,
and some Oriental carpets I picked up last time I was working

in Turkey. Marilyn knows what furniture is to go from here. She has the list. And we have a tight deadline. I'll be there a week from Friday or Saturday.''

"I'll get it done, Mr. Galea. And we appreciate the business,'' I said.

"Good,'' he said. "Now I must run. I have a meeting with the board of directors of an oil company. I'll be adding a new dimension to the skyline of Toronto soon.'' He smiled.

Marilyn Galea and I walked him to the front door. By this time he appeared to be in a bit of a hurry, but not so much that he couldn't stop to flirt. "I haven't mentioned how lovely you look this morning,'' he said to me as he took my arm. "I feel so much more confident my gathering in Malta will go well now that you have taken the house in hand.'' He started to go out the door, holding my arm until the very last moment.

"Martin,'' Marilyn said quietly. He looked back. She was holding his briefcase and his sunglasses.

He grinned at her. "What would I do without you, my love?'' he said, his arm briefly circling her waist, giving her a quick kiss on the cheek. "My guardian angel,'' he said, turning to me. "I'd be lost without her.''

Then with a boyish grin and a wave, he was gone. Marilyn's face softened as she watched him go.

It would have been a touching gesture had it not been for the fact that on his way out he brushed past me in a certain way. It is always edifying to be in the presence of greatness, but it is unfortunate that some of those who possess it are really revolting people. I turned my attention to his wife. If she had noticed the incident, she didn't mention it.

"You have an absolutely beautiful home, Mrs. Galea— Marilyn. You must be very proud of it.''

"My husband is an exceptional designer, I know. But it is the colors I love the most,'' she replied. "They remind me of Italy, of Florence. It is one of my favorite places in all the world. It is where I learned to love architecture, and I suppose set the stage for my life with Martin. When I told him that, he said he chose the colors for me," she said.

Then I got down to work, Marilyn very obligingly and competently helping me by taking down the measurements as I called them out. There were five pieces of furniture ranging from a huge mahogany sideboard to a large armoire that were to be consolidated with the shipment from the shop. Most of them were in the front of the house, not far from the door. I measured each one of them, estimated their weight to help Dave out, and then marked each with a yellow sticker with my initials on it to make sure there would be no mistake when Dave's men arrived to get the furniture. I was going on ahead to Malta, and Marilyn had pointed out to me that while the maid was home every day except Wednesdays, her day off, she and Martin were normally out during the day.

"I go to my club, every day, once I've gotten the house organized. I love it there. Do you know it? The Rosedale Women's Club downtown," she said, naming a very swank women's club that I had taken out a trial membership in a couple of years earlier during a period of forced inactivity shortly after my divorce.

It had seemed like a good idea at the time, getting fit in the company of women only. But after subjecting my somewhat zaftig figure and my grey jogging sweats to the scrutiny of women whose tights and headbands actually matched their leotards, and whose main topic of conversation seemed to focus on the latest color of nail polish, I had returned to my solitary morning jog. I was surprised that an obviously intelligent but shy woman like Marilyn Galea would be a member of such a club, but perhaps she was more gregarious in other people's company, or more likely she was simply to the manor born, which I was not.

I changed the subject. "Tell me more about your husband," I said. "He mentioned he is going back to his roots with this house in Malta. Is that where he is from originally?"

"Yes, it is. Galea is a very common Maltese name. He was

born in the town of Mellieha on the main island. His family was not well-off—his father had a little shop in the town. But Martin, Martin was born ambitious, I think. He and a friend of his talked their way into the international school in Malta and charmed their way into the homes of the international set. The principal of the school recognized his talent and helped him get a scholarship in architecture at the University of Toronto—Canada and Malta continue to have ties because of the old British Commonwealth connection.''

"Are his parents still living there?"

"No. Both of them died several years ago. Before I met him.''

"Have you seen the house?" I asked.

"Not yet," she replied. "I've never been to Malta. I'm looking forward to it, to seeing where Martin comes from, the village where he grew up. He doesn't talk about it much.''

"Will I see you there then?"

"No. This is a business trip. Martin is going to Rome for a couple of days to see to a project he's working on there, then he goes on to Malta. You know Martin." She smiled. "Always looking for the next big commission. He's gotten back in touch with a boyhood friend of his, who's also done very well for himself in the interim, and who hopefully will see that Martin gets connected to all the right people in Malta. Martin is entertaining some people as soon as he gets there. I'm not at liberty to say whom. But here, come and have a coffee with me in the kitchen. Would you like an espresso or a cappuccino?" she said, changing the subject abruptly.

"Sure," I said. I'd already noticed during the house tour that the kitchen was equipped with a commercial-sized espresso machine. It was an impressive space. White marble floors, brushed stainless-steel counters and cupboards, and the de rigueur, in that neighborhood, huge built-in refrigerator and six-burner professional stove. "Do you enjoy cooking, Marilyn?" I asked. You could run a small restaurant out of this kitchen.

"Not really." She smiled. "Coralee does most of the cooking," she said, gesturing toward the young woman who had opened the door when I arrived, and who was now chopping some vegetables at the far end of the kitchen. "Cooking has never been my forte, neither for that matter has housekeeping. Sheltered childhood!" She smiled again. I recalled her bluestocking upbringing.

After asking Coralee to make us cappuccinos, she led me off the kitchen to a small room. I say small, but it was probably the size of my living room. Here it seemed small. It was decorated quite uncharacteristically in a pink chintz, and seemed, and I do not mean this unkindly, a little worn. I noted with some surprise that the Indonesian Worryman I had given her the day before was sitting in a prominent place on the desk.

"This is my office," she said, noticing my glance about the room. The room was very neat, and I could see what looked to be financial ledgers, indicating to me that she was the one who looked after the smooth running of the Galea household. I found myself wondering why Marilyn Galea could not have taken on the house in Malta. She struck me as perfectly capable of managing the project as well as I could.

"The office was originally my mother's," Marilyn went on. "She died when I was very young, but I remember being in this room with her. Martin let me keep the room the way it was. You know how architects are," she said. "Even something so small as the placement of a bar of soap in the bathroom is a design feature, and one they must therefore control. It was a major concession on his part."

"This is your family home, then, is it?"

"Yes. We moved in after my father died about ten years ago. He'd roll over in his grave if he could see what Martin has done to it." She laughed. "But it seemed to be the sensible thing to do. Martin was just getting started, and building a new house seemed out of the question. Now I think we both like it." As she spoke she twisted her pearls, which I had the impression she always wore, and I knew, somehow, that the pearls had been her mother's, and like the office meant a very great deal to her for that reason.

Coralee brought us the coffee and we began to chat. I must say it never ceases to amaze me what we'll tell a relative stranger. Here I had just met Marilyn Galea and soon we were chattering away like old friends. At least I was chattering. She asked a lot of questions. I told her all about the shop—she was fascinated by the idea that I had just made up my mind to go into business and had done so.

I told her about meeting Alex Stewart when I moved into my little house in Cabbagetown, about how he had kind of adopted me, and how now, on a pension, he came into the shop every day to help us, out of the goodness of his heart, and certainly not because of the pittance we were able to pay him. How, even in his seventies, he was a whiz on the Internet and was probably, even as we spoke, online getting me an airline ticket to Malta.

I told her about my parents, my father a retired diplomat, about my two-year relationship with Lucas, who was, I told her, probably the nicest man on the planet. In short I told her everything. Well, not quite everything. I did not tell her that in the dying days of my marriage, when I was coming to realize that Clive's penchant for very young women and his distaste for an honest day's work were not a temporary aberration but a permanent condition, I had come dizzyingly close to succumbing to the charms of Martin Galea.

Common sense and good taste had won a moral victory then, but it was by a narrow margin, and it still caused me some embarrassment to think of the way I'd behaved. Above all, I hated to think that this down-to-earth woman, in whose kitchen I was sitting, knew anything about it. It was yet another reason why Martin Galea usually got what he wanted where I was concerned, with the one exception, of course. I really wanted him to keep his mouth shut about those unhappy days of my past, and Galea, from what I'd heard, was not above using what he knew about people to advance his career. Nothing so sordid as blackmail, to be sure, just a sense that there was a little tally of past sins to accompany the list of owe-me's.

While we were still chatting, my cellphone rang. It was Alex. "How do you feel about flying out tonight?" he asked. I muttered something. "I'm having real difficulty getting you connecting flights. Essentially from here you can get to Malta through London, Paris, or Rome. London is fully booked. In Rome they're having one of those regular strikes of theirs. There's a seat on an Air Canada flight that will get you into Paris in time to make an Air Malta connection to Luqa."

"Where?"

"Luqa—Malta's airport. I'd better get you some reading material on the country, I can tell. Will you go tonight?"

"Sure. No problem. I'll head home now and pack. Got a weather report for me too?"

"Of course. Winter. Rain gear a good idea, a jacket for evenings. But lots warmer than here. We're supposed to have an arctic blast in the next few days—minus fifteen or so at night."

"In that case, I'm on my way," I said, laughing, not realizing that even while I was thousands of miles away the Canadian deep freeze would cause me no end of trouble.

I said good-bye to Marilyn Galea and thanked her for the coffee and her help with the furniture. I told her that Thomson Shipping would be picking it up in the next day or so, and that Alex or Sarah would call her to let her know when. She gave me the names and telephone number of the couple who were the caretakers for the property in Malta, checked to see that her husband had given me the right set of plans, and made careful note of Dave Thomson's address and phone number, as well as that of Sarah and Alex.

Then I left her. I still have a vision of her standing in the doorway as I pulled out of the driveway. A tall, plain woman painfully shy but rather nice, married to a little boy—a disarming, talented little boy, perhaps, but a little boy nonetheless.

❧ TWO

*F*IRST THE ANIMALS, CREATURES OF *the Pleistocene. Driven*
before a great wall of ice that almost imperceptibly en-
croaches on their grazing lands, they move further and further
south, onto a narrow band of land, a bridge, that stretches
across the sea. But then the thunder of a great earthquake,
the waters rush in. The land bridge becomes a chain of little
islands, and then a very few. In this tiny archipelago, there is
no going forward and no turning back. Trapped on this rocky
shore, struggling for survival, they become, as the ages go by,
smaller and smaller. Stunted hippopotami, elephants the size
of dogs. Then silence, the Cave of Darkness, extinction.

But what is this? Digging in, cowering in the dark of caves.
Troglodyte! Will you move into the light?

I WAS IN SUCH A dazed state when I arrived in Malta, the
previous day a blur of activity that got me to the Paris flight
just in the nick of time, then to the Air Malta flight by the
same narrow margin, that I almost missed the hand-lettered
sign with the interesting phonetic treatment of my name.

MISSUS MCLEENTAK, it read, held by a rather nice-looking
young man in jeans and a Hard Rock Cafe T-shirt. Presumably
the age of mass media and production has brought us more
than the comfort of seeing T-shirts advertising the same es-
tablishment anywhere in the world, but at that very moment I
could not think what.

Actually the reason I almost missed it was that I was absolutely mesmerized by the appearance and antics of one of my fellow passengers on the Air Malta flight from Paris. He was dressed safari-style, whether because he thought Malta was the kind of place that required that sort of attire or as a matter of affectation, I couldn't know. In any event, he was wearing cowboy boots, khaki pants, one of those matching khaki short-sleeved shirts with an excess of pockets, and a wide-brimmed hat of the bush ranger variety, one side snapped up, that one associates with the Australian outback or the Serengeti. This one sported a leopard print band, and dipped over a pockmarked face, a bulbous nose, and florid complexion that indicated its owner should probably swear off the booze from time to time.

This fellow, whom I'd named for my own amusement GWH for Great White Hunter, had begun his performance even before the plane got off the ground in Paris. While everyone else was attempting to get seated, he was up and waving bills in assorted currencies in the direction of the cabin attendants. It seemed he wanted them to put the bottle of champagne—Dom, he called it—he'd brought on board in the refrigerator and to serve it to him at his seat. He was sitting with a lovely lady, he said in a stage whisper that could be heard halfway to Nairobi, and wanted to impress her.

The well-trained cabin crew, who had the good taste to regard the proferred money and the champagne as they would a basket of scorpions, explained to him that one was not supposed to bring one's own liquor for consumption on the aircraft. GWH apparently felt the rules did not apply to him. Finally the head cabin steward, realizing that GWH would be very disruptive to the comfort of the other passengers if they did not comply, agreed to take care of the champagne.

The "lovely lady" in question was an attractive middle-aged woman who appeared never to have met GWH, and was, I suspect, no more thrilled than I would be by this intimacy forced upon her by Fate in the form of the Air Malta computer.

In fact, she looked as if this flight was to be the longest three hours of her life. The aircraft was small, and had been overbooked, so it was absolutely full, even after some passengers volunteered, lured by the offer of cash and accommodation, to wait for a later plane. I myself had been tempted by the thought of a few hours in Paris and a nice afternoon nap after an all-night flight, but had decided to forge on.

In any event, I was seated across the aisle and back one row from the lovely lady and the GWH, and could tell that about thirty minutes into the flight, she was becoming desperate. At this point, in what I took to be a splendid gesture of Christian charity, a gentleman seated behind me, a priest in black robes and a cross on a long chain around his neck, told the cabin attendants that he would be pleased to change seats with her. The message was discreetly delivered and accepted with genuine gratitude, I'm sure, and the priest took his seat beside GWH.

I could see only the side of the priest's head, and thought rather uncharitable thoughts, considering his kindness, about his hairdresser. There was no part in his hair. Instead it hugged his skull, emanating in all directions from a tiny bald spot on the top of his head, perched like a polar ice cap on some small planet. At the front it looked from this angle as if his hair stopped just above his eyebrows, giving very much the impression of a man with a bowl on his head.

I was very tired from the overnight flight, and after reading the Paris papers for a few minutes and realizing that I had made the right decision to press on to Malta—there were reports of labor unrest and the chance of wildcat strikes possibly affecting the airport, and there had been bomb threats in the Metro—I fell asleep and did not waken until the "tables and chair backs in the upright position" announcement as we began our descent into Malta.

I peered past my seatmate by the window, straining to get a view of the island. Alex had told me that Malta is shaped like a fish—Alex knows the most amazing things—and that where I was going, Galea's house, was, if one assumed the top of the fish was to the north, just below the gill area. Not a particularly inviting location description and certainly not one I would expect to hear from the Maltese National Tourism Organization, but definitely descriptive. All I saw from the plane was a rocky and rather desolate island. It was raining, as Alex had predicted.

I did not see GWH and the priest exiting the aircraft, but they soon joined the rest of us at the baggage carousel. The priest had a duffel bag only, but the GWH had three large suitcases and a golf bag filled with clubs. There was the usual routine to get out of the airport, a red zone and a green zone, depending on whether or not you had anything to declare, and I headed for the green zone several steps behind the priest and GWH.

GWH was looking a little the worse for wear. He had had too much champagne, I suppose, and his khaki pants had slipped down below his paunch, so that he was now walking on the back hem of his trousers. He stumbled slightly, and the priest, who by this time surely deserved multitudes of credits in the hereafter, went to assist him. Both were stopped in the spot check in the green zone, but after sharing a joke with the priest, probably at the expense of GWH, the customs officers waved the priest through. GWH did not fare as well, and as I went through the outer door, I wondered if they would notice the metal detector amongst his golf clubs. It was the last I thought I would see of either of them.

It took me a few seconds to realize that Missus Mcleentak meant me, since I really hadn't expected to be met at the airport. I approached the young man and introduced myself.

"I'm Lara McClintoch," I said. "Are you looking for me?"

"Yes, ma'am," the nice young man said. "I'm Anthony Farrugia. My mother and father look after Mr. Galea's house for him. Mother thought it would be nice if I were to come and meet you."

"That is very thoughtful of you and your mother," I said. "Where to?"

He took my bag and led me out to a parking area and a very old car. An acid-yellow car, a British Ford of some kind, I think, conservatively twenty years old, and maybe closer to thirty. It looked well cared for, however, and Anthony's pride in it was evident.

"Nice car," I said and he beamed.

He loaded my luggage in the trunk and we got into the car. Alex's notes had warned me they drive on the left in Malta, so I was prepared for that. Not for what came next, however. Anthony put the car in gear and pulled away from the curb, then accelerated until the gears were screaming. Just when the smell of burning rubber or oil permeated the car, he pushed in the clutch, pulled it into neutral, put in the clutch again, and whipped it into third. He noticed me watching him.

"No second gear." He grinned. "Have to go like a bomb in first, then ease it into third."

"I see," I said.

At the exit of the airport, we roared around a corner in third gear, and I could hear my suitcase flying about in the trunk.

"Not good to slow down," he said. "It stalls."

"I see," I said again. Just then we went around another corner at breakneck speed, and with a thud the window beside me slid down into the door frame.

"Rats," he said. "It does that sometimes."

I tried to roll the window back up, but the handle spun uselessly in my hand.

"You have to pull the window up by hand," he offered. "I'll pull over and we'll do that."

"That's okay," I said. "I like the fresh air."

"Me too." He smiled.

"Mr. Galea gave me money to go out and buy a car for the house. I got a really good deal on this one," he said conversationally.

"Good for you," I said. "It's lovely."

"It belongs to the house, so you get to drive it while you're here," he said.

"I can hardly wait," I said. What I meant, of course, was that I'd rather ride a donkey than drive this car. We sat in companionable silence for a while, the damp air blowing in our faces.

"How old are you, Anthony, if you don't mind my asking?"

"Almost seventeen," he replied. Then after a pause, "But I've been driving since I was twelve." He looked sideways at me to try to ascertain why I was asking.

"Do you help your mother and father look after the Galea place?" I asked him.

"Sure. But only after school. I'm trying to do well at school so I can go to university. I want to be an architect like Mr. Galea. The Cassars are born architects."

"I thought your name was Farrugia. Who are the Cassars?"

"You haven't heard of Gerolamo Cassar?" he asked incredulously. "He was our greatest architect. He designed Valletta, the capital city, and the most beautiful buildings on Malta. My mother is a Cassar."

"Anthony," I said, "this is my first visit to your country, and my knowledge of it is woefully inadequate, but I'm looking forward to learning a lot about it while I'm here."

He digested that for a moment or two. "I think maybe I'll have to show you around, then," he said. "After school."

"I'd really like that," I said. "We sure can't see much now."

"Yes. You got here just in time. The fog is coming in."

He was right. As we traveled away from the airport, the mist got thicker until you could only see a few feet in front of the car and I had absolutely no sense of where we were going, nor how I would ever retrace my route. I had the impression, despite the rain, of a rather arid land, very rocky, with little vegetation. Everything seemed grey at worst, or at best, a kind of sere yellow.

After about twenty minutes or so, we made a sharp right turn and went up what appeared to be a driveway, lined with bushes and a low stone wall in what at closer distance was a rather pretty buttery yellow. Halfway up the hill, we reversed the pattern on the gears, coming perilously close to stalling, then rolled to a stop in front of a garage. An even older car was parked there.

The sound of the car brought a tiny woman with very fine features and a beautiful smile to the front door and out to the driveway. "My mom," Anthony said, although she needed no introduction. Their smiles, the kind that light up whole rooms, were identical.

"I'm Marissa, missus," she said. "Take the missus's suitcase upstairs, Anthony," she said. "And don't forget to give the missus the car keys."

I was about to offer to let Anthony keep the car, but I could tell—something in her eyes—that this would not be considered a good idea by his mother, so I kept quiet.

We entered the house. I'd had a chance to look at the plans and was beginning to recognize the Galea design trademark, so I was not surprised when the rather unpretentious facade opened into a spectacular space. The floors were all tiled in terra-cotta, and the walls, the pale yellow stone I'd seen in the driveway, had been stuccoed over in a pale ochre color. I knew the moment I entered the place that the furniture from the shop would be perfect here. It was a good feeling.

The design was open concept, only the stairway to the second floor segregating the kitchen from the rest of the space. There was a huge fireplace, and beside it a man directing a couple of workmen, who were putting finishing touches to the stucco, in a language that was totally incomprehensible to me. I knew from Alex's brief geography lesson that virtually all Maltese, young and old, are fluent in English, the result of almost two centuries of British rule and influence that ended only very recently. He had assured me that English was one of two official languages for business in Malta, so I'd have no problems. The native language of the island, however, is Malti, one of those minority languages that have survived over the ages despite invasion, repression, and active attempts to stamp them out, and it was this, I assumed, that the man was speaking.

As I approached, the older man tipped his cap and said, "Hello, missus." I took this to be Joseph, Anthony's father and custodian of the house. He had a pleasant, open face, the large hands of a laborer, and appeared to be considerably older than his wife, although perhaps years of backbreaking labor had added lines to his face.

Over in one corner of the large room there was what on closer examination I found to be a large amount of furniture protected by drop cloths. Beside it, rolled in plastic were several carpets. Galea had told me he wanted to use carpets to delineate the various living areas, and he had given me a carefully annotated list of all the carpets and where they were to be placed. I sincerely hoped I remembered how to distinguish a Tabriz from a Bakhtiari, or this would be trouble.

The back of the house was all glass, and there were no curtains in evidence. While I couldn't see more than twenty or thirty feet beyond the windows because of the fog, I assumed the bare windows meant there were no neighbors nearby. The windows would be protected from the summer heat of the Mediterranean by a terrace with a weathered brick floor and Greek columns. Large terra-cotta pots were already filled with flowers.

"I'll show you around upstairs," Marissa said, and I followed her up the staircase. There were three bedrooms on the second floor, all of them with large windows and a doorway onto a deck over the terrace below. Only one of the bedrooms, the largest, was furnished, and Marissa had seen to it that it was made up for me. There was a king-size bed, and an en suite bathroom with all the amenities. I wondered exactly where Galea was planning for me to sleep once he got there.

"You'll be tired from your long journey," Marissa said.

"I've left you something to eat, *fenek* and some bread and wine, and there is food in the refrigerator for your breakfast. I hope everything is satisfactory."

"It's wonderful, thank you, Marissa. And please call me Lara. We're going to be working together a lot over the next few days, and I hope we can be friends." She looked horrified at the thought of calling me by my first name. "I work for him just as you do," I said.

She seemed pleased.

"Tomorrow . . . It's the Sabbath, and Joseph and I normally do not work that day. We go to Mass . . . but I know there is a lot of work to be done before Mr. Galea comes."

"That's fine. You take the day off. I'll need some time to figure out where everything is here, and I'll do a plan so we can move the furniture in the easiest possible way. I'll see you on Monday."

"Thank you, Missus Lara," she said.

"Your son has offered to show me around Malta, after school. Is that all right with you?"

"Of course it is, but don't let him be a pest. He is so excited when someone from far away comes here, he can be a little, I don't know, clingy?" she replied.

"He's a really nice young man," I said. "You must be very proud of him."

"I am. We are," she replied. "In a way we have Mar— Mr. Galea to thank for that. Anthony was not doing well at school, always in trouble. Joseph and I, we didn't know what to do. Then Mr. Galea came to build this house. He has convinced Anthony he can be an architect. Now he has settled down, he works hard at school, he has a nice girlfriend."

"That's wonderful," I said, thinking there might be a side to Martin Galea I hadn't known. We headed downstairs, where Marissa showed me the dinner she had prepared for me. It looked good—a stew of some kind of meat with onions and tomatoes, and a large very crusty-looking loaf of bread.

She showed me where the telephone was, and put their

phone number beside it. "It sometimes works, it sometimes doesn't," Anthony said from behind us. "Can I take Missus Mcleentak out to look around Valletta after Mass tomorrow, Mum?"

"If she'd like to go?" she said, looking at me.

"That would be just great, Anthony," I said. "What time should I expect you? In fact, what time is it now? I'm still on Toronto time, I think."

"It's four-thirty," Anthony said. "I'll come and get you about one tomorrow?"

"Done," I said.

Joseph joined us in the kitchen. "Now, missus," he said, "you lock up the place after we leave. And don't you go walking around in the fog. There's a very big drop at the back of the yard here. We wouldn't want to lose you before my boy here can even show you around." He gave his son an affectionate pat and smiled at me. They were really nice people.

I walked them to their car, the three Farrugias and the two workmen, and waved as they left. They disappeared into the fog very quickly, then I heard the engine reverse and they came back up the driveway. Anthony leapt out and handed me the car keys with a grin and a wave. Then they were off a second time. I regarded the keys with unease.

The house did not seem all that welcoming now that they were gone. With so little furniture and none of the carpets placed, my footsteps made an unpleasant hollow sound as I walked about. There were also not many lights. The kitchen lights worked, but the ceiling lights in the main room were still wires hanging from the ceiling. There was one lamp, a desk lamp that had been plugged in and left on the floor, there being no desk to put it on. I had a feeling it was going to be a long evening.

It would still be late morning Toronto time, and I'd promised to check in when I arrived. I put through the call, and was glad to hear Sarah's crisp voice.

"I'm here," I said. "It's quite the place. How are things there?"

"I'm having a special day," she replied. "You know how it was freezing rain when you left? Well, this morning it's even colder. I had my car washed yesterday, and this morning the car doors were frozen shut, not just the locks, the door frames as well. Luckily I caught Alex at home, and he came in early and opened the shop. Please don't tell me it's eighty degrees in the shade where you are!"

"It's closer to sixty-five degrees, and it's raining and foggy, and I can't see twenty feet outside the window. The place is empty and there is hardly any light. Feel better?"

"Much." She laughed. "Misery loves company. Will you be okay there by yourself?"

"Oh, sure. It's just a little creepy, that's all. Any word from Dave?"

"He's having a tough time figuring out how to get the stuff there. Yesterday there was a strike in Italy. He says that's pretty normal. Now one of the public service unions in France is calling for a one-day strike that will virtually shut the country down for twenty-four hours. But he says not to worry, not yet anyway."

"That's encouraging. Be sure and tell me when to start worrying then."

"Oh, we will." She laughed. "Alex says to tell you he checked your house this morning because it's so cold. Everything is fine. No burst pipes or anything."

"Tell him thanks for me. We'll stay in touch until we get this job done."

I felt better talking to her, and realized I was hungry. I warmed up the stew as instructed by Marissa. It was close enough to dinnertime here. It was really very good. *Fenek*, I decided, meant rabbit. Rabbit stew. The bread was exceptional. It had a very crusty exterior, but the interior would almost melt in your mouth. I had to stop myself from eating the whole loaf, it was that good. There was a pleasant enough bottle of wine, local at that, to wash it all down. Soon I was feeling very mellow.

Dinner took up all of thirty minutes of the evening. It's amazing how slowly time goes by when you really just want to go to sleep but won't let yourself. I'm a firm believer that the way to get over jet lag is to adjust your activities to local time right away even if you have missed a whole night's sleep on the way over. I told myself I couldn't go to bed before ten, or maybe nine-thirty. And it was now only six-thirty.

I went upstairs and unpacked my suitcase. There were hangers in the closet, and the bathroom was fully equipped. There was even a nice, new, white terry bathrobe. Just like a fancy hotel. I had a shower in the white-tiled walk-in shower, and then with a towel around my wet hair and the bathrobe on, I eyed the bed. It looked very good—soft, down duvet, lots of pillows. I succumbed to the temptation.

A noise woke me sometime later. It was very dark, and it took me a few seconds to remember where I was. I could not identify the noise that had wakened me, but I could tell the wind had come up in the night. My eyes adjusted to the light a little, and I got up and made my way to the window. I did not turn on the bedside light. The house had a goldfish bowl feel to me, with no curtains or shutters, and I would have felt exposed by the light.

I stood at the window. I found the door to the upstairs deck was unlocked. That didn't make me feel good, but I stepped out onto the deck. It was a little chilly, but the fog was lifting, the wind whipping it in drifts across the yard.

As I peered into the darkness, I suddenly saw, or thought I did, at the far end of the yard, the figure of a man, standing very still. He was dressed in dark clothes, his head appeared to be hooded. I shrank back from the railing, my heart pounding. As quietly as possible, I backed into the house and closed and locked the door behind me. Then I went from room to room checking the doors to the balcony. All except mine had been locked. In the dark I made my way down the staircase and checked all the doors on the main floor. They too were locked. From the windows at the back of the house, I peered out into the yard again. I could see no one. The mist lifted, and the moon came out. There was no one there.

"It's your imagination, Lara, jet lag," I said out loud, my voice echoing in the empty room. "Go back to bed."

I didn't think I'd go back to sleep, but I did. I dreamed about a man in dark robes, beckoning me toward the edge of the abyss at the back of the yard.

❦ THREE

TEMPLES OF STONE, HUGE AND round. Megaliths, tons of rock carved with the most primitive of tools, moved without the wheel. What fervor, what piety drives you, the temple builders? It is I. Life, death, rebirth. Built in My image, below ground first, then above, stretched above the sea. Offerings, animal sacrifice, the acrid smell of burning herbs. Then suddenly, silence once again. Where have you gone, you wworshipped Me best?

"WHY IS HE SITTING LIKE that?" I asked.

"Who?" Sophia replied.

"The bus driver. Why is he sitting way over to the left, on the edge of the seat, and reaching back over to the steering wheel?"

"Because Jesus is driving the bus, not him," she said.

Alex had told me that Malta is a devoutly Catholic country, but I had no idea of the extent of it. Part of me, the cynical part, wanted to laugh out loud. Another side of me ached for the simple faith the statement and the act implied.

I was wedged in a seat designed for two between Anthony and Sophia, his utterly charming and sweet girlfriend, on a bus headed for Valletta, the capital city.

DESPITE MY DISTURBED SLEEP, I had awakened very early, and after a moment's hesitation, walked out on the balcony. The scene which had seemed so menacing in the night now looked quite different. As I stood there, the sun rose to my left, turning the rocks that had seemed so lifeless the day before to the color of honey. The sea—for the property, perched on the edge of a cliff, had a magnificent view over the Mediterranean—turned from black to yellow to finally the most beautiful blue, almost cobalt, over the space of several minutes. My vision of the night, a dream perhaps, now seemed preposterous.

I had a few hours to fill before Anthony was due to arrive, and divided them between the view and the work I had to do to get ready for Galea's arrival. I found the breakfast supplies Marissa had left for me—coffee, bacon, and eggs. The bread which I had enjoyed so much the day before was hard as a rock in the morning. I had learned something about Maltese bread, and the power of the food additives we put in ours. Maltese bread is made to be eaten the day it's baked.

After about an hour of resisting the temptation to check the back of the yard, I went out and nervously eyed the edge. There was, as Joseph had warned me, a sharp drop down many feet to the water below. Just in case, I looked for footprints, but the ground was very rocky. If someone had been there in the night, he had left no trace.

Back at the house, I took the drop sheets off the pile of furniture in the corner of the living room and checked it against the list Galea had given me. Everything appeared to be in order, and I found the place for each piece on the very precise plans he had given me. I unrolled a couple of the carpets and checked them as well. I also had made notes on the dimensions of the furniture still to come from Galea's house and from the shop. With all this information, I began to develop a plan to get the place ready for Galea's arrival.

The ceiling fixtures still needed to be installed in the living room, the stucco required repair in several places, and there was a fair amount of painting still to be done. A large tapestry was to go over the sofa, so it would have to be hung once the walls were ready, and before the furniture was in place. After a couple of hours work, I had determined how to proceed. It would be touch and go, but I thought we could see it all got done, as long as the shipment from home arrived sometime in the next three days.

Just after one, a very old orange and yellow bus came along the road and slowed down enough for Anthony, accompanied by a rather plump but pretty young woman, to get off.

He waved when he saw me. "This is Sophia Zammit, my girlfriend," he said, panting slightly after they had run arm in arm up the driveway. "She's going to come with us, if it's okay with you."

"Of course it is," I said. "Nice to meet you, Sophia." I handed the car keys to Anthony. "Perhaps you'd like to drive?"

"You don't mind?" he said, his eyes lighting up.

"Not at all."

But the car wouldn't start. After several tries, with his sunny disposition still intact, Anthony leapt out of the car and raced down the driveway waving his arms frantically. Another bus, even older than the first, pulled up, and the three of us ran to catch it.

Not for the Maltese the anonymity of a public bus service. I could only assume from the interesting decor that the bus was owned by its driver. I had noticed as the bus had approached us that the front of it was gaily painted with red flowers and several ornaments, the flags of various countries on metal decals attached to the radiator grille. The bus had a name too. Elaborately painted letters across the back declared it to be "Old but Sexy." It occurred to me that as I slipped inexorably into middle age, such a title might be the best I myself could hope for.

The personalized decor carried inside. Here there was a neon sign behind the driver, which from time to time flashed out the words "Ave Maria." Above the front window a plastic statue of the Virgin and Child surrounded by dried flowers and encased in a clear plastic bell swayed with the motion of the bus. Over to one side, however, closer to the driver, was a photo of a rather healthy-looking young woman who was definitely not the Virgin Mary. Malta and its people were beginning to develop a distinct personality to me.

In retrospect, I don't know what I expected Malta to be, if indeed Martin Galea's breakneck schedule had given me enough time to develop any expectations at all. Alex had given me the basic details—a group of small islands in the middle of the Mediterranean about sixty miles from Sicily and a little over 200 miles from Libya. Population about 350,000. Malta, the largest island, is only about seventeen miles long and nine miles wide. Gozo, the other inhabited island, is about a third the size. Comino, the third island, boasts a resort, but only a handful of permanent residents.

Alex had also told me that one of Malta's largest industries was tourism, so I think I expected the Mediterranean equivalent of a Caribbean isle—lots of sun, sand, and sea.

In any event, I was totally unprepared for what I saw. The countryside, naturally yellow from the rock that is its foundation, gives the impression of a painting in pastels. The landscape is punctuated by low walls that evidently trap enough soil and moisture so that there are large patches of green and some very pretty flowers. I did not see any rivers or waterways, and few trees of any height. Nonetheless, the place had a kind of rugged beauty I found quite enchanting.

We passed towns built entirely of the yellow stone, the skyline punctuated at regular intervals by the dome of a church. Horse-drawn carriages shared the road with buses such as ours and cars of all ages and descriptions. The island, like the bus in which we were riding, gave the impression of a society both ancient and modern.

After a while, the bus pulled into a terminal and I caught my first glimpse of Valletta. It is a completely walled city built almost entirely of the local yellow stone, but on a promontory of land higher than its surroundings. We walked across a bridge spanning a very large ditch—in a climate with more water I would have assumed it had been a moat. We passed through a gate and found ourselves in a square surrounded by shops, billboards, and the inevitable hamburger chain outlet.

It was here that Anthony commenced his grand tour of the works of his ancestor, Gerolamo Cassar.

"Gerolamo Cassar was our greatest Maltese architect, architect to the famous Knights of Malta," he began. He looked at me carefully for some sign that I knew who he was talking about. I did, but barely. The Knights of Malta were, if memory served me, the Knights of St. John, the Knights Hospitaller, who had been driven from the Holy Land in the fifteenth century and had eventually settled in Malta. This was the extent of my knowledge, but I, fearing there might be a test later, nodded and attempted to look knowledgeable. Anthony, apparently satisfied, continued. "It was Cassar who built this city. He was originally assistant to Francesco Laparelli, an Italian who had worked with Michelangelo and who was the architect of the Pope and the de Medici family in Italy.

"The Pope sent Laparelli here in 1566 to help the Knights build a new capital city after the terrible destruction of the island during the great siege of Malta by the Turks. Laparelli is said to have done a master plan for the city in only three days. After two years Laparelli left, and the work of building the city, and of designing its greatest buildings, was left to Cassar. Cassar first leveled the ridge on which we are standing to make a place for a great city, and then supervised the building of the fortification walls," Anthony said, gesturing to the city walls behind us. "He built the church across from us, the Church of St. Catherine of Italy."

With that introduction, we turned to the right and walked along to a large building with a green door flanked by two cannons and a uniformed guard at the entrance. The exterior was very ornately carved, and it had rows of large uniformly spaced windows and large cornerstones.

"This building houses the offices of the Prime Minister. It is one of the buildings Cassar designed, but it was remodeled later by another Maltese architect, Andrea Belli. Cassar believed that as this was a fortified city, the buildings in it should reflect that—dignified, with no embellishments like columns and carvings. Belli added the more ornate, baroque details— Mr. Galea said that Belli 'tarted it up'—but the design of the building is still Cassar's.''

As informative as this all was, I found myself working hard to suppress a smile. Anthony sounded as if he was making a well-rehearsed speech, a school presentation perhaps, every word chosen carefully for its effect, and memorized. His mother had said that Martin Galea had been a major influence on Anthony, and I could almost hear Galea's inflection, slightly tinged with pomposity, in Anthony's speech. Galea had shown Anthony around Valletta, I was quite sure, and I could almost imagine the two of them, Anthony hanging on every word, Galea basking in the young man's admiration. I hoped, for Sophia's sake, that a love of architecture and an affectation of speech were the only things about Galea that Anthony, immature in many ways it seemed to me, chose to emulate.

Anthony appeared to be looking to me for some comment, so in as serious a tone as I could muster, I told him that the building was handsome, tarted up or not, and he seemed pleased. After I had had a few minutes to admire it at some length, Anthony turned to retrace his steps.

''Let's take her to the Gardens,'' Sophia said. ''They're beautiful.''

Anthony did not wish us to be deterred from the Cassar tour. ''Later,'' he said.

But Sophia insisted. I could see she had a stubborn streak beneath the shyness. And she was right. The Gardens, the Upper Barrakka Gardens to be precise, were in themselves quite lovely, filled as they are with trees, shrubs, flowers, and sculpture. What made them special, however, was a spectacular view of Malta's famed Grand Harbour, surrounded by defensive walls, guarded at the entrance by what Sophia told me was the seventeenth-century Fort Ricasoli and further along

Fort Saint Angelo. The vantage point from the Gardens gave me an appreciation for the choice of site so long ago, a fortified city surrounded on three sides by water, with a huge natural harbor for shipping and for protection as well.

Continuing on with the tour, we doubled back and turned up a street that ran parallel to the main street where Anthony pointed out another building, the General Post Office, also a Cassar design, of course. As I stepped back to admire a particular feature of the building that Anthony was pointing out, I inadvertently stepped on someone's toe. I turned to apologize profusely, and found myself face-to-face with the strange fellow from the Air Malta flight the day before—he of the khaki safari gear, my Great White Hunter.

He did not appear to recognize me, which was fine with me, and after suitable expressions of regret on my part, and forgiveness on his, we parted company and the Cassar/Farrugia tour continued on. From the Post Office we went back to the main street via a little road called Melita Street. Republic Street, as the main street was called, was clearly the main shopping thoroughfare of the city, filled with shops and boutiques tucked into the fronts of some very old buildings, and we turned right, or away from the city gate, onto it.

A block or so further on, Anthony stopped to point out the National Museum of Archaeology. "Built by Cassar," he said. Then added in a more boyish aside, "It's now filled with pots and fat ladies."

Sophia glared at him, and he put an arm around her waist and gave her an affectionate squeeze. "Soph is studying really early history, not Cassar's architecture," he said. "She's interested in archaeology and spends a lot of time here. The fat ladies are statues that have been found in ancient sites around the island."

"I'm interested in archaeology too, Sophia," I said, "so you must tell me something about that later." She blushed but nodded and we moved on. Coming up the street behind us I saw the Great White Hunter again. I think he saw me too, but he gave no indication. In fact, he ducked rather quickly into the doorway of a shop.

A few yards further on we came upon a large church. Like the other Cassar projects, this one was of a very severe design, almost ponderous, but it had a certain solemnity to it I could appreciate. There was a little market set up in front of the church, and Sophia and I hesitated for a moment, both of us no doubt feeling the urge to shop, but Anthony, ignoring it, pressed on to the steps of the church. "This is one of Cassar's greatest projects, St. John's Co-Cathedral," he said. "It is not the first church in the city, but it is the largest and the most impressive. It's called a co-cathedral," he said with some pride, "because Malta, unlike most other countries, has two official Cathedrals. Unfortunately, the inside has been completely redone in the baroque style and is not Cassar's work," he said severely.

"Can we look inside anyway?" I asked. As charmed as I might be by Anthony's obvious enthusiasm for the accomplishments of his illustrious forebear, I wanted to see more of Valletta than this. "It would prove an interesting comparison, I'm sure, and would help to emphasize the finer points of Cassar's work," I ventured.

He looked somewhat mollified. "Okay, let's go in," he said. Sophia gave me a sunny smile that indicated she could see through my subterfuge but was quite prepared to go along with it.

The interior of the cathedral bears no resemblance to the austerity of the exterior whatsoever. It is in fact staggering in its ornamentation, almost every surface, every inch of the place, covered with arabesque carvings and gilt. The high altar is marble, silver, and lapis lazuli, the vaulted ceiling is covered in paintings, and the floor is emblazoned with elaborate marble tombstones. Both sides of the cathedral are lined with chapels; I counted eight or nine of them, linked by narrow little corridors.

As I wandered about, I saw in front of one of the prettiest

chapels which was enclosed with a silver gate, the man in the safari suit. He did not hear me approach, intent as he was on inspecting the interior of the chapel through the gate.

Not wishing to engage him in conversation again, I made to quietly move on past him, but the toe of my shoe caught in a raised stone in the floor and I stumbled. He turned quickly around and saw me. I assumed that he would think me a complete klutz what with my first stepping on his toe, and now stumbling around behind him, so I tried a wan smile. He tried to look as if he had not noticed me, a studied nonchalance I found amusing, and we both moved on. Obviously he was no more eager to talk to me than I was to him.

When I'd finished my quick tour of the cathedral, resolving to return when I'd have more time, I found Anthony and Sophia sitting in a pew near the back of the church, and we left together. We moved a little further along the main street and came to a pleasant square filled with tables and umbrellas and presided over by a large statue of Queen Victoria. On one side of this square was another large impressive building of a rather stolid nature that I was beginning to recognize. "Cassar?" I asked, pointing.

Anthony beamed. "You recognized it! It's the House of Representatives," he added.

I noticed Sophia looking longingly at a tray of sweets at one of the cafes on the square. "Can I treat to coffee and a sweet?" I asked. "In appreciation of a great tour?"

"We'll come back here," Anthony said. "There's one more building I want to show you," he said, gesturing further down the street. "The Mediterranean Conference Centre."

I was not paying much attention to Anthony at this point, partly because jet lag had set in once again, but also because I was mesmerized by the now familiar khaki hat bobbing among the Sunday crowds, heading in the direction Anthony had pointed. When I turned my attention back to the two of them, Sophia, sensing my fatigue, gave Anthony a warning nudge.

"Actually," he said, catching on, "a coffee would be great!" Despite my intentions, I turned back to where I had last caught sight of the hat, but it was nowhere to be seen.

As we selected a table in the square beside the House of Representatives, and I had a chance to sit down and really look around me, I began to forget the occasionally tacky shops and the advertising billboards, and to see Valletta as I think Anthony did, as a beautiful city of plazas, palaces, and churches laid out on an elegant grid. I could see that the plan and the style of Anthony's hero, the great Gerolamo Cassar, had been a pervasive influence; indeed, he had set the tone for the city and influenced its structure over the centuries since he had first envisioned and built it. It really was a magnificent achievement, and I was pleased for Anthony, for some inexplicable reason.

We ordered coffees and I, hungry for lunch, bought a couple of little pastry pies called *pastizzi*, filled with cheese and peas and onions. Both Anthony and Sophia ordered sweets, he a cheesecake of sorts, she something called a treacle tart. I, as the tourist and host, got to try everything, but found my new young friends' sweet tooth far exceeded mine.

While we were eating, I mentioned that I would like a good guidebook on the islands so I could see as much as possible in the time I was there. Anthony leapt up as soon as he was finished and said he knew exactly the guide I needed, and that he would get me one immediately. I insisted on giving him some money despite his protestations, and off he went.

Sophia and I sat enjoying the sunshine but saying little. She was very shy.

"I expect the guidebook will have a section on Gerolamo Cassar," I said as an opening conversational gambit.

She giggled. "I think you may be right. A long section, probably."

"He's a very nice young man," I said, sounding to my own ears, at least, like a doting auntie or something. Nothing like being with a couple of teenagers in love to make you feel old and tired.

"He is, isn't he?" she glowed. "Even if he does go on about Cassar."

"It's difficult to be an architect, you know," I said, continuing on in my aged auntie mode. "It takes years of study and dedication. Lots of people never qualify. And then it's hard to get commissions, to get started. And it must be very difficult to put so much of yourself into a design and then have people criticize it. I think you have to be pretty committed and focused."

She nodded. "I think he'll do it," she said.

"Are you married?" she asked in a moment or so, glancing at my ringless hands.

"Not anymore," I said.

"Have a boyfriend?"

I thought to explain to her that at her age you had boyfriends; at mine you had the chronic problem of coming up with a suitable description for the man, like partner, or significant other, or whatever. But I restrained myself.

"Yes," I said. "His name is Lucas, and he's an archaeologist."

"Oh!" she exclaimed. "Then you really are interested in archaeology!" I nodded.

"I'm studying history. You know they don't teach us much of anything in school about our own history, just everybody else's," she said, glancing over her shoulder at the statue of Queen Victoria in the square.

"I have this great new teacher. She's here from England, on a sabbatical, but she knows more about the history of Malta than anyone I've ever met. She's teaching us about the ancient archaeological sites—she says they are among the oldest and most important in the Mediterranean. I've been going to see them since I was a little girl and I had no idea! I can hardly believe what she's teaching us. We're even doing a play about Malta's history right from ancient times. The teacher calls it a tableau, or something. I have a small part in it.'' She smiled shyly.

"I think it sounds wonderful!"

"Do you, honestly?"

"I do, yes."

"She's giving a public lecture Tuesday night at the University. I really want to go, but I'm not allowed to go by myself. I can't ask my parents. The teacher talks about ancient gods and goddesses, and my parents would think that's heretical. Anthony says maybe he'll come, but I know he's not really interested in anything except architecture, and anyway he has to study every night if he's to get into the Academy next year. I don't suppose . . ."

"I'd love to come," I said. And why not? I thought. By that time the painting and electrical work at the house would be done and the furniture would be there, or at least on its way. A couple of hours off would be fine. "Just tell me where and when," I said.

Just then Anthony returned with the guidebook, and immediately showed me the section on Cassar. Sophia gave me a conspiratorial grin. Anthony, on learning that I planned to attend the lecture, suddenly announced that he too would attend. I told them I'd meet them there, and Anthony spread out the map that came with the guidebook and began to give me directions. He also pointed out other sights of interest, all designed by Cassar, of course, including something called Verdala Palace, not too far from the house.

Then we sat companionably together watching as the late afternoon sun began to turn the yellow stones of the buildings around us to gold.

As we did so, I got that feeling we all get occasionally, the feeling that we are being watched. I don't know why or how we know. Perhaps it's some vestigial remnant of an ability inherited from our earliest ancestors who lived in more dangerous times. But I think we are almost always right when we get this feeling. I scanned the crowd, and caught a glimpse of a now familiar figure near a column in the shade of the arcade that runs down one side of the square.

"This island sure is a small place," I said to my companions, trying to hide my unease as I pointed my fellow tourist out to them.

"Neat outfit!" Anthony said admiringly. Sophia rolled her eyes.

As we turned our attention to him, the Great White Hunter drew back quickly and vanished into the darkness of the arcade.

"Skittish too," Anthony said.

"Creepy," Sophia demurred.

I agreed with her. I also think that in addition to knowing when we're being watched, we sometimes have a sixth sense when a stranger wishes us ill. I had that feeling now.

I shook off my apprehension, however, as the sun and the beauty of the surroundings soaked in, and was actually reluctant to leave the square when the three of us headed back. The house looked much the same as it had when I left. Except for a dead cat, strung up and swinging from the branch of a little tree in the backyard.

❧ FOUR

FROM TYRE AND SIDON THEY come, the seafarers, children of Melqart, puissant protector of Phoenician sailors. Neither chart nor compass guides them, sights set on distant lands. Is it My temples, long abandoned, that beckon you from the safety of North African shores? Traders, craftsmen, keepers of the color purple, leave us alone. But leave your language, your alphabet, when you go.

IT TOOK ALL THE COURAGE I could muster to stay in the house that night, but I managed it. Indeed, by the next morning, I'd persuaded myself that the dead cat incident, as it became known in my mind, was a childish prank of some sort. An exceptionally cruel one, but a prank nonetheless.

Anthony had cut the cat down, as Sophia and I clutched each other, and we found a little patch of ground to bury it in. They'd stayed with me a while, but then Sophia had to get home, so I found myself alone. I spent the evening checking the doors and windows, peering out into the darkness, but most of all thinking about The Deez, my shop cat, whom I loved even though he was a rather standoffish little beast. In the end, mercifully, I slept.

The next day, though, there was an even nastier surprise in store for me.

Anthony had obviously told Marissa and Joseph about our problem with the car, because as soon as they and two workmen arrived on Monday morning, the men began to inspect the vehicle. Despite my protestations—the car could sit in the driveway forever, as far as I was concerned—it was decided that before work on the house could begin, the car would have to be repaired. After much gesticulating, sounds of annoyance, and shrugging of shoulders, one of the men, Eddie by name, headed off somewhere in Joseph's car.

"Have you found what's wrong?" I asked, hoping for an affirmative and a diagnosis that would not take long to fix.

"Part missing probably," Joseph replied. "If Eddie moves fast enough, he may get it back. For a price, of course."

I looked from Joseph to Marissa. "I'm not following this conversation," I said.

Marissa smiled at me. "We have a lot of old cars here. People grow very attached to them. Parts are scarce; sometimes they aren't even manufactured anymore. So they get stolen fairly regularly if you're not careful. We thought the place was far enough off the beaten track that it wouldn't be a problem. But I guess we were wrong.

"There are body shops around that miraculously always seem to have parts. Everyone knows who they are. So Eddie will visit a couple of them and get the part. It could even be the one we lost." She smiled wryly.

"Isn't that theft, or extortion, or something?"

"Probably. Here we call it the way things go. Joseph will clear some of the construction materials out of the garage so you can lock the car in at night."

"You know, the first night I was here I thought I saw someone out by the edge of the cliff. Someone wearing a hood. Perhaps he's our thief!"

"Did you now?" Joseph said. "Strange things go on here from time to time," he added. Marissa's usual sunny smile faded somewhat, but neither said anything more.

Eddie returned about a half hour later with a mechanic, and the two of them got to work. At first Eddie was very talkative: he told me that while he was at the body shop he'd also checked for a part that would fix the transmission, which is to say, give it a second gear. He'd had no luck. Someone had beaten him to one by *minutes*, he told me.

But suddenly there seemed to be a chill in the air, metaphorically speaking, and both Eddie and the mechanic grew silent. Soon there was a whispered consultation with Joseph, who in turn whispered to Marissa, who looked really upset. Joseph started clearing his tools and construction materials out of the garage, and Eddie headed out again, returning this time with a huge padlock which he went about installing on the garage door.

All of this was making me nervous, and by extension, annoyed. "We need to talk, Marissa," I said to her. "I want to know what is going on around here!"

"Let me talk to Joseph," was the reply. The two of them held another whispered conversation, Joseph finally nodded, and Marissa came back to me.

"The problem with the car was a bit more serious than we thought," she began.

"More serious than a stolen part?"

"A bit worse than that," she replied carefully. I waited.

"It's not so much a part missing. The mechanic said nothing was missing, actually. Some minor problem with the carburetor," she said. "It's just there was also a broken line, or something."

I watched her face carefully. She was frightened, I could tell.

"To the brakes," she said finally. "You . . . we were all lucky the car wouldn't start," she said. "I'm sure it's just because the car is so old," she went on. "But the mechanic says there is a possibility that the line didn't break, that it was cut."

I just looked at her. "It's fixed now, of course," she said, then burst into tears.

Anyone with any sense would have moved out of the house after this, I know, and I've often asked myself since why I stayed. It was partly my capacity for self-delusion, which is as strong as anyone's. I, like Marissa, preferred to believe the brakes were just old, not tampered with. In addition, I just decided, I think, that these horrible events were not directed at me. Furthermore, I had a job to do, and I didn't like the idea of telling Martin Galea his house wasn't ready for his important entertaining. Somehow I didn't think he'd find a dead cat and what was probably just an accident with the brakes a good excuse for not getting the house finished.

In any event, the job of getting the house ready took up more and more of my time and energy. I'd assumed, more than a little optimistically as it turned out, that by the time Sophia's lecture rolled around, the house would be shipshape and the furniture winging its way to me.

Instead, after the incident with the car, I put in a rather exasperating and anxiety-ridden couple of days as our work on the house not only did not progress as quickly as it should, but we actually seemed to be losing ground. Galea had said he'd arrive Friday or Saturday to inspect the place, and we were far from ready. I was getting worried.

The electrician, for example, was supposed to arrive Monday morning. However, he and most of the other tradespeople I encountered ascribed to a casual philosophy I'd call a Mediterranean version of mañana, and it was late Monday afternoon before he got there. Then what had seemed like a simple matter of installing a few ceiling fixtures had turned into a major wiring problem requiring several holes in the ceiling and walls to put right.

Next we ran out of the glaze for the stucco and had to match it. A good designer, for example my ex-husband on one of the rare days when he was actually prepared to work, would have matched it in a minute or two. Joseph, Marissa, and I took considerably longer, and in the end we agreed we'd have to redo one whole wall to get it right.

Even this would have been manageable. The really big problem was the shipment from home, and my early optimism that meeting Galea's deadline would be reasonably easy was fast beginning to fade.

A massive winter storm had blanketed much of the Great Lakes region and was now moving on to the eastern seaboard of the U.S. and Canada. Nearly twenty inches of snow had dumped on the Toronto area; temperatures had plummeted to way, way below zero; schools and offices were closed, as was the airport.

"We're completely socked in," Alex told me. I was in almost constant touch with him and with Dave Thomson as my anxiety levels headed for the stratosphere.

"Dave sent a truck out from his warehouse at the airport to pick up the furniture here and at Galea's place on Saturday afternoon. He'd found an Air Canada cargo flight headed for Heathrow that night that had room for the shipment. But it was so cold the truck blew a tire on the highway.

"Dave tried to find another truck but couldn't, then . . . Well, anyway, they never got here or to Galea's house and we missed that flight. Then the storm moved in. The airport authorities estimate they'll be back in business by tonight, so we'll try and find a flight then. Dave says don't panic yet!"

"Yet!" I grumped. But there was nothing I could do.

By late Monday night, Malta time, the situation didn't look any better. The airport might be reopening, but the flights were backed up and Dave was having trouble finding space for such a large shipment at such short notice. Furthermore, a pipe had burst in his warehouse out near the airport, and he hadn't been able to bring the two shipments there to pack them.

"I could probably get the stuff to Paris tonight," he said. "But I'm told there's going to be a countrywide transportation strike in France as early as tomorrow, and they're saying it may last several days. I don't want to risk getting the stuff there and then not being able to get it out again."

I knew he was telling the truth. I'd read the Paris papers on the way over and they'd said as much.

"So I'm working on something to Italy. Both Air Malta and

Alitalia fly to Malta from Rome. Hang in, Lara,'' he told me. ''I'll get it there somehow. As soon as I know which flight we've got, I'll get all the stuff picked up and packed in a container, and deliver it direct to the plane. I've already contacted a customs broker at the airport in Malta, and he's standing by to clear it through in a hurry and transport it to the house. You be ready to move fast. Mrs. Galea is being very nice about this, by the way.'' Then he added, ''But I haven't talked to the Great One himself yet. Can't say I'm looking forward to that conversation!''

By late Tuesday afternoon I was truly despairing of ever meeting my commitment to Galea. There was nothing more I could do that day, however, except worry, and I didn't want to disappoint Sophia, so I decided to go to the lecture and to try to forget all the aggravations of the past couple of days, for an hour or so, at least.

But there was the small matter of making my way to the University on time.

Marissa had given me rather complicated directions for taking the bus into the terminal and then another one out again. The bus route network in Malta seemed to operate on a hub and spoke model, with all routes radiating out from the Valletta terminal. This meant it was not possible to take one bus from the house to the University. On top of that the lecture was in the evening, and Marissa had told me the last bus service was about ten. I decided to drive. The car had been locked in the garage ever since it had been repaired, and I checked the padlock carefully to reassure myself it would be safe to use the car.

I knew from Marissa's instructions that the University was at the intersection of the regional road to Mellieha and the road to Balzan. When I consulted the map she had given me, it seemed to be almost due north of the house. The island was only eight or nine miles wide, and I prided myself on my sense of direction. I also prided myself on my ability to drive almost anywhere. My buying trips had taken me all over the world, and I'd found myself in pretty obscure places. I'd driven on the left and the right. Why, I'd even driven in Rome. And I was used to almost any kind of vehicle. I once rode a donkey up a steep slope to get to a village that had particularly lovely weavings. How difficult could this be?

As the saying goes, pride goeth before a fall.

I mapped out a route that took me to a place called Siggiewi, then Zebbug, to Attard, then Balzan, then on to the University. But I ended up on the road to someplace called Rabat. Cars roared past me on both the passing lane and on the inside shoulder; I dodged donkey carts and potholes the size of craters on the moon; I passed through towns that reminded me of illustrations in my childhood book of Bible stories; I whizzed around roundabouts; and I got totally, utterly, irretrievably lost.

I also learned that second gear is a really important feature in a car. Without it I either had to go very slowly, or speed along in third. Stalling was only a hairsbreadth away at any given time. I listened enviously to the sound of more fortunate drivers gearing smoothly up or down. I became obsessed with not slowing down.

Finally I got on a relatively well-kept road that unfortunately headed in the wrong direction, toward the aforementioned Rabat and something called Verdala Palace, which if I remembered Anthony's lecture was built by his idol, Gerolamo Cassar. That meant, at least I thought it did, that I was headed west, not north, but my innate sense of direction had totally deserted me so I couldn't be sure. I could only hope it would lead to something headed north, or at least a place name I recognized.

As I moved along this road, I overtook a car moving relatively slowly. There was an approaching truck, but it was still quite far away, and rather than slow down, I decided to go for it and pass the other vehicle. I floored it, roared past, then pulled quickly in front of the other car, in a way that, if I'm being honest, I would have to consider rather rude, if not a bit reckless.

I glanced guiltily at the driver as I passed the car. He was looking at me too. We were both surprised to see each other. It was the Great White Hunter yet again, and he was not pleased to see me.

Normally I think I would have found this a funny coincidence, but now, with the business with the brakes, there was an edge of menace to it, not the least because of what happened next. When the oncoming truck passed us, he geared down, then passed me much too closely, pulling in so tightly that I had to slam on the brakes, which mercifully worked in a manner of speaking. The car started to skid, and for a few seconds I thought I'd lost control of it, but I was able to pull over to the side of the road, where I sat for a few minutes listening intently to my heart pound. The Great White Hunter I couldn't see for dust.

It took me a few minutes to stop shaking. I kept telling myself I sort of deserved it, what with my rush past him. But to be forced off the road? I could hardly believe what had happened.

While I sat there, a man on an aged bicycle pedaled by, and I flagged him down. He was a pleasant person who gave me new directions, briefly explaining the intricacies of navigating around Malta: which is to say, road signs, where they exist, are only relative. One gets a general sense of the direction one is going, then sticks to it, ignoring signs for towns and sites along the way.

It was good advice and I managed to find the University, then most fortuitously a place to park. I got out, pulled up the window on the passenger side which had done its trick of falling down into the door at the first roundabout I encountered, then eyed the car. I sincerely hoped I would not return to find it minus several critical body parts. A young boy offered to watch the car for me—such a nice car, he said—for a small fee of course. I paid him on the spot, walked into the hall, flinging myself—there is no other word to describe my hasty and inelegant entrance—into the seat that Sophia and Anthony had saved for me just as the speaker mounted the platform and moved to the podium.

"Who will speak for the Goddess?" she began, a tall, big-boned woman with wispy, greying hair, owlish glasses, a less than stylish print dress, and what my mother would call sensible shoes. Not that my mother would be caught dead wearing sensible shoes herself, mind you.

The lights in the hall dimmed, then were extinguished, a single reading lamp on the podium the only light in the room, casting eerie shadows on the wall behind the speaker as she spoke.

"Who will speak for the Goddess? Try now, if you can, to set aside the kind of world we know today, and imagine yourself living in the world of six thousand years ago. To do so, you must leave behind you all those technological wonders we take for granted. Lights, cars, running water, telephones, television, computers. You must also forget all you know about the world around us: what causes the rain to fall, lightning to strike, the wind to howl, a bright orb to rise in the sky and then disappear into darkness, plants to grow, and most especially, for a child to be born and for people to die.

"Imagine yourself a fisherman, perhaps, or a sailor, setting out from your shelter in a cave or a mud-brick hut on the island we now call Sicily, to cast your nets on the sea, or ply your trade along the coast.

"As your small craft nears these islands, you catch your breath in amazement and perhaps in fear. For rising from this rocky terrain you see huge structures that you can scarcely believe are made by human hands, bigger and higher than anything you have seen before, maybe thirty feet or more in height, towering from the cliffs above you.

"You may wonder who built them, or even how they were constructed. But you do not ask yourself what they are used for, or to whom they are dedicated. Because when you and

your ancestors before you try to explain the unexplainable, when you turn to a deity for succor, inspiration, or an explanation of the mysteries of nature around you, the god you turn to is female. She is the Great Goddess, giver of life, wielder of death, and for at least twenty-five thousand years and arguably much, much longer, She has provided the focus for human existence.''

The speaker's name was Anna Stanhope, Dr. Anna Stanhope, Sophia and Anthony had told me. Principal of a posh English girls' school, she had taken a sabbatical to come to Malta to study the Neolithic Age on the islands. While here, she had taken it upon herself to enlighten Maltese students as to their own history, and had taken a part-time teaching assignment at the school Sophia attended. As she spoke, I sat in the darkness and tried to concentrate on her words.

But it was difficult work trying to keep my mind off the unsettling journey I'd taken to get here. Try as I might, I could not keep from thinking about the incident with the Great White Hunter, a man I'd regarded as something of a buffoon when I first laid eyes on him on the plane. Now his ridiculous outfit and pretensions of grandeur had taken on a more sinister cast. Could it have been he who killed the cat and tampered with the brakes? Did he know where I was staying? Had he followed me home from the airport? That seemed a ridiculous idea, and anyway, he'd been in no shape to do much of anything, and he'd been delayed in customs.

Furthermore, it couldn't have been he who killed the cat. I'd seen him several times in Valletta, and I didn't think he'd have had time to get to the house ahead of us. Did that mean he had an accomplice? The hooded man at the back of the yard?

The more I thought about it, the more difficult it was to assume that it was a coincidence that our paths had crossed so often. Could I recall seeing anyone else from the airplane since we'd landed? GWH's original seatmate, his ''lovely lady,'' for example? The priest? My own seatmate, an executive with Renault, I think he'd said. No, not one of them. Only the Great White Hunter. Why? I told myself to stop thinking about it. I was driving myself crazy.

"Twenty-five thousand years! Since the end of the last great Ice Age! Not one of the great religions of today can claim a fraction of that! From the steppes of Russia, through the caves of France, all through what we now call Europe and beyond, humankind worshipped the Goddess. How do we know? For one reason, for every phallic symbol or male statue we find in these times, we find many, many more triangles or female statues. All over the ancient world, people buried their dead with tiny statues of the Goddess, they dyed the bones with ochre, the color of blood, symbol of life and of the Great Goddess.

"It is here in Malta that Her worship reached its peak, its most creative expression. Here the Goddess became the presiding deity of every aspect of life. At least forty temples, the oldest freestanding structures in the world, older than the Great Pyramid of Egypt, older than Stonehenge, were built to honor Her. Hagar Qim, Gigantija, Tarxien, names you know well.

"The tools that built these massive structures have been found. Remnants of the huts and cave dwellings of the workers and worshippers have been uncovered. What we do not find from that time period is archaeological evidence of weapons. What does this mean? Quite simply that these people lived in peace with their neighbors, in harmony with nature, secure in the workings of the universe. That they knew their place, part of the cycle of birth, death, and rebirth. That they understood the interrelationship of all things. That they saw life and all things of it as a circle, not a line.

"But even as She flourished here, Her worship was under threat elsewhere. . . ."

Maybe he was following me. Maybe right this minute, as I sat in the darkness, he was watching me, or outside watching my car, I thought. Or perhaps he was back at the house doing something even more awful than before. Try to get a grip, I told myself. Your imagination is running away with you. Think this one through logically.

I tried to do that. Either it was a coincidence that our paths kept crossing, or it wasn't. Either way, there had to be some rational explanation, a missing piece of information that would make it all make sense.

"What happened to the Goddess? Where did She go? Around about the fifth millennium B.C.E., a new group of people moved into the area which later became known as Europe. These people, some historians have called them Kurgans, brought a different belief system, a different religion. They worshipped what have come to be called sky gods, gods not of the Earth as the Goddess was, but rather deities, usually male and warlike, who ruled humankind from another place, a place without. Like Mount Olympus, for example, or the Elysian Fields, or more recently and perhaps closer to home, Heaven.

"Gradually these people, warlike like their gods, began to take over. In some cases, they lived in coexistence with the people of the Goddess, but by the time of the ascendancy of Greece, and even earlier, active attempts were made to stamp Her worship out, attempts that would ultimately be successful. Here in Malta, isolated in many ways from the rest of the Mediterranean world, the Goddess ruled supreme, omnipotent, long after Her worship had vanished elsewhere. Longer, but not forever. Suddenly, about 2500 B.C.E., the part of Malta's history that belongs to the temple builders abruptly and mysteriously ends."

Maybe, I thought, I needed to know more about the places where I had seen him, the places built by Gerolamo Cassar. I had the guidebook Anthony had chosen for me, and had already started reading it, in part because I thought he might quiz me later and I didn't want to appear to be a total ignoramus where his country was concerned, but also because I was beginning to find the history of this tiny island absolutely fascinating. If I could do some study on the places Anthony had taken me to, I might find a connection. At the very least, it should take my mind off the morbid thoughts I was having about the Great White Hunter and his intentions toward me. I resolved to do that.

"While we may not know exactly what happened to the Goddess here in Malta, we can find hints as to what happened elsewhere in the stories, the epic poems, the mythology of those times. Many say myths are born of fantasy, but I believe they often have an historical basis, and that a careful reading will give us clues to the political and religious events of the day.

"And many tell of the replacement and subjugation of the Great Goddess and those who worshipped Her by 'heroes' of invading peoples. By the time we reach the world of classical Greece, we have an active attempt to rewrite the story of the Goddess to justify the new order as defined by the Greeks, and to denigrate the old. In the stories of that time, we have numerous examples of the conquest of centers of Goddess worship. We find these in the stories of Zeus and other members of that quarrelsome pantheon of Gods of Mount Olympus.

"Zeus' rape of Europa, for example, probably tells us of an invasion of Crete, where the Goddess was worshipped for centuries. Think also of the story of Ariadne of Crete, whose name means holy or sacred, and who was probably an earth Goddess. She helped Theseus slay the dreaded Minotaur on his promise that he would carry her away with him. He did, but then he abandoned her on the island of Naxos. There are many stories of this kind—the beheading of Medusa by Perseus, Apollo's attempted rape of Daphne—all representing invading peoples' conquest and assimilation of centers of Goddess worship. The Goddess had been tamed.

"Oh, not gone entirely, of course. Tamed but not obliterated. She can be found, if you look for Her, but hidden, the dangerous other. In Greek mythology, She is demoted to mere demonhood: She is Charybdis, the bottomless whirlpool who *drags sailors to their deaths, and Scylla, the six-headed sea monster whose lower half rests in a cave and who springs up to snatch hapless passersby. On Gozo, Malta's sister isle, She is Calypso, the mesmerizing siren goddess who diverts Odysseus from his purpose for seven years. In the Old Testament She is Leviathan, and the serpent in the Garden of Eden. Still later She is the dragon slain by St. George. And in our own times, we find vestiges of the Goddess, much diminished, in the Virgin Mary.*

"What did we lose when we lost the Goddess? We lost our place in Nature, our sense of the sacred circle, of the Cosmic whole of existence. We underwent one of those major shifts of perception, a paradigm shift if you will, that came to govern how we saw everything. We began to see the universe in what has been called binary polarities, or opposites, and we thought one polarity better than the other. Like good and evil. Or male and female, from which came sexism. Black and white, from which came racism. We also moved from a belief in a relationship between all parts of creation to a belief that we were, like our gods in whose image we believed ourselves made, something apart from nature.

"From there it was a very small step to wanting to master Nature, and believing we could do so. Master? Perhaps conquer is a better word for it. And if Nature could be conquered, so could other people.

"And from there it was only a tiny step to Hiroshima."

She paused. *"Who will speak for the Goddess?"*

For several seconds after Dr. Stanhope stopped speaking, you could have heard the proverbial pin drop. Then she turned and abruptly left the stage. Pandemonium erupted. I looked over at my young charges. Sophia's eyes were shining. Anthony looked thoughtful, his usual cheerful face altered by a somewhat puzzled frown. Everyone spoke at once. Some applauded, others left, offended, still others shouted outrage. Regardless of whether you agreed with her or not, Dr. Stanhope had made an impression.

The three of us made our way out of the noisy crowd and over to the car. The young boy was still there, smiling happily, and the car looked fine. That was one problem taken care of, but there was another.

"I got lost," I said to Anthony.

"Yes," he said. "Everyone new here does."

"Can you direct me back?"

"Sure. How about we take Sophia home, and then go on to my place? Mr. Galea's house isn't far from there, and it's easy to describe the route."

"Thanks. Would you like to drive as far as your house?"

"Sure." He grinned.

So that is what we did, and I got home without incident. None of us had much to say on the way, all lost in our own thoughts. Sophia gave me a hug at her place. I could see a man, her father presumably, silhouetted in the window waiting for her. Then Anthony gave me very careful directions from his home, seeing me off with a cheery wave.

As I carefully checked that all the doors and windows were locked, I thought how friendly and accommodating all the Maltese I'd met had been. Indeed, the first exception might be Martin Galea when he found out I hadn't got the job done.

Then I thought about the foreigners I'd become acquainted with, in a manner of speaking. Dr. Anna Stanhope, who'd probably insulted half the population of Malta in the short space of an hour or two by implying their religion was responsible for most of the world's ills, including the atomic bomb. To say nothing of her opinion of the Blessed Virgin Mary.

Next the Great White Hunter. He obviously didn't like me at all. Maybe even, I'd have to admit, he was trying to kill me. And for what reason I absolutely could not fathom. Surely not for stepping on his toe! Perhaps for some reason I did not understand, I was the Hunter's prey.

And then there was the unknown. What had Dr. Stanhope called it? The dangerous other. The hooded figure at the back of the yard. Was he just a car parts thief? Somehow I didn't think so.

All in all, I could only hope the Goddess was looking out for me.

FIVE

WHAT DO YOU THINK I am? A mere pawn in the battle for control of this sea called Mediterraneo? Your Hannibal, am I to admire his audacity in challenging Rome? Elephants in the Alps? Do you not hear it, the thump and groan of the Roman galley, the clang of the Roman legion? They are coming. Soon those among you who have ruled here, who have used My tiny island for your forays across the sea, you who have taken My people as slaves, will know what it is to be a slave. Go home. Your cities are in flames. Delenda est Carthago. *Carthage must be destroyed!*

JUST WHEN I THOUGHT NOTHING else could go wrong, Thursday Joseph went AWOL. Well, perhaps not exactly AWOL. Marissa probably knew where he was, but she wasn't saying. Her pale, tired face and slighty teary eyes when she told me her husband wouldn't be coming to work that day forestalled any questions I might have liked to ask.

To be fair, he'd seen to it there was lots of help. A handful of cousins stood by, ready to unload the furniture the minute it arrived. It wasn't the same, though. I missed his quiet and somehow solid demeanor and perpetual air of calm. I even missed hearing him call me missus, a practice he persisted in, despite his wife's having come to call me Lara with ease. Even Anthony did so when his parents, who would not have approved of such license, weren't around. Still, Joseph would have been a definite asset on this rather harried of days, the one when, at last, the furniture was due to arrive.

One would think that by this time I might have noticed that the alignment of whichever celestial bodies were responsible for the events in my life was hurtling me down a steep and slippery slope. At the time, though, I thought Joseph's disappearance merely another in a series of rather vexatious events, all part of the project at hand.

To my mind, every day brought its particular trial. The problem of the previous day, Wednesday, for example was water, or rather the lack thereof, as I discovered when I went to shower the morning after Dr. Stanhope's lecture. This brought Nicholas, the plumber. I was always surprised by the British-sounding names attached to people who were obviously Maltese, like Anthony for example, but I shouldn't have been. The last British barracks closed for good in 1979, and the British influence was still pretty pervasive.

Nicholas, a greying man with considerable paunch, insufficient teeth, and what I took to be a perpetually grave and worried air, tsked and clucked his way around the house until the source of the problem was found. This took two hours—and four holes in the walls.

"The paint is barely dry on the repairs to one disaster before it's time to mix some more," I whined to Marissa.

"Why don't you go and do some sight-seeing?" she replied. "We can look after this." I took this to mean I was fussing and getting in the way. Actually, with the exception of the adventure of Tuesday evening, the days were beginning to be remarkably the same. Every morning I'd survey the progress and discover the next disaster. Repairmen would be summoned, and I'd spend the rest of the day and well into the evening literally watching paint dry. And listening to the one decent tape I'd been able to find to play on the antiquated tape player—the workmen preferring late seventies disco music—a collection of Italian arias sung by a Maltese soprano, Miriam Gauci. Fortunately it was a wonderful tape.

There was my research, of course, on the Great White Hunter, a project I began as soon as I got back to the house after Dr. Stanhope's lecture, stimulated by the fear of another encounter with that dreadful man. I sat on the edge of the bed with the guidebook and a map spread out, and tried to figure out if in fact it was mere coincidence that I kept running into him. One thing I learned very quickly: Malta had the most amazing history. Almost everyone seems to have come to Malta at some point. It might be more accurate to say everyone and everything because even animals escaping the Ice Age crossed over a land bridge that linked Malta to Europe and possibly to Africa, back in the mists of time. For a while it seemed to be impossible to find any connection between my peregrinations and those of GWH, other than the somehow unlikely assumption that he, like Anthony, was a fan of Gerolamo Cassar, but in the end it proved reasonably simple.

Anna Stanhope would probably have said that the most important age for Malta was that of the temple builders, and if longevity counts, she would be right. The temple builders may have been on Malta for as many as six hundred years, and after they left, just about everyone in the Mediterranean used the island for some purpose at some time. The Phoenicians used it as a base, as did the Carthaginians. Hamilcar, Hannibal's father, is said to have surrendered to the Romans there, for example. The Greeks were there, the Romans, even St. Paul, who is said to have been shipwrecked off Malta's coast.

But if one were to look for the most prominent influence on the island, in terms of its landscape, its customs and practices, arguably this title would belong to the Knights. And it was here that I began to see some consistency in the places I'd seen GWH.

The story of the Knights began, I learned, in about 1085 when a group of monks known as Hospitallers began to minister to Christians who required medical attention on pilgrimages to the Holy Land. It soon became evident, though, that what these pilgrims really needed was protection from the so-called Infidel, in other words the followers of Islam, much more so than medical attention. Thus the Knights of the Order of St. John of Jerusalem came into being, an order that offered care and service to those in need, backed up by knights prepared to do battle if need be.

Gradually the Ottoman Turks began to gain the ascendancy in the Holy Land and the Knights of St. John were driven out of Jerusalem by Saladin, then out of Acre, then Cyprus, at which point they got to Rhodes. Here they stayed a while, only to be driven out again, this time by Sulieman the Magnificent. Sulieman allowed them to leave Rhodes, but this time they had no fallback position. They had nowhere to go.

Charles V of Spain, at the time Holy Roman Emperor, had various lands in his possession for which he apparently felt no great need. The island of Malta was among them. At first the Knights were not interested—they thought the island disagreeable at best—but in the end, what choice did they have? Beggars can't be choosers. It was that or Tripoli, which was even worse, and they couldn't argue with the rent: one falcon a year for Charles, the real Maltese falcon. After seven years of negotiation, they agreed to go to Malta, and most of Christendom heaved a collective sigh of relief, homeless knights being an embarrassment to all. Henceforth the Order came to be associated with Malta, and they built the great cities and fortifications that are so much a part of Malta today.

What was relevant for my research of the day, however, was that while Anthony had emphasized the architecture and the current use of the buildings: the Post Office, the Prime Minister's residence, and so on, the original use of every one of these places we had gone, and everywhere I had seen GWH, lurking in that way he had, led back directly to the Knights: either the inns or auberges in which various orders of the Knights had lived, their cathedral, their hospital, and so on.

The question was: So what? It was all very interesting, but it didn't get me anywhere. GWH was as entitled as anyone to visit those places, and maybe he was just a student of that particular period of history. In the end my research was just about as rewarding as the rest of my evenings at the house.

After the repairs and the research, the daily phone call to Toronto to check on the furniture shipment was about as exciting as it got. Dave Thomson had been right about France. A national transportation strike had shut the country down. Toronto International was still experiencing delays because of the weather, and when I wasn't bored, I was in a state of high anxiety.

"Anthony told me about the lecture you went to last night. It sounded . . . interesting," Marissa said rather hesitantly after a particularly prolonged bout of complaining on my part. She probably thought she was taking her life in her hands to talk to me, my just having had a hissy fit on the subject of the water problem.

"Actually, it was," I said, cheering up slightly. "Whether you agree with Dr. Stanhope's point of view or not. I had no idea a little island like this one could sustain such a rich and fascinating heritage!"

"It does." She smiled. "One of the temple complexes the professor told you about isn't far from here—Hagar Qim and Mnajdra. They're very close by car."

"I'll bet!" I said, remembering my harried drive of the day before in crystal clear detail.

"Really!" she affirmed, then giggled. I guess Anthony had told her how lost I'd managed to get. I'd given him the edited version on the way home, omitting the part about the Great White Hunter. Tourists trying to find their way around this tiny island seemed to be a grand source of merriment for the locals.

"How far is it, exactly?" I asked.

"It's exactly a mile . . . or thereabouts," she said, not being quite as precise as I'd hoped. "You could actually walk if you wanted to."

I thought this a much less stressful mode of travel than the car from hell, so soon I headed out with Marissa's carefully drawn map in hand.

She was right. It was relatively easy. I just had to keep the sea on my right.

Walking is a wonderful way to see a new country and for a little while I was able to enjoy, indeed revel, in the sights and sounds and smells of a new place. It might have been the dead of winter at home, and an exceptionally harsh winter at that, but here it was already spring. There was warmth in the air and fields of poppies everywhere, bright flashes of brilliant color against the subdued pastel of the terrain.

Several times I stopped to look at tiny mauve and white flowers—I had no idea what they were—bravely clinging to existence in the thin and arid soil. I followed a rough path along the edge of the cliffs for a time, then turned inland to pick up a footpath that arched to the north and then angled back toward the water, passing just inland of the temple complex.

You could see the huge stones that formed the temple walls, megaliths indeed, their color bleached almost white in the bright sunlight, long before you reached the site. Maltese temples are circular in shape, made from huge limestone blocks, each weighing several tons, I should think. Some of the stones are covered with what look like pockmarks, put there by ancient craftsmen. The temples reminded me a little bit of the shape and grandeur of Stonehenge or some of the other stone circles you see in Northern Europe and Britain, but the Maltese temples are much older, and their design seemed more complex to my eye: circular chambers that lead into other circular chambers to form either a trefoil or a cinquefoil, three or five rounded chambers or apses leading off a central area. I knew from Dr. Stanhope's lecture of the previous evening that these temples are the oldest freestanding stone structures in the world, and the huge statues of the Goddess that once rested there, probably the first freestanding statues anywhere as well.

I recalled Dr. Stanhope had said these complexes were built

between about 3600 and 2500 B.C.E., by people who had neither copper nor bronze, and who used only blades made from
local stones or from flint mined in Pantelleria over 125 miles
away, an incredible feat when you thought about it. She had
also said the temples were designed in the shape of the Goddess Herself, although I had difficulty conceptualizing what
exactly that meant.

I wandered about the site for a while, marveling at the work-
manship, enjoying the shade provided by the massive stones.
An old woman also resting in the shade smiled at me and
gestured in the direction of a path that led toward the sea. I
followed her pointing finger and walked down a long stone
causeway to a second site nestled on a snug promontory on a
steep cliff well over a hundred yards above the sea. I took this
to be Mnajdra.

Walking through the portal flanked by large stones, I suddenly felt I was indeed in a sacred place. From time to time
we come to places which contain a special power for us.
Where each individual feels this power, this mystery, probably
says more about the person than the place. I consider myself
fortunate to have been touched by this feeling more than once,
not, as life would have it, in the monuments deemed spiritual
by our society, but instead in the ancient remains of past civ-
ilizations.

Mnajdra was such a place for me. I thought about the people
who built it, 11,000 of them at the height of the temple building phase Dr. Stanhope had spoken of; how they had chosen
this site, perhaps because it also spoke to them; how they had
eked out an existence on these rocky shores while seeking to
transcend their physical existence through the concrete expression of their spiritual longing in the carving and placement
of each of these stones.

I suddenly understood what Dr. Stanhope had meant about
entering the body of the Goddess each time you entered a
temple. Viewed from the sky above, I realized, a smaller
chamber at the top would be Her head, the rounded chamber

in the middle Her encircling arms, the much bigger chamber at the entrance Her large belly and thighs. The body of the Great Goddess of Malta, I knew, was large, like her Paleolithic forebears, a symbol of fecundity. Fat Ladies, Anthony had called them.

Outside again, I found a place with a breeze, overlooking the site and the sea, and sat, lost in my thoughts. More than anything else I thought about Lucas. His specialty was Mayan archaeology, of course, but he had a wonderful sense of exploration and delight in new experiences, and I thought how much he would have loved it here.

He would have known, without being told, how the temples were constructed, what kind of roof had covered them, and he would have had a theory about each and every component and artifact. I'd noticed a pitted stone monument at Hagar Qim— I'd assumed it to be an altar—on which was carved what could have been a spinal column but more likely was a plant of some kind growing out of a pot. Lucas would have told me all about tree cults, I'm sure, or about something similar from his part of the world. I could almost see him standing there, tall and slim against the sunlight, his long dark hair streaked with grey, dressed in black jeans and T-shirt as he almost always was. I could picture the way he'd look at me as he spoke, the shape of his arms as he pointed out the features of the sight.

I suddenly missed him so much, I could feel a constriction in my throat and a burning behind my eyes. I could only hope that halfway round the world at his archaeological site, he was thinking of me at that moment too.

These chains of memory were broken by the sounds, faint above the sound of the sea below the site, of giggling school-girls, Sophia among them, who soon hove into view on the causeway above me.

At the head of this delegation, in print shirtwaist dress and straw hat, was the redoubtable Dr. Anna Stanhope. Sophia saw me immediately and rushed to give me a hug, introducing me to five or six young girls with her, and then to Dr. Stanhope.

After a minute or two of polite chatter, Dr. Stanhope sent the girls into the temple, reminding them what to look for, and then sat down on a stone near me.

"Nice place you've found here," she said rather breathlessly, wiping her brow with a lace handkerchief, which she then delicately put down the front of her dress like a Victorian spinster. "Hot," she added.

"It is," I agreed. "But it's a wonderful place and I should thank you for bringing me here."

She looked surprised. "I attended your lecture last night," I explained.

"Did you? Did you like it? Set some of them back on their bottoms I daresay." She hooted.

I had to smile. "I believe you did," I agreed.

"I'm a feminist, you know. A placard-carrying, bra-burning, raving feminist. Came to it rather late, I'm afraid. But you know what they say. Better late than never. Or more likely, there's no fool like an old fool." She hooted again. She wasn't that old, actually. At close range she appeared to be in her mid-fifties.

"Explains a lot, though. Feminism, I mean. Why I never got the senior academic posts I wanted. Why I had to work so hard to get my papers published while my male colleagues, most of them louts, soared through academia.

"Best I could do was head mistress of a girls' school. But I'll get my revenge. Inculcating feminist values in hundreds of little British schoolgirls." Another laugh.

"What brought you to Malta?" I asked, changing the subject. I consider myself a feminist too, but there was an edge to this conversation that I didn't want to deal with.

"Sabbatical," she replied. "I've had a few in my day, of course. Never been able to get away before, though. Lived with my mum. I've been—what's that horrid expression?—primary caregiver, that's it. She died last year. I was sorry, of course. We'd been so close. But I felt . . . free I guess, for the first time. I'd heard my dad talk about Malta when I was a little girl. He died fifteen years ago. That's when I moved back in with my mum. He'd been stationed here during World War Two—terrible time they had here, nearly starved to death you know, the Maltese, until the British broke the blockade.

"Anyway, my subject is history. And this place has a fascinating one, not the least of which is its place as a center of Goddess worship. So here I am. How about you? Canadian, I expect. The accent."

"I am," I said. I told her about my project in Malta, and how I expected it to be completed in a few days, but that I might—the thought was forming as I spoke—stay on a few more days to look around. We talked in a desultory fashion for a while, the heat of the afternoon making us both a little languid, and then we sat in companionable silence enjoying the site.

As we did so, a man appeared on the causeway above us. With all this talk of feminism and Goddess worship, he seemed a little out of place, and indeed he was the first male I'd seen since the ticket taker at the entrance. The man was attractive, almost movie star good-looking actually, well dressed in a nicely designed lightweight suit, Italian cut I'd say, dark complexion and hair, and he wore those reflecting sunglasses. He reminded me a little of Martin Galea. As we sat, he slowly scanned the site, his gaze resting on Dr. Stanhope and me for only a second. That done, he took off his sunglasses for a moment and carefully polished them. Then he walked around the perimeter of the site and was temporarily lost from view.

"Time to get going," Dr. Stanhope said, hefting her large frame from the stone. "Come along, girls," she cried. It sounded like "gulls" to my North American ears. The giggling schoolgirls gathered round.

I walked back up the causeway with the little group, Sophia at my side. The girls had started at Mnajdra first, the reverse of my visit, so I said good-bye and started back to the entrance.

"I don't suppose you'd like to help me with a little project?" Anna Stanhope called after me as I turned to leave. "The gulls and I are putting on a little play for some visiting dignitaries in a few days. My stage crew of one broke his leg waterskiing, silly fool. Do you think you might give us a hand?"

"Say yes," Sophia mouthed at me.

"Yes," I said. "I'd like to." Sophia smiled her placid smile.

"Jolly good. Next rehearsal Saturday afternoon, three o'clock at the University. In the auditorium, same as last night."

"I'll be there," I said.

AS I LEAVE THE GODDESS'S sanctuary, I turn back for one last look. The sun is low in the sky.

I find myself the apex of a perfect triangle. I think if I raise my arms to shoulder height in front of me to form a sixty-degree angle with my body, with my left hand I point to Dr. Stanhope, with my right I point to the man. It is a pattern that will repeat itself.

For a few seconds, we are frozen in perfect symmetry, but then I turn to go and the triangle breaks apart. I see the man begin to walk toward Dr. Stanhope, but do not look again.

I feel a vague twinge of memory. Something about the eyes, when he took off his sunglasses for a moment. Or perhaps the way he walks. Was it recently I knew him, or a long, long time ago?

Somewhere in the brain, a command to retrieve data is sent. Billions of neurons spring into action; minute electrical impulses sprint through the mamillary body and round the hippocampus. Dendritic spines stretch out like tiny hands to meet each other; synapses crack across the voids.

The command is encoded low priority. I will not remember in time.

• • •

THE NEXT MORNING THE PHONE rang very early, long before dawn. I groped my way to it and heard what I thought was a honking Canada goose. It was, it turned out, Dave Thomson with a dreadful cold, calling me on his cellphone from what sounded like the end of the main runway at Toronto International.

"We did it!" he croaked. "It's on its way. Four hours start to finish. Warehouse is still a mess, so we picked up the stuff at the store in one truck and at the house with another. Packed it right on the frigging tarmac outside the hangar. Freezing cold, let me tell you. The wife says I'll catch pneumonia. But it's on its way. Skyliner Cargo. It'll be in Rome in less than seven hours. We've got an hour's turnaround. Everybody's standing by. It'll be on the two p.m. for Luqa. Let Azzopardi know for me, will you?" he said, naming his Maltese broker. "Docket 7139Q."

"Dave, you really are the best." I laughed. "I'm sticking with you for life."

"Another satisfied customer," he honked. Then, "By God, this was a squeaker. I'm going home to bed."

I knew I'd never get back to sleep, so I put on a pot of coffee and watched the early morning light. Most places are enchanting at this time, none more so than Malta, where the early morning light was as beautiful as I'd ever seen it. I was beginning to love the place, idiosyncracies and all.

Later as I waited for the workmen to arrive, sans Joseph, and had left a message for Mr. Azzopardi on his answering machine, I did my own house inspection. I tried the taps: the water came on, hot and cold. I tested the switches: every light worked. The walls were free of holes, the paint matched perfectly to my eye, the woven hanging looked wonderful in the living room. I checked the kitchen cupboards: glassware, flatware, and dishes all lined up in satisfying rows, ready to be called upon at any time.

And best of all, the furniture was on its way.

"We might just be all right here," I said to the empty rooms. "We might just be all right."

By 4:45 that afternoon I was in position at the door, clipboard in hand, as a phalanx of small trucks—Mr. Azzopardi must have commandeered every small truck on the island for the occasion—came along the road and up the driveway one at a time to unload. The cousins stood by ready to unload and install.

"Two carved mirrors. Upstairs hallway," I said.

"Teak dining table and six, seven . . . eight chairs. Dining area to the left.

"Wrought-iron and glass table, four chairs. Verandah at back.

"Antique etagere, second floor, far end."

And so it went. Until the very end when there appeared a large oak chest. The cousins stumbled with its weight.

"What's this?" I said. I checked the list again. "This is supposed to be a sideboard, not a chest."

I looked the piece of furniture over. The yellow sticker with my initials on it was plainly visible.

"They've sent the wrong piece!" I said in exasperation. "I don't believe this! What am I supposed to do with this?"

I wanted to kick it, valuable though it might be. Instead, I turned the key and flung the lid open with considerable force.

SOMEONE SCREAMS AND SCREAMS. IT is a voice I think I recognize. A tiny rational part of the brain sends a high priority message to seek a match and finds one. The voice belongs to me.

Martin Galea is dead. Very dead. Body stuffed awkwardly into the chest, a brown stain on the front of the impeccable silk shirt. Eyes staring toward eternity.

For a few seconds time stands still for me.

ARIADNE

❦ SIX

*R*OMA LOCUTA EST. *ROME HAS spoken. Benign, perhaps,
Pax Romana. But still, another imperial interloper on
My shores. You drink My wine, eat My honey. Your villas,
baths, and fortifications dominate My lands. Causa finita est,
you say? Case closed? No, not quite. You too will leave us.
Barbarians are soon at your gate. Pax Romana no more. Europe will sleep. I, Malta, My island, will sleep as I watch over
it.*

"COULD WE GO OVER THIS one more time, please, Miss
McClintoch?" Vincent Tabone asked. Detective Vincent Tabone of the Maltese police, I might add.

I nodded numbly.

"You came here to get the deceased's house ready for a
social event of some kind. One that was to be attended by
what you have referred to—forgive me, you have corrected
me on that point already—that the deceased had referred to
as important people. You don't know who these people are,
nor when the event is or was to be."

"That's right," I said, nodding again.

"You knew the deceased was coming to inspect your work
soon, but you didn't know exactly when he was due to arrive."

I nodded.

"Was that a yes?" he asked, looking up from his notebook. I nodded again.

"You were responsible for seeing the furniture was packed and shipped, then placed in the house, but you weren't sure until today when it would arrive."

I nodded again. I thought if this questioning kept up much longer, I'd be doing serious injury to my neck.

"There was a piece of furniture in the shipment that shouldn't have been there, and it just happened to contain the body of the deceased. It was marked with a yellow sticker with your initials in what you say is your handwriting, and you don't know how it got there?"

"Right again," I said.

"You've been staying in the house for . . . how long? . . . six days. The first night you were here you thought you saw someone at the end of the yard, but you don't know who, or even if there really was someone there. You also found a dead cat, and someone *may* have tampered with the brakes on the car, but you have no idea who or why?"

"Yes," I said. I could also have told him there was a man, dressed in a safari suit, who had tried to run me off the road because I'd stepped on his toe. But what would be the point?

He looked at me for a long time, then sighed loudly.

"Another day of joy, adventure, and achievement in the service of the Maltese people," he said.

"I beg your pardon?"

"Don't you have some expression for days which are not going well?"

"Sure. At the shop we say 'just another day in paradise.' Is that what you mean?"

"Exactly," he said. Amazingly, he smiled at me. Despite myself, I smiled back. It was the first friendly gesture that had come my way since I'd arrived at police headquarters in the town with the rather charming name of Floriana. Charm had been sadly lacking in its inhabitants, however, until I had met Detective Tabone. While the police may have been prepared to concede Martin Galea's right as a native-born Maltese to come home to die, they were not pleased with the foreigner who had had the bad taste to find his body.

For the first time since I had arrived there, I relaxed a little, and was able to look closely at him, trying to take the measure of the man. He was slim, tall by Maltese standards, with greying hair, an arresting, shall we say, moustache, and an air of fatigue about him, not so much from the lateness of the hour, I thought, as the chronic weariness of seeing too much of the seamier side of life.

"We don't get a lot of this kind of thing, you know. Oh, there's no question people kill each other from time to time. Domestic situations, usually. Find the culprit right away. And people like to throw bombs in doorways every now and then. Blood feuds of some kind, politics at the heart of it most of the time. But people don't normally get killed by the blast that often. We have more trouble with fireworks factories blowing up as a matter of fact. That seems to happen pretty regularly."

He tossed his pen and notebook onto the desk. "I expect it's the wife," he said. "It usually is. *Cherchez la femme*, you know."

"Marilyn Galea? I find that hard to believe. Too quiet, timid even."

"Ah, but it's often the quiet ones . . ." We both thought that one over for a minute or two, before he continued, "And you know what they say about women in Malta. That when St. Paul was shipwrecked here, he rid the island of poisonous snakes by transferring the venom to women's tongues!"

"No, I didn't know that," I said, in what I hoped were suitably acid tones. Perhaps, I thought, I should introduce this man to Anna Stanhope and watch her have a go at him.

Then, thinking how more than anything, I just wanted to go home, I said, "Is she coming over? To claim the body and make arrangements for . . . you know?"

"I expect she might, if we could find her to tell her. Gone missing, it seems. Hasn't been seen since sometime yesterday.

Cherchez la femme, as I said. Anyway, why don't we call it a day? It's nearly midnight, and there isn't much more we can do until we get the coroner's report. If we get the coroner's report, that is.'' He sighed loudly again.

I wondered what that meant. I didn't want to ask.

"You wouldn't be thinking of leaving Malta in the next day or two, would you? No? Then I'll get someone to drive you back to the house. I think it'll be good to have you staying there. Who knows, maybe the mystery guests will show up, one of them with a sign saying 'I'm the murderer.' Or someone who confesses to killing Galea because he wasn't considered important enough to be invited to the party. You never know!'' As he spoke, he watched my face, and evidently thought better of his attempts at humor. "I'll get someone to watch the house at night, if it would make you feel better,'' he offered. I told him it would.

AFTER CHECKING EVERY DOOR AND window in the place, and peering intently into the backyard to see if the hooded creature was there, I sat in the dark in the living room of Martin Galea's nearly perfect house, and thought about the day. Had it not been for the fact that this was all the result of a murder, it would have seemed rather funny, in a Monty Python kind of way.

After my initial screaming fit, my northern temperament reasserted itself, and I got a grip, admittedly tenuous, on myself. This could not be said for the others. I have never heard such a din. Everyone was screaming and yelling. Marissa took it all particularly badly, overcome by a really serious attack of hysteria, which ended only when she fainted dead away. The cousins, the truck driver, everyone was crying and waving their arms around.

I headed for the telephone. I had no idea how to reach the police, of course, so I tried to get an operator.

I got a recording of some sort, which in my shaken state I tried to engage in conversation. I assumed it was telling me in Maltese that all the lines were busy, that my call was important to them, and that I should stay on the line. Then there came extremely loud and raucous music, disco style, seemingly everyone's favorite in Malta. On this occasion it was disconcerting, to say the least.

Finally, after what seemed an eternity, an operator, a man, literally shouted something in Malti.

"There's been a terrible accident," I said, rather inanely.

The operator switched to English and yelled, "What do you want?"

"The police," I yelled back.

"Where?" he shouted.

Where what? I thought. "How should I know?" I yelled.

"Malta or Gozo?" he yelled again.

"Malta." Another round of rock music. I thought he had cut me off. Finally I was connected to the police and told them as best I could that there was a body in a piece of furniture. You can imagine how this was received. I was asked where I was, and couldn't describe my location. "Wait a minute," I yelled.

"You don't have to shout," the policeman said peevishly.

I went to fetch the calmest, or perhaps I should say least hysterical, of the cousins, and got him to talk to the police. Finally they arrived. A doctor was called for Marissa, and I was escorted to police headquarters in Floriana, where I was treated as a major nuisance, until at last I was taken to Vincent Tabone. All of this, including Tabone's interrogation, had taken many hours and I was feeling more than a little sorry for myself when I got back to the house.

It was nearly one in the morning, so my first thought was that it was way too late to call anyone. But then I remembered the time difference and realized it was dinnertime back home. But there was the question of who to call. It is one of life's revealing moments when one considers who, out of perhaps dozens of acquaintances and friends, one knows well enough to call when one has found a corpse, a murdered corpse, stuffed in a piece of furniture.

Calling Lucas was out of the question. As much as I might need him right now, he was out of reach, probably sitting in a tent eating astronaut food from a plastic bag, oblivious to my situation.

I considered calling Clive, my ex, on the theory that a heated argument, even over the telephone, would be therapeutic. Even talking to his new wife, the rather fatuous but extremely rich Celeste, might do the trick.

In the end, I called my neighbor, Alex. I first met Alex when I moved into the neighborhood after my rather acrimonious separation and divorce. He adopted me somewhat in the way he takes in various stray cats and dogs from time to time. I credit his avuncular concern and friendship with getting me through a bad patch in my life. In turn, I have fended off more than one foray by his other neighbors who feel his rather ramshackle house and jungle-like garden are not in keeping with the image they have of our part of town. They're right, of course. His place is a bit of an eyesore, but who cares? Alex is a genuine eccentric, and I don't know what I'd do without him now, nor how Sarah and I could manage the store without his help.

When I told him what had happened, he clucked over me in a soothing and satisfying way.

"Haven't heard a word of this here yet, although I'm sure we will soon enough. I'll expect police enquiries, shall I? You tell me Mrs. Galea—Marilyn, is that right?—has gone missing, and is the prime suspect?"

"Yes. Did Dave mention whether or not she was at the house when his men got there?"

"No. I waited for his team to pick up the furniture last night but didn't talk to him personally. They came around eight or eight-thirty, I'd say. We were open late last night anyway, and they came before we closed. Dave left a message on the answering machine at the shop. Said the furniture was on its way to you, it was late and he was going to bed. Bad cold or flu, by the sound of him. We didn't bother him at all today. We figured we'd hear from you if there was a problem.''

"No doubt he'll be bothered soon enough, if he hasn't been already.''

"No doubt. Maybe I should call and warn him he can expect a call from the police.''

"You know what, Alex? I think I'll call him myself. Something went very wrong with that shipment, and maybe Dave can enlighten me in some way.''

"Okay. But you take care. Leave the detective work to the police this time, will you?''

"I will, Alex. And thanks for being there!'' I said.

I called Dave at his home. His wife answered.

"Hi, Sandy, it's Lara. How's Dave? Is it possible for him to come to the phone?''

"Hi, Lara. How's Malta? Warmer than here, I hope. Did the shipment get there all right?''

"It got here,'' was all I could think to say.

"Dave's got a cold. It's settling in nicely. The way he's carrying on you'd think he had dengue fever, mind you. You know how men revert to babyhood the moment they get even the most minor of ailments! He's asked me to screen all his calls. You are, in fact, the only person he said he'd talk to. Hold on a minute, I'll get him.''

Dave came on the line, and I gave him a short version of events and told him to expect a call from the police.

"Good Lord!'' he exclaimed.

"Can you tell me anything about the shipment, Dave? Did you notice the switch in the piece of furniture? Was the chest particularly heavy? Who was there when your men got to the house? Anything strike you as unusual, anything at all?''

"We did everything in such a hurry, Lara. I don't know . . . I'll have to ask my team who let them into the house. I didn't think to ask at the time. I did notice that one piece wasn't measured with your normal military precision. But the yellow sticker with your initials was on it. I checked every piece for that. And you know, the description—chest, sideboard—not much difference really.

"I think I thought that maybe Galea had changed his mind about which piece to send, although it did cross my mind that maybe you'd come under the legendary Galea spell and lost it for a minute or two. You wouldn't be the first woman that happened to." His laugh turned into a coughing spasm.

"Very funny, Dave. The guy is dead. Stabbed."

"You're right. I'm sorry. It's not funny. I should have known something was wrong. I guess I screwed up. Big time," he said morosely.

"I don't think you screwed up, Dave. Presumably the murderer switched them. The police here think it was Marilyn Galea."

"That little mouse? Tired of all his philandering, no doubt. Still I wouldn't have put her down for it, would you? And you'd think divorce, while it might take longer, would be a more socially acceptable alternative, wouldn't you? Most of the money's hers, from what I hear. Isn't it just as likely to be a jealous husband, or a colleague whom Galea beat out for a big commission? There must be a few of those. He got a lot of commissions.

"Come to think of it, I do recall a couple of the guys complaining that some of the furniture must be filled with bricks, or something. But they were all heavy wood pieces, and we didn't open anything. I just amended the waybill accordingly. We were really rushing to make the flight. I . . . hold on a sec, Lara, Sandy's waving at me."

He put his hand over the mouthpiece for a second or two. "Gotta go," he said. "Police at the door, as you predicted. Thanks for the warning. We'll talk soon."

"Just one more question, Dave. Was the furniture always in your sight from the time it left the Galea house? I mean, could he have been killed somewhere other than at his house?"

"Doubt it. The guys took it directly from the house and loaded it on the truck. They came straight to the airport. There was no time for a coffee stop, or anything, and they told me they came direct. I don't think there was a time when at least one or two of us weren't there during the loading. And anyway, why would anyone come all the way out to the airport to stab somebody? And what would Galea be doing out on the tarmac or in the hangar?"

What indeed? It was looking more and more as if Tabone was right. Galea was probably killed in his own home. And yet . . . I couldn't imagine Marilyn Galea stabbing anyone, much less her own husband. She had seemed very nice to me. But what did I know? Perhaps I just felt guilty because I'd once contemplated having an affair with her husband. A middle-class Presbyterian upbringing stays with you forever.

IT WAS NOT UNTIL THE next day that I figured out what all the loud sighing was about when Tabone talked about the autopsy. I was back in Floriana the next morning, going over the same old stuff one more time. Marissa, looking very pale and sad, was leaving the office when I arrived. She gave me a wan little smile as we passed in the corridor. I'd seen Anthony and Sophia in the waiting room as I came in. He was utterly crushed, I could tell, by the death of his idol and mentor, she in her own quiet way, was a pillar of strength. It occurred to me that Anthony, an only child, and a very much adored one, was seeing life in the raw for the first time. Sophia on the other hand possessed a maturity that far exceeded her young life.

In any event, as I was reading the typed version of my statement, prepared for my signature, the telephone rang.

"What have you got?" Tabone grunted upon answering it. There was a pause.

"That's it?" he asked incredulously. Then a few seconds later, he slammed the phone down and spoke to no one in particular.

"It appears Martin Galea was stabbed. With something

sharp. Brilliant, wouldn't you say? But perhaps you figured that out for yourself just looking at him," he said, turning his attention to me and glaring in my general direction. I said nothing.

"Well, what would you expect from a loaner?"

"A loaner?" I asked hesitantly.

"Our former coroner, Dr. Caruana, has retired. He's a prince. Really knew his stuff. We're hoping to hire another one, Maltese, but in the meantime, we have a Frenchman, on loan. One of their rejects, if you ask me. He complains constantly about the primitive conditions under which he has to work here, and of course, he's right. We have a long way to go in that area. Can't do all the fancy tests other labs can. True in the medical area too. When Rosa, our eldest, was badly hurt in a car accident, my wife and I flew her to Italy for tests and treatment. Took every cent we had. No, more than that. We borrowed from several relatives, and we'll be paying them back forever. But it was worth it, let me tell you.

"Caruana wasn't bothered by it, though. He did his autopsies the old fashioned way, and he was always right. This French fellow obviously relied on fancy equipment in the past, and he's definitely not so good at the basics. Complains about everything, including, and maybe especially, the food here. I hate spending any time with the man, but obviously I'm going to have to.

"We're having a devil of a time getting a permanent coroner. But what can you expect? Coroners, like policemen, are civil servants. Very badly paid. You get what you pay for, except of course in my case, where my contribution far exceeds the paltry sum I'm paid, wouldn't you say?"

"Absolutely," I agreed. He smiled at me.

"Sorry. Totally lost it there, didn't I?"

I decided I liked Tabone. He had a sense of humor, bizarre and occasionally brittle though it might be, and he didn't seem to take me very seriously as a suspect, despite my involvement in the whole affair. He also didn't seem to share his colleagues' distrust of, and dislike for, foreigners.

"Is that all he said? The coroner, I mean. That Galea was stabbed with something sharp?"

"Just about. Well, one more thing. He estimated the time of death at about noon or one p.m. yesterday, give or take an hour or two. He bases this on the fact that rigor mortis had not yet set in, which it would normally start to do within five or six hours, and the fact that the last meal in Galea's stomach—pardon the details here—was breakfast, bacon and eggs. The poor fellow didn't get time for lunch before he expired.

"I expect this means that either Galea was killed in Rome wandering about the cargo area for some inexplicable reason, then stuffed in some furniture that just happened to be his, and which just happened to be heading for his new home in Malta, or alternatively that he and the murderer both stole on the cargo plane, and Galea was murdered mid-Atlantic. Perhaps—now here's an idea—the pilot killed him, in a fit of rage because he was a stowaway. How likely do you think these alternatives might be? Ludicrous, would you say?" he asked contemptuously. "Maybe our loaner is getting into the embalming fluid in his desperation.

"But I suppose we must work with what we have, and it does give me ideas. I'd better check with the Italian authorities and the airline to see if Galea was on a flight to Rome. Not that I have much in the way of resources, of course. Most of my staff are on security detail."

"Security? For what?"

"It's not terribly well-known for security reasons, but our prime minister is hosting representatives from a number of Mediterranean nations next week. He wants to get Malta into the European Union. It's an uphill battle, of course. The Opposition party opposes it. They think a little country like Malta will get swallowed up by the Union in one tiny bite and our economy will be ruined, and they may be right. Who's to say really? I for sure have no idea whether it's a good idea or not. In any event, the PM soldiers are on for the cause. He's hoping to get the support of countries like Italy and Greece to get us into the Union. So he'll wine and dine a few of them and see where it gets us.''

''Would these be people important enough to warrant an invitation to Martin Galea's new house, would you say?'' I asked.

He looked at me thoughtfully. ''Interesting question, my dear Miss McClintoch. Very interesting question indeed.''

THE REST OF THE DAY passed quietly enough, except for one very strange incident. After my meeting with Tabone, and reluctant to return to the house, I ventured by myself into Valletta. I needed to change some travelers' checks into Maltese lire, and I had promised myself a return visit to St. John's Co-Cathedral. Ostensibly, my reason for going there was the painting I'd heard was in the cathedral museum and had missed on my previous visit, a Caravaggio, and to see more of the cathedral, unhurried by Anthony's relentless quest for buildings designed by Gerolamo Cassar. The real reason for going there at this particular moment, however, was, I think, an idea that a visit to this magnificent place of worship might put the horror of the previous day in perspective somehow.

The sun was shining brightly when I went into the dim interior. Once again, I was amazed at how every inch of the interior was ornamented in some way. I found the painting I wanted to see, the quite magnificent ''Beheading of St. John,'' and then I just wandered around some more. A large tour group had left the cathedral shortly after I arrived, and I had the place more or less to myself.

In the little chapel to the left of the main altar was a staircase that led down to the cathedral crypt. The guidebook Anthony had purchased for me indicated that visits to the crypt were only possible by writing for an appointment well in advance, something I had obviously not done. On my previous visit, the gate at the bottom of the steps had been held shut with a padlock and chain, allowing only a tantalizing glimpse of the crypt through the gate. This time, however, I could see that the padlock was open. I don't know whether it was the lure of the unlocked gate, the thought of seeing something usually forbidden, or perhaps a bit of an obsession, recently acquired, with the hereafter, but after looking carefully about me, I went quickly and quietly down the steps and let myself in.

There is something about crypts that demands silence, the coolness, darkness, and damp so akin, perhaps, to death. I walked very quietly into the depths, trying not to disturb the inhabitants, several of whom, I noticed, had been Grand Masters of the Knights of St. John, in their final resting place. For a moment or two I thought I was alone, until in the very back, at a dead end, I came upon the Great White Hunter himself, crouched low examining one of the tombs very intently. I don't know why I was surprised. GWH was where he always was when I saw him, hanging about in the presence, here literally, of the Knights. Surprised I was, however, and I obviously startled him. Perhaps he had been concentrating so hard he hadn't heard me at first. When he did, he turned, looking at me as much as anything like a cornered animal, fear in his eyes.

"I'll give you thirty percent," he said.

"Thirty percent?" I said, mystified.

"All right, then. Forty."

I just looked at him.

"Fifty/fifty. I'll split whatever we get with you. It's the best I can do. I have expenses, you know." His voice was a hoarse gasp.

"What are you talking about?" I exclaimed.

He looked at me intently, and then straightened up, keeping his eyes on me at all times.

"Then it's not you," he said.

In my confusion, I took this to be an existential query of some sort and replied, "Of course it's me. Who else would I be?"

He lunged past me, pushing me roughly against a stone

tomb and hurtled up the stairs. I heard his footsteps receding quickly above me. I stood there alone in the crypt for several minutes, listening to some water drop against damp stones, my shoulder aching from the contact with the wall, totally baffled by the encounter.

It would be some time before the significance of this event became clear to me.

❤ SEVEN

BUT HERE, WHAT IS THIS? Shipwrecked soul, cast upon My shores. Paul, they call you, Saul of Tarsus, follower of the Nazarene. I see Cathedrals rising from My rocky soil. My strength ebbs before it, the Word that rings across the ages. Love thy neighbor. Subdued, silent, but not defeated, I remain. They will worship Me again.

THE FOLLOWING DAY THE ENORMITY of what had happened finally caught up with me. Until then, I had been reasonably pleased with the way I'd been holding up. I did not wish to think I was becoming inured to the sight of violent death— this was not, regrettably, the first time in my life I'd discovered a murder victim—but by and large I had felt rather untouched by events. I knew that the planets were out of alignment somehow, but I merely sensed a kind of detached surprise. Indeed, I had put my feelings about finding Galea roughly on a par with my perplexing encounter with the Great White Hunter.

That morning, however, a black cloud had descended upon me. The dreary rain outside mirrored the inner workings of my psyche. The fog that swirled around the yard had somehow worked its way into my body. I felt as if my eyes and ears and all my inner workings were clogged with cotton wool. I could not get out of bed.

Marissa and Joseph, who had reappeared as suddenly as

he'd left, arrived late morning. I heard them come in and call out for me, but I could not summon the energy to reply.

They came looking for me, and soon their two heads poked around the bedroom door. I waved at them in a languid fashion, extending my hand only inches beyond the edge of the duvet, which was pulled up to my nose, to do so. Apparently they did not like what they saw. I heard, but could not understand, their whispered consultation in the hall outside the bedroom and as they descended the stairs.

Soon I heard footsteps on the stairs once again and Marissa came into the room with a tray.

"Sit up, please," she said in a tone of voice I assumed she normally reserved for Anthony at his recalcitrant best. I did what I was told. She was younger than I, but the tone apparently works for both children and people of all ages in a state of shock.

"Drink this," she ordered. I shook my head. "I've talked to the doctor, and if you don't drink this and eat something, he's coming over." I decided I was not in the mood to meet a Maltese doctor, however lovely and competent he might be, so I drank it down. It was tea, very hot, with lemon and enough sugar to supply the day shift at a candy factory. I had visions of it drilling its way through my teeth. But it worked. I felt better almost immediately. Then there was toast and jam and a little cheese.

"Good!" Marissa said. "Now you can have a bit of a rest until it's time to get dressed. Anthony and Sophia will be here to pick you up about two."

"Pick me up for what?" I managed to say.

"Don't tell me you've forgotten. You promised to help Dr. Stanhope with her play. Sophia is counting on you," she said severely.

I had completely forgotten, to be sure, and I didn't want to leave my bed. Somewhere in my battered psyche I knew that everyone had decided it would be good therapy for me to do this, but I didn't feel like it a bit. I knew I couldn't let Sophia down, though. I had come to feel real affection for her. I also understood that fussing over me was good therapy for Marissa, who looked dreadful, puffy-eyed and exhausted, so I suppose we struck an unspoken bargain of sorts. I agreed to go.

It was a very damp day, so of course the car wouldn't start. Anthony was not to be deterred this time. He made me sit in the driver's seat, and then he and his father pushed the car down the incline of the driveway. It started just as I steered around the corner at the bottom. Anthony was pleased with the result. I did not feel my relationship with the car was improving over time.

We, Anthony, Sophia, and I, made our way to the University. I tried to memorize the route for future reference, but I was having difficulty concentrating on anything. Anthony, acting on his mother's instructions, no doubt, dropped us right at the door and told us he'd be back for us about six.

Many of the students had already gathered when we arrived, and Sophia was pulled into the crowd immediately. I sought out Dr. Stanhope and reported for duty.

"Right," she said. "You'll be wanting a briefing. The play we are putting on is a history of Malta from Paleolithic times to the present. It's done as a series of vignettes. I don't suppose you've ever been to a *son et lumière*, sound and light show?"

"Sure," I said. "The Forum in Rome, Athens, the Pyramids of Giza, Karnak on the Nile—I kind of collect them. They are held after dark and use music and dialogue along with lighting to tell the history of a place—they light up particular areas of an historic site where an important event took place."

"Exactly. Well, this is a little like that, except that we actually light the girls as they speak. They represent the people from different eras, all the nations that have come and gone in Malta, with commentary on historic events. We did it this way because our budget for elaborate sets is just about nil, and there are only fifteen girls in the class participating. Not exactly a cast of thousands.

"For our original production, the students designed and made their own costumes to illustrate various time periods, and we even got the boys in the school involved making props. In shop class they made the kind of implements that were used to build the temples, for example. Everyone pitched in to make the backdrop. The students painted scenes from Maltese history on huge sheets of paper. The first one was a picture of Hagar Qim, the second the ramparts of Valletta, the third the Grand Harbour. You get the idea. The assistant principal came up with a fast way to change the sets."

"It sounds very ambitious," I said.

"Well, it is. The students worked very hard. But I think they needed a bit of a stretch, and frankly their knowledge of their own history was appalling, just appalling. I made them do all the research and write the script. Originally I tried to get them to do it from the point of view of the women of each era, but it was too difficult for them. Too much under the thumb of the men around here, if you ask me. Then I hit upon the idea of telling the history from the point of view of the Great Goddess, sort of like having the spirit of Malta speak, and it's worked out really well.

"Your young friend Sophia is proving to be quite a good little writer, by the way. Wrote her own part, and several others. Anyway, we put it on about a month ago here in the auditorium. Huge success, I must say. Standing ovation. The girls were thrilled."

"So you've extended its run, I take it?"

"Extended. . . . Ah, yes, show business talk, I surmise. Yes, for one performance only. After the show here, some muckety-muck in the Prime Minister's office, Mr. Camilleri I think he said his name was, asked for an appointment with me. His card made him out to be the Prime Minister's chief public relations officer.

"Told me the PM was entertaining some foreign dignitaries and he thought the play would be just the thing. Well, I have to admit it was all pretty flattering. I asked the students what they thought, and they were just blown away by the whole idea.

"Camilleri had some ideas to jazz it up a bit, of course. You know these PR types. Anyway, at some point a week or so ago, he hit upon the idea of putting it on at the site, Hagar Qim or Mnajdra. That's why you saw us there a couple of days ago. We were location scouting—is that the term? We've decided Mnajdra is the place. We'll put chairs—there'll be about twenty-five people—about where you and I were sitting the other day, facing the temple entrance; we'll use the ruins as a backdrop; and we'll light certain portions of it to illustrate the history. The inside of the temple will be, in effect, our backstage.

"Our fallback, of course, the rain location, is here in the auditorium. We'll keep the sets at the ready. But it would be quite a lark to do it at the site, don't you think?"

"I think it sounds terrific. What can I do?" I asked.

"We need a sort of stage manager. You know, get everyone to the right place at the right time, in the right costume. That sort of thing. The vice principal had that role, but I think I told you he broke his leg waterskiing. Why anyone would want to roar across the top of the water on a couple of sticks is beyond me. He was practicing for a jumping competition. At his age! I would have credited him with more intelligence. But there you have it. Boy stuff. Way too much testosterone!

"The lighting for this production will be key. Had a bad moment there. Only had one bloke who knew anything about electricals—I certainly don't—the school caretaker. He's in hospital. Fell down the back stairs at the school Thursday evening after everyone had gone. Claims he can't remember what happened. But we know what happened, don't we? We know he's down in the boiler room having more than the odd nip or two at regular intervals during the day. Drunken old sod!

"I thought we'd have to call the whole thing off, but the Goddess is watching over us. Sent us a savior. Right at one of her sacred places. Mnajdra. A very nice gentleman has come forward to help out. Knows all about the stuff. And oh . . . here he is. . . ."

"Signore Deva, how wonderful!" she gushed as she turned toward her savior. It was the man I'd seen at Mnajdra a couple of days before.

"Signore Vittorio Deva, Ms. McClintoch."

"Signore," I said.

"Please, signora, call me Victor. I am at your service, ladies. I will leave you now to see what lighting and sound equipment will be available here, if I may?"

"Isn't he just darling?" Dr. Stanhope asked me after he'd left.

"Just darling," I agreed. "Did you sign him up at Mnajdra?"

"No, in fact we just chatted for a few minutes. He asked me questions about the historical significance of the site. He was very interested in what I told him about Goddess worship, and what we were up to, the play, I mean. Then yesterday morning I heard about old Mifsud falling down the stairs. . . ."

"Mifsud?" I interrupted.

"The caretaker. He's a mess. Nasty bump on the head, cracked ribs, broken ankle. I didn't know what to do. I went to get a spot of lunch at my usual place, and in walked Victor . . . Signore Deva. We chatted again. I told him what had happened. He was ever so sympathetic . . . and delicate. Let it be known he'd be glad to help if I asked him, but that he wouldn't presume without my asking. Such a gentleman!"

"Indeed," I murmured.

The rest of the afternoon passed quickly, and I momentarily forgot my problems, partly because the place was an absolute din. I was coming to realize that in Malta, shouting is a normal conversational level. Soon I was shouting too. I used my shop organization skills to get all the costumes lined up in order, and made annotations in the script. Signore Deva—Victor— for all his unctuousness, seemed to know his electricals, to use

Anna Stanhope's expression—and he made some recommendations for additional purchases.

"I took the liberty of visiting the site this morning, my dear Dr. Stanhope, and I have some ideas I'd like to discuss with you, with your permission, of course."

"All right, Victor, but remember, we have an extremely limited budget for this production," she said.

Victor looked wounded. "My dear Anna, if I may be so bold as to call you that? Yes? It would be a privilege—no, an honor—for me to be permitted to contribute in this small way to your most prestigious event. Please allow me the pleasure of purchasing the necessary equipment at my personal expense!"

I thought Deva was rivaling the tea Marissa had made for me earlier in the day for cloying sweetness, but Dr. Stanhope was all atwitter. She agreed immediately, and off he went to make his purchases. I'll admit I could see why she was smitten. He was a very attractive man, mid- to late forties, I'd say, lovely Italian suit, impeccable manners, if a tad old-world, and very, very smooth.

There were a couple of other adult members of the team. Mr. Camilleri, from the PM's office, had donated the services of one of his staff, a woman named Esther, a pleasant enough person who didn't seem to do much, but presumably she'd be doing protocol duties the day of the event. There was also a young man by the name of Alonso, the older brother of one of the girls, who acted as general gofer and handyman. Whenever brute strength was called for, Alonso was called upon to provide it. He moved furniture, lugged racks of costumes, and even went out to get everyone soft drinks—some very sweet fruit-flavored concoctions.

Anthony and Sophia took me home. There was a police car in the driveway when we got there, but there had been one there off and on since Galea's unfortunate arrival, so I thought nothing of it. When I went into the house, however, I was in for a little surprise.

Vincent Tabone was there, and he, Marissa, and Joseph all had fingers held to their mouths in the universal "hush" sign. I was led upstairs to one of the empty rooms and found it empty no longer. A cot had been set up in one corner of the room, and on it, sound asleep, was a tall man. I say tall, because his feet protruded past the end of the cot. We went back downstairs to talk.

"Sergeant Robert Luczka of the Royal Canadian Mounted Police!" Tabone pronounced the name *Looch-Ka*, with an emphasis on the first syllable. "He's come over to assist in the investigation of Martin Galea's death, Galea being a Canadian citizen now and all. And the possibility that he was killed in Canada, or Rome, of course. The sergeant arrived today.

"He's on a very small per diem. Budget cutbacks, apparently. So I thought bringing him here would accomplish two things: save him some money, and provide you with protection. Good idea, don't you think?"

"Great," I said. What else could I say?

"A Mountie!" Tabone exclaimed. "A real Mountie! I never thought I'd get to work with a Mountie!"

Indeed. And I never thought I'd have to live with one either.

THE NEXT MORNING I AWOKE to the smell of coffee and bacon. It irritated me more than I can say, for reasons I cannot explain. I think it was because I was beginning to consider the house mine in some way. Not literally, of course. I have never expected to make enough money at my business to ever own such a wonderful home. But my furniture was in it, and when I go buying for the shop, I only buy objects I love. I had handpicked every piece Galea had selected. I'd also worked so hard, and worried so much, to get it ready. But most of all, the house was beginning to feel like an orphan. Martin Galea dead, Marilyn Galea missing. No children. Marilyn was an only child, I knew, and if Martin had relatives anywhere, he had never mentioned them to me. I wondered what would happen to it. I felt the Mountie did not belong here.

I took my time going downstairs, not looking forward to my first conversation with the man. I was determined, I have to admit, not to like him. When I got downstairs, he rose immediately, poured me a coffee which he placed at a neatly set place on the counter, and stuck out his hand. He was tall, as I predicted, with light brown hair with a balding spot, blue eyes, and a lopsided smile.

"Rob Luczka," he said. "Pronounced L-o-o-c-h-k-a and spelled L-u-c-z-k-a. Ukrainian. You, I know, are Lara. It's nice to meet you."

"And you," I said between clenched teeth. How could someone be so cheery first thing?

"Here, let me get you some breakfast. Marissa has left us lots of good stuff. How do you like your eggs?"

"In the carton," I said. "I'll just have some toast and coffee, thanks."

"You need fuel to get through the day, you know. I'm cooking you some bacon. No, how about an omelet? That's a good idea," he said, answering his own question.

My God, I thought. There's going to be another murder victim before this is over. I'll kill him for sure. But I said nothing. He served up quite a passable omelet actually, and once I had that and some coffee, I felt I could face a conversation with him with some equanimity.

"So you're here to assist with the murder investigation," I said as my opening gambit.

"Yes, sure. Pretty cut-and-dried, though, I'd say. Most likely suspect is Galea's wife. What's her name?"

"Marilyn," I said. "And I don't think she did it. Didn't you see the autopsy report? Said he'd been dead for only a few hours."

"I've seen the report. Tabone showed it to me. Somewhat . . . basic, shall we say? I mean I don't wish to criticize another jurisdiction's work, but . . ."

"Tabone didn't think much of it either," I admitted.

"The point is, it's been mighty cold back home. Sub subzero. I figure Galea could have been dead for much longer than the coroner here thinks. We already know that the furniture was loaded outside, it was minus fifteen at the time, and we checked the cargo line for the temperature of their cargo bays—they were embarrassed to tell us how cold they were, actually. So I figure Galea was just thawing out about the time he got here. That would account for the report.''

''But you're here now,'' I persisted. ''Presumably you weren't sent here because it was an open-and-shut case. You or your superiors must have thought there was some doubt.''

''Not really. We were sent a copy of the autopsy report, so we had to look into it.''

''So when do we start?''

''Start what? And if it's what I think it is, who's we? I'm the policeman, you are the shopkeeper, the one in whose shipment the body turned up, I might add.''

''Fine. Go out investigating by yourself. You'll get lost five minutes out of the driveway, I assure you. And were you planning to take the car? I can't wait to hear all about it!''

''Do I take it that you think that because I'm a Ukrainian from Saskatchewan I can't find my way around an island this size? I'm a Mountie, remember. I track criminals through roaring blizzards, just like on TV.'' He grinned.

''But of course,'' I said. ''Let me get you the car keys.''

❦ EIGHT

Normans, Hohenstaufens, Angevins, Aragonese, Castilians—a blur of rulers, mostly absent. My tiny islands pass from hand to hand, pillar to post, sometimes the spoils of war, other times, more happily, to seal the marriage contract, yet others, a forgotten outpost in some despotic sovereign's empire. Will freedom never come?

"I HAVE A COUPLE OF pieces of news I think you'll find interesting," Vincent Tabone said, looking across his desk at Rob Luczka and me. My anticipated moment of triumph at seeing Luczka off in that splendid car was denied when Tabone called to say he was sending a squad car to the house. The factor mitigating my disappointment was that I was invited too, the Mountie's opinion of shopkeepers doing detective work notwithstanding.

"I've heard back from the Italian authorities," Tabone continued. "Martin Galea got to Rome on Canadian Airlines flight 6040. His car, a Jaguar—I'm impressed!—was found in the long-term parking area at Toronto International Airport. The Italians no longer require disembarkation cards at Fiumicino Airport—a mistake if you ask me. If they did, we could compare the signature on the card with the signature on the offer to purchase the land where he built the house just to confirm it was Galea on the flight. Not that we need to. We know he got here somehow. We've also contacted the airline. Galea was prebooked in seat 15B. But the flight was full, lots of large Italian families traveling together, and there was a bit of a computer glitch. A few seats in that area were double-booked. There was a seat for everyone, apparently, but a lot of trading around on board. It was a 747—over 400 people. I've never been on one, but it sounds unnatural to me! We'll try to contact the person who was supposed to be sitting in 15A, to see if we might get a positive identification, but frankly, I'm not hopeful.''

"So that means what?" Luczka mused. "Maybe his wife killed him in Italy—what's her name again?"

"It's Marilyn," I burst out. "M-A-R-I-L-Y-N. Not what's her name! Not 'the wife.' Not *la femme*. Marilyn. She may be plain and very, very shy. She may have so much money you want to despise her. But I've met her. I like her. And she deserves better than this . . . this automatic presumption of guilt on both your parts!" I was almost sputtering. Both men looked sheepish. "What if something dreadful has happened to her too?"

Tabone cleared his throat. "Perhaps I should have added that I also checked on Mrs. Galea—that is to say, *Marilyn* Galea—and there is no indication she was on the plane with him. There's no boarding pass, no ticket in her name either."

"You said there were two items of interest," I said, somewhat mollified. "What's the second?"

"The second is equally interesting, I think," Tabone said. "The information you requested on Galea's will has come through from Canada, Rob. The bulk of his estate, as one would expect, is left to his wife, but, and this is the interesting part, he leaves the sum of $100,000 to the Farrugia boy—Anthony."

"I think that's great!" I exclaimed. "It's to pay for him to become an architect, for his tuition and everything. Who'd have guessed Galea would be that generous?"

"Very generous indeed," Tabone agreed. "But I think one would have to ask the question: Is this really for the boy's

education? Galea was what—thirty-seven?—when he died.
Surely he would have expected to live longer than that. If he
wanted to pay for Anthony's education, why didn't he just
offer to do so?

"So the question remains, and the answer is very critical:
Where and when did he get killed? If he was killed in Rome,
then Marilyn Galea probably didn't do it. If he was killed in
Canada, then the Farrugias are no longer suspects."

"You'd think the 'when' could be verified, wouldn't you?"
Luczka asked. "God knows I'm no pathologist. I can't understand anything of what they're doing with DNA evidence
these days, but if I remember anything of my elementary fo-
rensics class a few years back, it is only in crime novels that
it's possible to pinpoint the time of death to an hour or two.
I know what your pathologist says about rigor mortis. It normally begins to set in about five to seven hours after death, is
fully set in after about twelve hours, and passes off again. But
temperature makes a big difference to the rate. And as far as
the breakdown of tissue after death—I think they call that
autolysis—there wouldn't be much difference between five
hours and say, fifteen, which would put Galea back in Toronto
when he died. And autolysis takes place at a slower rate when
the body is cold.

"So let's, for the sake of argument, say Galea was killed
in Toronto. His body could even have been frozen for all I
know. The weather was certainly cold enough. And it seems
to me it would be relatively easy to find out whether the body
had been in freezing temperatures over a period of several
hours, as you and I discussed yesterday, Vince.

"If I remember correctly, cells rupture when a body is frozen, sort of like frostbite really. You wouldn't necessarily be
able to tell just looking at the body, but the fractured mem-
branes should show up under a microscope if someone knew
what to look for. Even if the body hadn't been at subzero
temperatures long enough to freeze completely, you could look

at tissue samples from the extremities, the fingers and toes, because they would freeze first.''

''Ah, but that requires, as you so delicately put it, someone who knows what to look for. At the present time, we don't have that,'' Tabone replied. ''But I take your point. I'll make arrangements for the coroner to send some tissue samples to a lab in Italy, and we'll see what they say. But what about the stomach contents? Bacon and eggs. Breakfast. And we know that's the last meal they give you on an overnight transatlantic flight.''

''This may come as a surprise to you, Vince, but we North Americans eat breakfast food any time of the day or night. I don't think that necessarily proves anything.''

Tabone nodded as Rob continued. ''You might also have someone do some tests on the chest he turned up in, if it hasn't been done already. It's been well handled, I know, so chances of finding clear prints are slight, but I've got a copy of Galea's fingerprints that I brought along. Got them when he applied for a visa to come to Canada. In the meantime,'' Luczka said, ''I think I'll have a bit of a look around, if it's okay with you, Vince. Try out a little old-fashioned detective work. Find where Galea was from, who he knew, that sort of thing.''

''I know where he's from,'' I piped up. ''At least I think if I had a look at a map the name of the town would come back to me. Marilyn told me that day I went over to measure the furniture. I remember the word made me think of honey—the Greek word for it, *meli*.''

''Mellieha?'' Tabone asked.

''I think that's it,'' I replied.

''Well, you may be right. Because it says so right here on his file.'' Tabone grinned at me.

I glared at him. ''What else does the file say?''

''Parents both dead. No known relatives. Emigrated to Canada about eighteen years ago. That's about it.''

''Will you give us a lift back to the house so we can get the car?'' I asked. ''And directions to Mellieha?''

"Of course. Call me when you get back and tell me what you've found. And you will be careful, please, driving in Malta. We have many, many accidents. Remember what they say about Maltese drivers. We don't drive on the left or the right. We drive in the shade! And by the way, try not to get lost!"

AND SO IT WAS THAT the Mountie and I set off to do detective work. He wanted to drive, but the car, egalitarian in its perverseness, wouldn't start for him either. I took over, he pushed, and I waited for him, engine running, a few yards past the end of the driveway. I noticed he was limping slightly as he approached the car, but I was feeling too irritable to ask him if he was okay.

He got in and started looking for a seat belt. "There aren't any," I said.

He looked annoyed. "There should be a law!"

"There is, but it only applies to cars manufactured in 1990 or later, Anthony tells me. This, as you can see, is just a little bit older than that."

"Like about twenty years!" he responded. I put the car in gear and revved it up to the max. We tore down the road, engine screaming, until I was able to make the shift to third.

"Nice car," he said. I looked at him sideways but could not tell if there was irony in his words. We hit the first roundabout. There was nothing coming, so I didn't gear down. The window beside him fell down. "Very nice car," he added, as the handle spun uselessly in his hand.

I had had a good look at the map before we left, and I had chosen a route that picked up the road to Rabat, then angled up to the northwest corner of the island where the town of Mellieha was located. We whipped past the sign for Verdala Palace around where the Great White Hunter had run me off the road, and I idly wondered where he was, and whether he was trying to negotiate another surrealistic deal with someone, perhaps a total stranger like me. Fifty percent of what, was the question.

As I had learned from my earlier outing in the car, I ignored the directional signs and kept angling along in the general direction of Mellieha. It gave me a great deal of satisfaction to sense the Mountie beside me studying the road map with a perplexed air, but regrettably he was keeping his confusion to himself. He did wince perceptibly, however, when a mini minor shot past us on the shoulder, and again when someone passed on a hill.

Once part of a prehistoric land bridge that linked it to what is now Italy, and also, perhaps with Africa, Malta is shaped a little like an oval platter with the northwest side tilted up, and the south and east down. Its western end is bisected by alternating parallel ridges and valleys cutting across the island from coast to coast. Our route, which took us out of the lower south and east, climbed for a while. As we crested the top of the first ridge, I could see, still miles away, the sweep of a large bay on the far side of the island, the water a silver ribbon against the dark outline of the shore. If my calculations were correct, it should be St. Paul's Bay, where St. Paul was supposed to have been shipwrecked, and thus converted the island to Christianity.

From here, sometimes the road followed a valley, relatively green and terraced to preserve precious soil and water, sometimes it crossed another craggy ridgeline and we could see the coastline for a few minutes again.

Finally we reached the large bay. It was at the coastal edge of one of the island's largest valleys, and it looked as if it had been formed during an earthquake or a volcanic eruption millions of years ago when the sea washed into one of the depressions between the ridges. Moored at the edge of the bay bobbed several beautifully colored fishing boats, their bright paint in sharp contrast to the subtle yellow stone of the buildings that hugged the shoreline.

From here the road curved along the edge of the bay, then

up onto another high ridge. It was not long then until we came to the edge of a town, and a sharp turn in the road to the right put us on the main street looking downhill toward a large cathedral.

"Mellieha, I think," I said, pulling into a parking space, and then looking about me at what appeared to be a rather prosperous little town.

"I believe you, but I have no idea how you got us here." The Mountie sighed.

"Tell me again about tracking criminals through raging blizzards," I said in dulcet tones.

"Must be the absence of snow." He grinned. Obviously it was not possible to irritate this man easily.

We were parked very near to the top of the main street, and when we got out of the car, there was a wonderful smell of baking. "Could it be lunchtime?" the Mountie said, his eyes lighting up. We followed our noses to a small building on the curve in the road into town. We'd found the local bakery.

There was a lineup of Maltese women, some in jeans, but most in black skirts, white blouses, and black cardigans. Several of them were carrying trays covered with tea towels. The Mountie, obviously the irrepressible type, asked the woman ahead of us what she had on her tray. Several of the women turned and smiled at his question.

"Timpana," she said, lifting the tea towel to show us a casserole covered in pastry. "Sunday dinner," she added.

"We bring it here on Sunday to have it cooked," another woman said, "when the baking is finished for the day." She showed us her platter, a traditional roast beef dinner just waiting to be cooked. As we talked, a couple of women left, their string bags filled with several of the round crusty Maltese loaves.

"People have ovens in their own homes now," a younger woman said. "But it's still a nice tradition. We get to have a bit of a visit while our supper cooks."

"Does this mean there is nothing to eat here unless you

bring your own?'' the Mountie asked in a disappointed tone.

"You can come to my house for supper anytime,'' one of the young women said, and the rest giggled loudly. They beckoned us to go ahead of them into the dark interior. There was a counter on the left and a large brick oven at the back of the room. Arranged on a tray at the front were what looked like individual pizzas covered in a rich, dark sauce. We each ordered one and ate it right on the spot. They were delicious: lots of garlic, olives, and anchovy paste would be my guess as to ingredients, sprinkled with fresh herbs. The Mountie ordered a second right away. One of the women smiled and patted his arm.

"I don't suppose any of you would remember Martin Galea?'' I asked them.

"The man who was killed?'' one of the younger women asked.

"Yes, that one.''

They looked suspiciously at me. "I knew him in Canada,'' I said. "Very well-known architect. I . . . We, thought if he had family here, we'd express our condolences,'' I lied. This seemed to allay their suspicions, but I could feel the Mountie's law-abiding eyes boring into my back.

"There are lots of Galeas around here, but I don't remember anyone called Martin,'' one woman said. She spoke to the older women and asked them something in Maltese. They all shook their heads. One woman added something, and the others all nodded.

"You should go and see *il Qanfud*, the . . . What's the name in English? The . . . Hedgehog,'' the woman said.

The Mountie and I looked at each other. "Where might we find this . . . Hedgehog?'' he asked. The woman pointed us down the hill to an old man sitting in a chair outside one of the shops.

"Take him a beer. His favorite is Cisk lager. He'll talk your ears off,'' one of the women said. They all laughed.

"A bit crazy, but harmless enough,'' another added.

"What would we call him, if not Hedgehog?" I asked.

"Grazio," one woman replied. We thanked them and started down the hill toward the Hedgehog.

"Why would you call someone a hedgehog?" the Mountie asked no one in particular.

"Beats me. But beer sounds like a good idea," I replied.

"You're driving," he said severely. "Although come to think of it, I'm not sure how you tell the drunk drivers from any others on the road. Takes a policeman's breath away, the way they drive around here."

We stopped and bought six cold Cisk lagers, and approached the man with a degree of caution. The Hedgehog was sitting in a battered lawn chair at the foot of a flight of stone stairs leading to an upper part of the village. He was wearing a very old plaid shirt, a tattered tan cardigan, and rather rumpled beige trousers, bare feet thrust into old sandals. He wore dark-rimmed glasses with very thick lenses, had grey hair and a rather grizzled appearance. "Hello," I said in what I hoped was my nicest voice. "Is your name Grazio?"

"Who's asking?" he said suspiciously.

"My name is Lara, and this is Rob. We're looking for the family of someone we knew back in Canada, and the women at the bakery told us to look for someone by the name of Grazio who knew just about everybody," I said in an ingratiating tone.

"I doubt they called me Grazio," he said. "More likely they called me *il Qanfud.*"

"That's true," I said. "Would you like a beer?"

His eyes lit up. "Take a load off your feet, dearie," he said, gesturing toward the steps behind him, "and tell me who you're looking for."

"How'd you get a name like Hedgehog?" the Mountie dared to ask as we plunked ourselves down on the steps near the old man.

"*Skond ghamilek laqmek,*" he replied. "Your nickname reflects your behavior. Or something else about you," he added. We both nodded sagely.

"We're looking for friends or family of Martin Galea," I said, pronouncing it, as Martin had, Ga-lay-ah, with the emphasis on the second syllable.

"What kind of name is that?" he grunted. "Here we say Galea." He pronounced it Gal-ee-ah, with emphasis on the first syllable. "And Martin, that sounds British to me," he said, flicking his hand in dismissal. "I'm a Mintoff man. Don't like the British."

Rob and I looked at each other and then him.

"Gal-ee-ah would have left here at least fifteen years ago," I said. "He went to Canada and became a famous architect."

"Did he now? Is he the dead Galea?" the Hedgehog asked. "The one who turned up in a box?"

"Yes," we said in unison.

"Saves the expense of a coffin, I guess. So why do you want to know about him?"

I gave him my by now standard response about consoling the family.

"I don't know a Martin," replied the old man, apparently satisfied by my explanation. "There's lots of Galeas, though. Pawla *ta' Hamfusa*, Pawla the beetle. There's Mario *il-Kavall*, the mackerel. And long ago there was a young man, Marcus *ta' Gelluxa*, the young bull. *Il-mara bhall-lumija taghsarha u tarmiha.*"

"What?" we both said.

"For him, a woman is like a lemon. You squeeze her and throw her away," he cackled.

"That's the one!" I said.

"Was he now? Marcus was quite the youngster. His mother died when he was just a baby, but he charmed all the women in the village, and they all mothered him. He was also quite the hustler. Do just about anything to get ahead in life. Knew everyone's weaknesses, and was not above using that knowledge if it got him ahead. Played all the angles, always on the lookout for an opportunity,'' the Hedgehog said, swigging his beer. ''Can't blame him for that, though. His father died when he was just a lad, and he kind of had to look after himself. He got in with the wrong crowd for a while.''

''I heard—his wife told me—his father owned a shop here.''

''Owned? I think not. Worked in one, though. Just like Marcus to exaggerate,'' the Hedgehog said.

''No other relations?'' I asked.

''Not really. Nobody who'd admit it now anyway. He and his pal Giovanni *il Gurdien*, Giovanni the rat—such a pair, although I've always believed Marcus figured out Giovanni before some of the rest of us. But he left the village too. So you tell me he's famous. An architect. Nothing would surprise me about Marcus Galea. Giovanni did just fine for himself too. Although how he could do what he did! It makes me sick!''

The Mountie and I looked at each other again. The conversation got more confusing the more the Hedgehog drank. ''What might that be?'' Rob ventured to ask.

''Most recently, you mean? Switched to the Republic party as soon as it got elected. Ran in the next election. Got to be a Cabinet minister right away as a reward. Typical! External relations minister, no less. Turncoat! And that's the best I can say about him. Him I don't want to talk about.'' The Hedgehog looked as if he might spit out his beer, but then he thought better of it, no doubt not wanting to waste so much as a drop.

''Always liked Marcus the young bull, though, I'll admit. Certainly turned out better than some of the rest of them, like Giovanni and the other one, Franco *ta'Xiwwiex*, Franco the troublemaker, from Xemxija. He grew up to be a gangster.'' The old man giggled. After another swig, he added, ''Although there's lots of folks around here don't think too highly of Marcus either, not after what he did. At least, as far as I know, he never changed his politics!''

We all sat in silence, thinking this over for a while. Rob

opened another beer and offered it to him, asking casually, "And what was it he did that people didn't like him for?"

The Hedgehog swilled his beer. "Ran off and left the little Cassar girl in a bit of a mess, didn't he? At least that's what everybody thinks. Always wondered whether Joe *tas Saqqafi*, Joe the roofer, knew. He should have been called *ta' Tontu*, the stupid, if he didn't," he cackled.

I was starting to get the general drift of the conversation. "So Martin—Marcus—Galea left the Cassar girl—was it Marissa Cassar?—in the family way so to speak, did he?"

"Exactly!" he said. "Quite the scandal it would have been, if Joe *tas Saqqafi* hadn't come forward and married her. They moved to the other end of the island right away, but we heard about the boy, born shortly after the wedding. She was the prettiest girl in the town, you know, quite the prettiest girl in the town. Might have helped her out myself, if I'd known," he snorted. "Is there another beer, dearie?"

"Why don't you keep the rest?" Rob offered. "We should probably be on our way. Thanks for helping us out."

"Are you sure you have to go?" the old man asked. "I could tell you about lots of other people around these parts, you know."

"I'm afraid we do. We have an appointment in Valletta," Rob said. "But thank you, and enjoy the beer." We left the Hedgehog happily hugging his bottle, and went back to the car. I was so despondent about what we'd learned—everyone I liked seemed to have a motive for murder—and convinced in some irrational way that it was the Mountie's fault, that I could not speak to him as I drove back.

He made a couple of attempts at conversation, chattering away into my black silence. "Got all the bases covered, these fishermen," he said, as we made our way past St. Paul's Bay with its lovely fishing boats. "Named the boats after saints, but do you see they've got eyes painted on the prows? They're the eyes of Horus, the Egyptian god. If one god doesn't protect them, the other one will." He laughed.

Then later, "It does speak to the fact that this is a very religious country, doesn't it? If what we've learned today is true, it would be pretty disgraceful for a good Catholic girl to get pregnant with the father nowhere to be found. I guess this means Galea is Anthony's father, if I followed the conversation. Which I'm not sure I did. I have a hard time understanding these people, even though they're speaking English. Marissa Cassar is left high and dry by Marcus Galea, who's a friend of the foreign minister, a fact that may or may not be relevant. Joe the roofer rescues her, and they move to the other end of the island and have a son. Anthony's seventeen, I think Marissa told me, and Tabone just said this morning that Galea emigrated about eighteen years ago.

"We can't be sure they're the same people, though, can we? Joseph Farrugia is a tradesman but not necessarily a roofer. It would sort of explain the hundred thousand for Anthony, though, wouldn't it?"

His stream of consciousness thought patterns roughly paralleled mine, but still I couldn't bring myself to take part in the conversation. When we got back to the house I left him there and walked for a couple of hours along the bluffs. I felt heartsick. Whichever way I looked at it, someone I liked appeared guilty of a most terrible crime.

When I got back to the house, I could tell the Mountie had been busy cooking. I walked in the door and began to make my way up the stairs, still not speaking. I got about halfway up, when he said, "I've cooked us a nice supper."

"I'm sorry," I said with my back still turned to him. "I am feeling so rotten about all this. I feel as if at best I'm digging up things from Marissa's past that I never should have known, and at worst, I could be sending her to prison."

"I know you do, and I know that my being here is making it worse, for which I am sorry. But nothing of what we learned today makes her a murderer," he said gently. "Come and eat."

I might have been able to keep going up the stairs if I hadn't looked back at him. He was wearing an apron and waving a spatula in my general direction, and I had to smile. He poured me a glass of wine, and then served up a very respectable bowl of spaghetti in a meat sauce made with spicy sausage, and a green salad. He'd even sliced up oranges for dessert.

"You must have gone shopping while I was out," I said.

"I did," he replied. "Found a nice little grocery store, but regrettably I have no idea where I was, nor how to find it again!"

After dinner, Rob called home. He had, he'd told me, a sixteen-year-old daughter, Jennifer. While I tried not to listen, I could not help but hear the tone of the conversation, which was not a happy one, and Rob was in a foul mood when he rejoined me. "Kids," he muttered, then sat in a black silence for several minutes.

"Do you have kids?" he finally asked.

"Nope."

"My girlfriend Barbara moved in with us just a few weeks before I came over. She's having a tough time with Jennifer, who won't do anything she asks and is generally raising hell while I'm away. What a mess."

That's probably, I was thinking, because you threw her mother over for some bimbo who's barely older than she is. I said, however, "Perhaps Jennifer could go and stay with her mother for a while."

"Hard to do," he said. "Her mother died when Jen was seven. Cancer. I've brought her up by myself. She needed a mother, I know that, but . . . I don't know. Either she's going through a bad phase, or," he sighed, "I've botched her upbringing. Totally," he added.

Even though I hadn't voiced my caustic thoughts, I felt dreadful. I really had to stop, I thought, judging all men by my ex-husband's standard. "I'm sure it's the former," I said. "It's a long time ago, of course, but I can still remember that being a sixteen-year-old girl is no picnic."

He looked at me. "Thank you for saying that," was all he

said. Then he rallied, "How about a liqueur? I found some of that in the grocery store too."

We sat in the living room, filled with my furniture, and I chatted away, answering his questions and making up, I hoped, for my silence earlier in the day and my recent uncharitable thoughts. It was, I suppose, one of the more pleasant police interrogations I've been through. I told him about the shop, how Galea had sent me to Malta, about the party that would never happen. I told him about Anna Stanhope's play and all the preparations for the performance. I told him all about trying to get the house ready, and all the funny, and not so funny things that had happened. I told him about Nicholas the plumber, the electrician, the paint job, and how, at the very last minute, Joseph had gone missing.

"I wonder where he went," I said, not really expecting an answer.

"I'm afraid I know the answer to that one," he said slowly.

I looked at him.

"Joseph went to Rome."

☥ NINE

WANDERING KNIGHTS, RUDELY WRENCHED FROM your most holy temple, Jerusalem. Pursued across the Mediterranean by a wave of history you call the Infidel. To Rhodes, only to be exiled again. To where? Will no one give you sanctuary? Here—My tiny island, the fee one falcon. A home at last, the Knights now mine. But not a haven. You are not yet safe.

WHATEVER HIS SHORTCOMINGS IN LIFE, in death Martin Galea seemed, like Imhotep, designer of Egypt's first great stone building, the step pyramid of King Zoser, to be headed for deification. In eulogizing him as one of Malta's greatest sons and counting him among the world's greatest architects, Malta's English-language media seemed incapable of mentioning Galea without comparing him to Frank Lloyd Wright or Mies van der Rohe. His youth on the island, his rising above poverty and adversity, his flight to America and triumphant return as prodigal son took on almost mythic proportions.

It was no different back home, I discovered, in speaking to Sarah and Alex. Reporters and editors had gathered Galea to their collective bosom, his all-too-human frailties lost in the hyperbole that surrounded his design achievements, his talents appearing god-given, if not god-like, in proportion.

How galling it must have been to those who had seen his darker side: those design colleagues and competitors who had endured his less than gracious demeanor in victory and his scathing and personal criticism of their work; the cuckolded husbands who had given Galea commissions only to find the price tag included their wives; the abandoned mistresses tossed on some emotional slag heap after gambling and losing in a high-stakes and soul-destroying game. All of them were in some way the detritus of a life arrogantly and carelessly lived. And perhaps none of them had suffered more from Galea's casual cruelty than the young woman abandoned like some lost Ariadne by a callous lover.

I sat alone in the kitchen with Marissa the next morning. I had arranged to meet her early on the pretext of settling the house accounts. Neither of us had any idea what would happen now that Galea was dead and his wife was missing, and I needed to know how much money was left in Malta for house maintenance. I'd decided, at Rob's suggestion, that I'd have to try to contact Galea's solicitors and make arrangements for the house and the Farrugia family, as well as for Dave Thomson, whose shipping bills had not been paid before Galea's untimely demise. We went over the accounts and discussed how I planned to proceed. Then, as delicately as I could, I told her what Rob and I had learned the day before in Mellieha. She looked out the window for a long time before she began to speak, but when she did the words just poured out of her.

"I waited for him for a long, long time," she began. "Long after I married Joseph, long after Anthony was born. I thought we were a couple, you know. We'd been together for at least three years. I helped him with his schoolwork; he'd never have got the scholarship without me, and I thought he would come back for me as he'd promised, to carry me away with him to an exciting new life in America. But of course he never did.

"He asked me to run away with him, you know. To elope. I can remember his excitement as he described what we would do. He said we'd write my parents after we got to Canada, when we were married, and that when he'd made his fortune, we'd bring them over too. He had very grand plans.

"But I thought it would kill my father. I was an only child, much adored and a little spoiled, a bit like Anthony, perhaps. I could not bring myself to run away. And I wanted to have a wedding. A real wedding. So Marcus went alone. He said he'd write, send me his address as soon as he got settled, but the letter never came. For a while I deluded myself into thinking that something terrible must have happened to him, but in my heart I think I always knew this wasn't so. He never knew about Anthony. I didn't know myself until after he had gone.

"Joseph saved me from a terrible disgrace. He is very kind, you know. But more than that, he is direct and dependable. Over time I have come to value these qualities a very great deal.

"Joseph was a widower. His wife and baby daughter died one winter of the flu, a freakish accident really. For several years after that, he remained alone. He was a friend of my uncle, my father's younger brother, and I guess he heard what happened from him. My father, when I told him about the baby, went into his room and closed the door and stayed there two days. After that he never was the same.

"When Joseph made his offer of marriage to my father, I was reluctant at first to accept. I still expected a letter from Marcus and believed that when he heard about the baby, he would come back to marry me. My father hit me, slapped me across the face, when I told him I wanted to wait for Marcus. It was the first and last time he would ever strike me. I left his house that night and never returned. My father died six months later, my mother shortly after that.

"And so I married Joseph and we moved to Siggiewi. Anthony was born soon after. Joseph is a good man, but life has not been easy, moving to a new town so far from home. Oh, I know by American standards it is not very far, but it seemed a great distance to me. It took a long time to reestablish ourselves, for Joseph to get work. Joseph worked pretty steadily around Mellieha where he was known. When we moved he had to start all over again, and jobs were very slow coming in the early years. Here people deal with those they know, relatives and friends. But we've managed. I did what I could. I sold my lace embroidery work, and worked for a while part-time in a store.

"We were very happy when Joseph got several months' steady work on this house. We were a little worried about what would happen when the project was finished, but then one day, Joseph came home and told me the owner was looking for a couple to watch over the property for him, caretakers of sorts. He suggested we both go and present ourselves to the owner and apply for the job.

"I know you are thinking that it is strange that I didn't guess by now who the owner was, but Joseph never referred to Marcus . . . Martin by name. You may think it is even more strange that Joseph didn't know who Anthony's father was. But we never spoke of such things. Joseph always said that our lives before we married were to be considered a closed book, never to be reopened. He said we both had loved other people, but that we were now a family. So I have never asked him about his first wife, nor ever talked about Marcus to him. Joseph has always been the type to keep to himself; he hates gossip, so while there was talk around Mellieha, it never reached his ears.

"Can I describe that day to you? Anthony, Joseph, and I, all in our Sunday best, drove over to the house to meet the owner and see if we passed muster as potential caretakers. Sometimes I wonder what we must have looked like, the four of us standing in a little circle outside the house, only Anthony oblivious to the little drama that was unfolding. How the Fates must have laughed at the three of us, each coming almost simultaneously upon a sudden realization that would change our lives forever. Marcus knew right away, I'm sure of it, about Anthony. I could tell from the look he gave me, the way he looked back and forth between the two of us. And Joseph knew too, somehow.

"Marcus offered us the work. Joseph said we'd think about it. We had the most terrible row that night. Joseph said there was no way we'd accept the job. I said we had to, that I wanted a decent life for my son. In the end, he agreed. What choice did we have? God knows, we need the money. And Marcus has never touched me, not once. He never even shook my hand.

"No, what he did was much, much worse than that. It was not me he wanted, it was Anthony. He wanted a son.

"Anthony has not been an easy child to raise. He has his father's restlessness, an almost frightening need for affection and approval, ambition way above his station in life, and at times a lack of sensitivity to those about him. But I think he is, at the heart, a good boy, and Joseph could not have loved his own son more.

"Marcus started spending time with the boy whenever he was in Malta. He took him around the island explaining all about the buildings, taking him to fine restaurants and buying him fancy clothes—all the things Joseph and I could not do. And gradually he began to drive a wedge between Anthony and his father . . . Joseph, I mean.

"I don't blame Anthony. How could I? I was just as dazzled by Marcus Galea when I was his age. Anthony talked incessantly about Marcus, and finally announced he wanted to be an architect. I don't think I ever noticed how good Anthony is at drawing. I was as proud as any mother at the pictures he drew for me, and I thought some of the chalk drawings he did of the streets around our town were quite lovely, but I didn't see the talent there. Marcus did.

"The idea of sending Anthony to study architecture was so far beyond our means that it was ludicrous. But then Marcus came to the house and offered to pay for Anthony's education. He said he would speak to the dean of a school of architecture in Rome where he'd lectured, and try to get Anthony accepted there. But then he suggested that a preferrable alternative would be the University of Toronto where he had graduated and where he was on the Board of Governors. He said that Anthony could live with him and his wife while he was at school to save money. Anthony was thrilled by the idea of going to America. I could see it in his eyes. But I watched the light go out in Joseph's.

"I looked at Marcus standing there with his smug little smile and his expensive clothes—my God, his sunglasses probably cost more than Joseph could make in a month!—and I hated him. Really, truly hated him. He knew we wouldn't say no, that we would not jeopardize our son's future!"

She sat looking down at her hands for a moment or two, unable to say more.

"But you could have said no," I said quietly.

"And what good would that have done?" she burst out. "Anthony is a lot like Marcus. He would have gone anyway, wouldn't he? Marcus would have paid his way, and we would have lost Anthony forever."

"Does Anthony know Martin Galea is his father? Have you told him?"

"No!" she said vehemently. "I never will!" Then turning and grasping my arm very tightly, she said to me, "Please promise me you won't tell him. Promise me!"

"I promise, Marissa," I said slowly. "But you will have to tell him eventually, you know."

She just looked at me.

"We know Joseph was in Rome on Thursday, Marissa. He may have some explaining to do should we find Galea was killed there."

"Joseph didn't kill him. He didn't even know he was there."

"Then why was Joseph there, Marissa?" I asked.

"I have no more to say," she replied bitterly. "Nothing. I have promised. But Joseph would not—could not—kill Marcus Galea."

There was no changing her mind. Not then. I left her sitting there, silent and morose. I would have liked to sit there with her, try to persuade her that to talk about Joseph was better than saying nothing, but I had other responsibilities to consider, a young friend I couldn't disappoint.

WE WERE TO BEGIN OUR setup for the performance at Mnajdra, meeting first at the University, and then traveling together by chartered bus to the site. I'd promised Dr. Stanhope, and more importantly Sophia, that I'd be there. When I arrived at the auditorium—Rob having dropped me off there on his way to Tabone's office in Floriana—there appeared to be an altercation of some sort taking place outside the door to the building. A group of people was shouting and gesticulating at someone, and that someone turned out to be Anna Stanhope. It took me a while to ascertain what all the shouting was about, but it soon became clear that it was a group of parents objecting in the strongest terms to some of the redoubtable Dr. Stanhope's more feminist teachings. Clearly, they did not want their daughters taking part in the performance. Dr. Stanhope was seriously outnumbered, with only Victor Deva beside her, wringing his hands and making a gesture as if to shoo people away. Mario Camilleri, the PR type from the Prime Minister's office, tried valiantly to calm the crowd, but being singularly unsuccessful, opted instead to pull Anna and Victor back into the building for safety.

I could see Sophia in the crowd with a man, her father presumably, although I'd only seen him in profile in the window the night we drove her home. He had a firm grip on her arm and was trying to pull her away. Sophia's mouth was set in a stubborn line, but I could see she was wavering. A couple of her fellow actors were starting to move away with their angry parents.

It was beginning to look as if the sound and light show was not to be. Then the crowd suddenly began to clap and drew back to allow a silver-grey limo to pull up to the steps in front of the University building. Someone I could hear, but could not see very well from my position near the back of the crowd, began to speak rapidly and energetically in Maltese. No matter that I couldn't understand a word, I found the voice compelling, the plummy tones of an orator, and I could feel the mood in the group begin to shift. Sophia's father let go of her arm and she edged her way to my side.

"Who is that and what's he saying?" I whispered to her.

"It's Giovanni Galizia, the Minister for External Relations. He's telling them that he, unlike some others, has a vision for Malta in which we play a prominent role in the Mediterranean, that he believes we must take our place on the world stage. He says others may be content for Malta to be a mere pawn in European politics, but he believes that after this performance all the world will know of Malta, that the leaders of Europe, many of whom do not appreciate Malta's glorious history, will be here to learn of it, and that they, as parents, and their daughters will help bring prosperity to all Maltese." Sophia looked at me and made a face.

I laughed. Just the kind of speech you'd expect from a politician, I thought, but I had to give him credit. This was not the kind of crowd I'd have liked to have taken on. Galizia apparently moved into the crowd to press the proverbial flesh, although I still couldn't see him. Soon, the limo pulled smoothly away, and even though you could not say the parents were all smiles exactly, the crowd began to disperse. Mario Camilleri, for some reason, glared at the back of the retreating car.

"Who are these others Galizia referred to, by the way, the ones with no vision? Or was it just political rhetoric?" I asked Sophia.

"He means the Prime Minister, Charles Abela," she replied. "I think maybe the two of them don't get along. Abela is sick, recovering from surgery. The deputy Prime Minister has been filling in for him, but Galizia is acting as if he has the job," she added. "He probably hopes Abela will have to retire, but it looks as if he'll recover completely and be back at work soon."

"That would explain why Mario Camilleri wasn't looking too keen. I assume he's on the side of the PM in this feud." Sophia nodded. "How do you think this episode happened in the first place?" I asked. "What set the parents off like this? Surely not just the girls talking about the play at home."

"Well, there's no question they aren't very keen on Dr. Stanhope's teachings. But we think it's Alonso, Marija's brother. We think he's spying on us and telling our parents," Sophia replied. "But we need his help, so there's not much we can do." I personally doubted that he was spying. Alonso was just a nice big teddy bear of a boy, I thought. I put it down to schoolgirl paranoia, perfectly understandable in light of events.

Just then Anna Stanhope, who'd beaten a hasty retreat when the crowd got ugly, returned rather pale and flustered. I assumed she had been frightened by the experience, but it soon became apparent that she was unfazed by the parents, but quite unbalanced by the presence of Victor Deva, who was being his usual overly charming self. Her appearance had changed too. Instead of her usual dull shirtmaker dress and sensible shoes, she was wearing a skirt, a pink blouse with a ruffled collar which displayed a fair amount of her more than ample bosom, and rather more stylish sandals. Her hair seemed wispier than usual, and she had taken the time to apply makeup with what seemed to my eye to be a somewhat unpracticed hand.

I decided she was totally besotted with Deva, who in turn fluttered about her paying her extravagant compliments and rushing to help her every time she tried to do something. I rather unkindly decided he was an aging Lothario out to get Anna Stanhope's money, but the flaw in this was that I wasn't at all sure she had any money for him to get, and secondly he had bought a lot of lighting equipment which couldn't be cheap. I concluded there was just no accounting for tastes.

Deva and Alonso, the gofer and suspected spy, lifted three heavy crates of lighting equipment and my two wardrobe con-

tainers onto the bus, and then we all got on and headed for
Mnajdra, the girls chattering happily as we went. Anna Stanhope and I sat together, with Victor Deva and Alonso across
from us. Anna and Victor exchanged meaningful glances from
time to time.

"That was quite the scene with the parents," I said.

"Nasty lot, aren't they?" she said. "Dinosaurs, mindless
slaves to religion, if you ask me. Should be ashamed of themselves, stunting their daughters' development like that. Got me
sacked from my part-time job, you know. Now they're trying
to stop the play. They're very much against my teachings
about the Great Goddess. They think it gives their daughters
ideas—makes them uppity. But the point is, it's true: Malta
really was a major center of Goddess worship for many centuries. Oh, I know there are archaeologists who dispute that,
most of them men, of course. But why, I ask you, when you
find dozens, hundreds even, of female figures and symbols like
the triangle, and only a handful of phallic symbols, why on
earth would you conclude their god was a man?

"The temples here are extraordinary, and they have found
as many as thirty Goddess figures, some of them ten feet high.
You can't argue that some more advanced civilization passed
through here and built the temples, because there are no temples that date to the time these were built that are even re-
motely like them. They are absolutely unique. You'd think the
Maltese would be proud of that. And whether they like it or
not, there is a very long tradition of worship of a Great Mother
Goddess throughout the Mediterranean that extended long after the temple builders of Malta, to the era of recorded history—to Roman times essentially.

"She was worshipped under many different names, and the
rituals may have varied, but the pattern of Her worship is
strikingly similar."

"Which is?" I asked. This was all new to me, as it obviously was for the parents of Malta.

"The Great Goddess, representing the power of nature, is

usually associated with a child, usually Her own, divine but of lesser status. This child never attains real adulthood. He remains forever a youth. But he often becomes the consort of the Goddess as well as Her child. The young god dies, disappears from earth. The Goddess, in extreme mourning, searches for him all over the earth, and often as far as the underworld. While She searches, life on earth goes awry. Because She is the power of earth, crops don't grow, animals and men cease to procreate. Finally a divine deal is struck. The youth, the so-called dying god, is reunited with his mother/consort for a part of the year, and must spend the rest of the year in the realm of the dead.

"And so we have these divine pairings, Great Goddess and dying god, through much of ancient history. Inanna of Sumer, Queen of Heaven and Earth, and her Dumuzi, Ishtar or Astarte with Tammuz, the warlike Anath with Ba'al in Mesopotamia, Isis and Osiris in Egypt, Aphrodite and Adonis in Greece, Cybele and Attis in Rome. Their sacred marriage and the god's death and return represent the cycles of Nature, and provided the basis for earthly kingship for many centuries. Earthly kings took their right to rule through the institution of the sacred marriage to the Goddess: They became, in effect, the earthly embodiment of the dying god. The power of the Goddess diminished over time, of course, and gradually the patriarchal gods took over, but this does not take away from the tremendous power the Great Goddess exerted over life for millennia.

"If people here think learning about this tradition gives their daughters 'ideas,' then so be it. I think it's a good antidote to all the Adam and Evil kind of stuff they get in church schools. Neanderthals!"

"You're not teaching anymore, but you're going on with the play, I take it."

"The show must go on, don't they say? I don't much mind about the teaching job. I'm on sabbatical and I can survive without the income. But I think the play's important, and so, obviously, do the girls. They've rebelled, as you can see, and turned up despite their parents. Warms my heart, I'll tell you."

"What happened to the temple builders, by the way?" I asked, thinking about the scene in the play about the temple builders where the music is supposed to end abruptly and the lights go out quickly.

"You mean did a group of parents put a stop to the temple building?" She hooted. "Seriously, nobody really knows. All activity just stopped. Maybe famine, drought, a plague of some sort. One of the great mysteries of history!"

When we got to Mnajdra, we found the site had been closed off to all but our group and a number of workmen who were erecting a large awning designed to protect the guests while they were watching the performance. Several members of the police and army were watching over the proceedings. Security for this performance was going to be very tight, that was clear. A guard met the bus and checked off each of our names as we disembarked, then all our cases, mine with the wardrobe and all Victor's electrical equipment, were opened and searched.

We got to work. We did a quick run-through of one of the later scenes in which two of the girls represent women trying to find enough food to feed their families during the German blockade of the island during the Second World War. I knew the story of Malta's heroism during the war: The day after Mussolini joined forces with Hitler, the bombing of Malta had continued until the island acquired the dubious distinction of being the most bombed out place on the planet. Such was its strategic importance in the Mediterranean that in a two-month period, twice as many bombs fell on Malta as fell on London in a year at the height of the blitz.

Rationing began in 1941, the island completely cut off by the Axis blockade. In August of 1942, two weeks before the island would have had to surrender, five out of an original convoy of fourteen Allied ships limped into the Grand Harbour with supplies. For its heroism, and in recognition of the terrible suffering the islanders had sustained, Malta was awarded the George Cross, the only nation ever to receive it.

I knew that the islanders had suffered terribly, on the brink of starvation, bombed day and night from Italy. But I had never heard the story so poignantly told, seen as it was now by these students, and even though I'd heard the scene before, I was again quite moved by it. It was one of the parts that Sophia had written.

"This scene is quite wonderful, you know," I said to Sophia. "You have a rare talent for this. Maybe you should think about a writing career."

She blushed. "Thank you. Dr. Stanhope said that too. I'd really like to try to write. But my father wouldn't let me. He thinks I should get married soon and stay here and raise a family. He's not too keen on Anthony either. If he goes away to school, my father won't let me go with him. It's a problem," she sighed.

I'm a firm believer in the Prime Directive, whether it's applied to intergalactic journeys or to the kind of travel the rest of us do: that is, that you should leave a place the way you found it and not do anything to affect the future. I realize this rule would severely restrict the activities of the Anna Stanhopes among us, to say nothing of the missionary zeal of various religious organizations and those nations with aspirations to empire. But there it is. I could not help feeling, though, on hearing Sophia's words, that the world had not changed much since Marissa Cassar had decided to do what her father wanted rather than following her heart, and that a little education about the Great Goddess might be just what Sophia and her friends needed.

I left Sophia to help Victor, who was working away at his lights. I could see he really was good at "electricals." I helped him string wires as the girls rehearsed and he worried a great deal about the exact placement of the poles. Camilleri and his assistant, Esther whatever her name was, were also helpful. They'd arranged for the grassy area in front of the site to be cleared and smoothed out so chairs could be placed there, and for the hydro people to string a temporary line all the way from the restaurant at the entrance to the temple site way up the hill. Most of the time, though, they fussed a great deal about the comfort of the guests. Camilleri watched as a couple of heaters were placed in the tents, since evenings were still cool.

"We'll have a bar set up for them at the back of the tent," he explained to me. "Champagne, caviar, the best, of course."

"Of course," I murmured.

"After the performance there will be a state banquet at the Palace. We're out to impress these people, to convince them we can play in their league, so to speak."

Mr. Camilleri had seen to it that a temporary storage shed had been set up out of site behind the temple, so we were able to leave a lot of our equipment and the costumes there. After the rehearsal, we all piled back on the bus and headed into Valletta. I had been planning to walk back to the house, but Anna suggested I accompany them. "Victor is not entirely happy with the music we are using to open the show," she said. "He has an idea, a modern Italian composer, that he thinks is just the ticket. Such a cultured man!" she said rather breathlessly. "Anyway, if you haven't seen the market, it's kind of fun, and if we hurry we can get there before it closes. Why don't you come along?"

Since I had been trying all day to avoid thinking about the conversation I'd had earlier with Marissa and what the implications of what she'd told me in connection with the murder of Martin Galea might be, I decided to go.

The open-air market in Valletta is situated in the steeply sloped, narrow, and aptly named Merchant Street. The street is closed to vehicular traffic almost every morning, and vendors set up temporary stalls right down the middle of the street, from which they sell everything from tapes to T-shirts to towels. That day it was very crowded, and while we all started out together, I soon lost track of Victor and Anna, Sophia and the rest of the girls, as gradually we all went our separate ways, our paths crossing from time to time as we looked around. I saw Marissa and Joseph in the crowds, but they didn't see me.

I was inching my way along, close to the buildings on one side of the street, when suddenly I felt a strong arm reach out of a doorway, grab me, and pull me into the darkness. It was the Great White Hunter again. "We've got to talk!" he croaked. "There is something you should know, something wrong. You, the others, danger!"

He was unshaven and reeked of alcohol and sweat. At close quarters, his jaunty hat was stained, as was his shirt. In the closeness of the doorway, I felt almost ill in his presence. I wrenched my arm away and made a run for it. Convinced he would follow me, I dodged through the crowds in the marketplace, looking for someone I knew.

I finally stopped and looked behind me, but couldn't see him. By now the fright was passing, and I could feel myself getting angry. "Enough of this!" I said to myself, and then, determined to be the hunter rather than the hunted, I started looking for him to give him a piece of my mind.

At first I couldn't find him, but then I saw his hat bobbing along in the crowd about a block and a half ahead of me. I followed as quickly as I could but gained very little ground because of the crowds. I did manage to keep him in view, however, and saw him turn down a side street. I reached that corner just in time to see him enter St. John's Co-Cathedral, the place where he and I had already had our baffling conversation in the crypt.

By the time I got to the church, a tour group was slowly filing in, delaying me enough that there was no sign of him when I got inside. I moved quickly through the chapels on the left of the altar, but could not find him there. The gate to the crypt, I noted, was chained this time. Trying to keep my eye on the main doors as best I could, I looked in the vestry and then moved to check the chapels on the right-hand side of the church. He wasn't there either. I couldn't be absolutely certain he hadn't left while I was checking the chapels, but there was still one place to look: the cathedral museum.

I paid the entrance fee and quickly walked through the first room where the Caravaggio was exhibited, then along a hallway and up a flight of stairs to a room with huge tapestries covering all the walls, and a choice of left or right. I listened carefully but could hear no sound. There was no one in sight, neither staff nor visitor. I chose to go to the right, since left led to the exit, and walked along a narrow hallway with windows on one side overlooking the street. I paused for a second or two to look out, and found myself overlooking the market. The vendors were beginning to take down their stalls, so the scene was even more chaotic than before, but I did catch sight of Anna almost directly below, and a little further down Marissa was talking to someone that I assumed was Joseph, although I couldn't see his face.

I left the window, turned right at the end of the corridor, and came to a room, a dead end, with another display of tapestries and some glass cases filled with illuminated manuscripts. Once again there seemed to be no one there. I quickly circled the room to make sure GWH was not hiding behind one of the cases, checking for telltale bulges in the tapestries that would reveal his hiding place, but he was not there. I retraced my steps, looking out the window again. Anna and Victor were studying a tape at one of the stalls. Sophia and Anthony were chatting on the far side of the street. I could not see Marissa or Joseph.

I cut through the room with the tapestries and headed toward the exit. I found myself in a room filled with memorabilia of the Knights of Malta. Elaborate robes were displayed in high glass cases, and on the walls were crests and other items significant to the Knights. I didn't see him at first, because the room was ill lit, presumably to protect the exhibits.

He was standing at the far side of the room, and watching him through one of the glass cases, I could see he was assiduously studying a suit of armor. I walked quietly up behind him, determined to frighten him as he had frightened me. But the Great White Hunter, whoever he was, had saved his worst encounter with me for last. He was dead, shot in the head, but still standing, locked in a ghastly embrace with the suit of armor, his body impaled on the Knight's long sword.

AHRIMAN

☿ TEN

IT IS COME. THE OTTOMAN fleet. Thirty thousand men strong. Beacons flare along the coast, My people scurry for shelter. In vain. The stench of death is everywhere. Ditches fill with putrifying corpses, headless bodies float on crosses in the harbor, the water red with blood. But still the Knights, stubborn, no, reckless, in their faith, hang on.

Is it possible? That flag? The Knights' Cross? Is the battle won? Will there be peace at last?

"WOULD YOU LIKE TO TELL me about it?" the Mountie said in a studied casual tone as he handed me the chopping board, knife, and a bunch of parsley and gestured to me to start chopping.

It was late in the day following my discovery of the body in the museum. I had gone for help, of course, and had once more found myself at police headquarters in Floriana. This time, however, it was Tabone's day off, and I was forced to endure a questioning that bordered on interrogation from another policeman who evidently felt Tabone's belief in my innocence misplaced. In retrospect I suppose it was understandable, this being the second dead body I'd found since arriving on these shores. The more he badgered me, however, the more closemouthed I got, refusing to tell anything other than the details of how I'd found the body. I said nothing about the episode in the market, nor my other encounters with the deceased, deciding to wait until Tabone's return even if it meant a night in jail. I did learn one thing while I waited. The police had no more clue than I did as to the identity of the body.

It was the wee hours of the morning before Tabone could be located by telephone, and I was allowed to leave in the custody of the Mountie. Rob had brought the car and drove me home, and I'd have to say he showed a tact I wouldn't have credited him with in that after asking me if I was okay, and hearing my rather prim answer that I was, he'd not bothered me for information on the way to the house. I went straight to bed when we got there, and slept pretty well all day, not awakening until almost dinnertime.

When I went downstairs, Rob was already starting dinner preparations. He'd put on his apron and a pair of those demilune reading glasses through which he was peering at a piece of paper, a recipe presumably, on the counter. It gave him a rather endearing air, I had to admit.

"What are you making?" I asked in a feeble attempt to avoid his question.

"Something called beef olives if I have understood the name correctly," he replied. "Beef sliced very thin, then rolled and stuffed with ground pork, hard-boiled eggs, tomatoes, and spices. It's cooked in a red wine, onion, and tomato sauce. I decided to try to make something local. A very nice woman in the grocery store gave me detailed instructions," he added, gesturing toward the piece of paper on the counter.

"You do very well with the women in the stores here," I said, recalling the women in the bakery in Mellieha.

"Don't I?" he replied, grinning. "Found the same grocery store as before. The proprietor and I are old friends now. I'm starting to get the hang of finding my way around here. You ignore the signs, I take it. Just because you think your route takes you to Siggiewi, for example, doesn't mean you follow the signs for Siggiewi. You just head in its general direction. It's sort of like a bypass on the thruway right?"

I nodded.

"And the rules of the road. Technically, I know, one should yield to the right. I say technically, because as near as I can tell, no one yields to anyone or anything. But once you enter into the spirit of it all, approach driving with a kind of *joie de vivre*, shall we say, and as long as you don't mind the odd dent or two, it begins to work for you.

"I'm also getting used to the car. In fact, I'm wondering why Ford and General Motors ever felt the need for second gear! Now, after that pleasant diversion, perhaps we should get back to the subject at hand," he said, peering at me over the top of his glasses.

"Which is?" I tried, assiduously lining the parsley up in neat little rows and starting to chop.

"Which is, the corpse in the safari suit, of course."

"Why would you think I would have anything more to add to what I've already told the police?" I asked, the knife frozen in mid stroke.

He looked at me for a moment. "I'd like to say it was intuition honed by twenty-five years of dazzling detective work, but the real answer? Let's just say you shouldn't take up poker. You don't have the face for it. And . . . how do I put this delicately? You seem to be developing the bad habit of finding murder victims, or being associated with them in some way. And not just in Malta either."

"I assume that in addition to Martin Galea and the guy in the safari suit, you're referring to an incident in Mexico a couple of years ago."

"I am."

"So you've been checking up on me."

"That's my job," he said mildly.

I could hear a certain tone creeping into my voice. "And your conclusion?"

He looked across the counter at me. "I've just handed you the sharpest knife in this kitchen. You could, if you chose to, take that as a solid vote of confidence."

I really didn't know what to think of this man, but I willed myself to relax. He smiled at me. "So what do you have to say?"

"There's nothing much to say, really. I first saw the man in a safari suit on the plane from Paris. He was causing a bit of a scene. Wanted to bring his own drinks on board. I saw him later at customs. I did notice one thing: He had a metal detector stuck in with his golf clubs. He does stick out in a crowd. There aren't too many people running around this island in that getup."

"Not many people with golf clubs either," the Mountie said. "I'm told there is only one golf course on this island. But go on."

"The next day I kept running into him, sometimes literally—I stepped on his toe—around Valletta. Anthony was taking me on a tour, and we kept ending up at the same places as this guy—the Archaeological Museum, St. John's Co-Cathedral, and so on."

"These are all normal tourist spots, I take it?"

"They would be, I think. Anthony was showing them to me because they were all designed and built by the architect Gerolamo Cassar, who he says is an ancestor. "

"Is that it?"

"No. There's more. I was trying to drive to the University. I got lost near a place called Verdala Palace, and you know the car . . . I went past him very quickly, but then he tried to run me off the road."

"Did he now? Whatever for?"

"I thought at the time it was my terrible driving. But really I have no idea. I didn't see him for a few days after that, until after Galea turned up, and then, while I was looking around the crypt in the cathedral . . ."

The Mountie raised his eyebrows and looked at me sceptically.

"I don't know why I went there. Perhaps I was a little obsessed with death, and maybe I was entitled to be, under the circumstances.'' I glared at him. ''In any event he was there, and we had this bizarre conversation. He looked very strange, frightened, I'd say, when he saw me, and offered me thirty percent.''

''Thirty percent?''

''Of what, I know you're thinking. Whatever it is, or was, we got up to splitting it fifty/fifty.''

''You bargained with a stranger for something that you have no idea what it might be? You are nuts!''

''It wasn't like that. I was tired and a bit out of it, so I just stood there looking surprised, I should think. He took this to mean his offer wasn't good enough, I guess, and revised it. It's a technique, I've been thinking, that once perfected, could be used to real advantage on my buying trips,'' I said, trying to make light of the matter.

''I think he finally figured out that I had no idea what he was talking about, because he ended up by saying, 'Then it isn't you!' or something like that,'' I continued. ''And then he gave me a good push out of the way and dashed out of the crypt. That's the last time I saw him until yesterday.''

''In the museum.''

''Well, no. Actually in the market. He grabbed me and pulled me into a doorway, told me we had to talk, there was something wrong, danger for me and for others.''

''And this dangerous thing was?''

''I don't know. I ran away. But then I got mad, and followed him into the cathedral, and from there into the museum. You know the rest. Do the police know who he was?''

''Not yet. There was no ID on him. No wallet, passport, money. You have any idea what his name is?''

I paused. ''I am trying to recall if the flight attendants referred to him by name. I think maybe they did, but I'm not sure I can remember it.''

''Accent?''

''American. California, maybe.''

''So what have we got here? An American in a strange outfit

flies here from Paris. He's got a metal detector with him, so presumably he's looking for something metal. He may, or may not, be a fan of Gerolamo Cassar, but more likely he's a tourist, visiting historic places of interest. I say that despite the fact that he would appear to be a little, shall we say, nervous, or even possibly paranoid. And his name is . . ." He looked at me and the name clicked into place.

"Graham. They called him Mr. Graham."

"Well done!" Rob smiled. "I'm calling Tabone. Here, stir this from time to time, will you?" he said, gesturing toward the skillet.

He came back a few minutes later and checked on my work. It really smelled delicious, I had to admit, and apparently my stirring technique was acceptable, because he appeared satisfied.

"Tabone is suitably grateful for the name. He hadn't narrowed it down to Mr. Graham yet. As for the murder I'm here to investigate, I also told him about our visit to Mellieha. I expect he'll be asking Joseph in for a little chat shortly. The good news is that Tabone's been able to convince the former coroner, Dr. Caruana, in whom he places much more confidence than in his successor, to come out of retirement just this once to help us out. We should start getting some more satisfactory answers as early as tomorrow or the day after. And"—here he smiled at me—"with any luck your friend Joseph will be off the hook."

"And my friend Marilyn will be back on, I suppose. Has she turned up?"

"Nope. No sign of her. I talked to my chief before you got back. We've had men with dogs out searching the ravine behind the house, and we've gone over the house and his car in the airport garage with a fine-tooth comb. No blood in the car anywhere. Only the fingerprints you'd expect in his car and his house. His, the maid's, and lots of other prints we assume are hers. We have his prints from his visa application, and Tabone has also sent a copy of the real thing from here. There aren't many prints on the steering wheel. He wore driving gloves most of the time, I'm told. Anyway, the short answer to your question is that there is no sign of Mrs. Galea."

He served up the beef with a green salad and poured a very passable Maltese Cabernet. As we ate we talked about our experiences as tourists on this charming island, and we seemed, for a brief moment or two, to be establishing rapport.

Inevitably, however, the conversation turned to the two murders.

"Don't you think it's odd that two foreign visitors turn up dead—murdered no less—on this tiny little island within a few days of each other?"

"Tabone said much the same thing. He said the place was going to the dogs, or words to that effect. Two visitors murdered, and a couple of priests attacked someplace—Mdina, I think he said. You'd think priests would be pretty safe in a place like this, wouldn't you? All these churches!" he mused. "But if you're thinking there might be a connection, very unlikely, I'd say."

"I don't know why, but I can't shake the feeling that they are linked in some way, that if we followed the threads, worked our way through the two cases, we'd end up at the same place, somehow."

"I'm here to investigate Galea's death and I'm going to stick to that. Investigating Graham would be a waste of time, in my opinion," he said. "I mean if you're looking for a link between Galea and Graham, the only obvious link is you. You knew Galea, you were on the same plane as Graham, you're the one who kept bumping into him. I didn't come here to investigate every crime on the island!"

I could feel myself getting really irritated. "And why exactly are you here?" I asked in a faintly accusing tone. "Do they usually send a sergeant from the RCMP every time a Canadian gets killed abroad? What is this, a reward for good behavior or something? Got some information on your chief he'd rather you not report?"

He looked at me for a second or two. "Consolation prize, more likely," he said finally. "I've been on disability leave for a while. Had a bit of an accident. I thought I was closing in on some big-time drug dealers. It turns out they were closing in on me." I just looked at him, and after a pause he continued.

"We had a bit of a confrontation, of the automotive sort. The trouble was, I was driving a squad car, they were driving a truck. I don't remember much except the headlights coming at me broadside. I woke up a few days later in hospital. I was a bit of a mess. I'd like to say 'you should see the other guy,' but the other guy got away. I had a lot of time to contemplate the state of the universe, whether to stay on—on the force, I mean—and I guess I will. I'm due back soon, but I guess I'm in for a desk job. I hope I'll get used to it," he said tersely.

"But to answer your question more directly: The Maltese authorities asked for some help with this one. There really wasn't anyone available, but I guess they thought I was well enough to muddle my way around an island sixteen miles long."

"I'm sorry," I said, feeling like a jerk. I'd noticed he was limping a couple of times, and I'd just never thought about it. I wondered why this was the way it was between him and me. I always assumed the worst about him, and then found out that quite the opposite was true. "I was being a bit of a pig."

"Forget it," he said. "I was being a bit of a pig myself. To give your musings the attention they deserve, let's assume there is a link somehow between the two. What would Graham be doing here that would get him killed?"

"I kept wondering if all the places where I saw him have something in common, other than Gerolamo Cassar, I mean," I replied. "I did a little research and found they do. Although what it all means, I'm not sure."

"Go on," he said.

"Well," I said, drawing a deep breath, "Anthony emphasized the architecture of Valletta, overemphasized it, I'd have to say, because of his enthusiasm for his subject. He took me to see many of the buildings designed by Gerolamo Cassar, but other than mentioning briefly that Cassar had studied with some other architect—Laparelli, I think he said—who was the Pope's architect, he didn't say much about him. But Cassar was the architect to the Knights of Malta, or more formally, the Sovereign Military and Hospitaller Order of St. John of Jerusalem, Rhodes, and Malta, the so-called Knights of St. John. Malta was their home for about 250 years.

"The Knights were organized into what were called *langues*, languages or tongues. There were eight originally, named for the countries the Knights originally came from. *Langues* were headed by *piliers* or priors and were accommodated in their own inns or *auberges*. The Head of the Order was called the Grand Master."

"And so?" Rob said.

"So, all the buildings Anthony took me to were originally buildings belonging to the Order. The Prime Minister's office: originally the Auberge of Castille et Leon; the Post Office, the Auberge d'Italie; the Museum of Archaeology, the Auberge de Provence. The House of Representatives was the Palace of the Grand Master. Verdala Palace—it was near there that I had the little incident on the road—was once the summer house of the Grand Master."

"And the clincher," I said, "is St. John's Cathedral. That was the Knights' own church, and the crypt is where many of the Grand Masters are buried!"

"And your point is . . . ?" the Mountie said.

I glared at him. "I'm not really sure. But every place I saw Graham was related in a very direct way to the Knights. There are lots of stories about the Knights, both the Knights of St. John and the Knights Templar, those whose job it was to guard the temple in Jerusalem. There are all kinds of rumors of great treasure of incomparable worth hidden by the Knights, like the Chalice, for example, and more than that, lots of conspiracy theories, that some of the Knights went underground, so to speak, and are now in very powerful positions, except that we don't know who they are." I knew as soon as the words came out of my mouth that they would not sit well with this particular law enforcement officer.

He looked at me rather disdainfully. "I've read about those. What's that Italian semiotics professor—Eco? He wrote a book about that."

"*Foucault's Pendulum*?"

"Right. That's the one. Great book, or should I say, great work of fiction. Surely you are not talking about secret societies that rule the world unbeknownst to us! Are you saying that Graham, if that's his name, was killed to protect the conspiracy, or something? That he was stuck on a Knight's sword as a sign, no better still, a warning?"

It did sound rather ridiculous. "Not really, I guess," I said lamely.

Just then, almost as if to spare me further embarrassment, the phone rang. It was Alex, checking up on me. I told him about the most recent developments, and I could hear the concern in his voice. "I hope you aren't investigating the murders, Lara. Leave that stuff to the police," he said severely.

"I know. There's a policeman right here, as a matter of fact. So don't worry, Alex." I was about to say good-bye, when I thought of something else.

"If you can, do some of your wonderful research and find out what a Mintoff man is. It's been bothering me ever since I heard it."

"I know the answer to that one already," Alex replied. "I visited Malta a few times when I was in the merchant marine, you know. It was a stop on a route from Southampton to Piraeus via Malta, Cyprus, and, in the old days, Beirut. The Grand Harbour was one of our ports of call. Splendid place, although there was always the Gut, of course."

"What in heaven's name is the Gut?"

"Let's start with your first question." He laughed. "Mintoff would be Dom Mintoff, head of the Labour Party, and the Prime Minister of Malta for many years. Became PM in the mid-fifties, if I recall. A Mintoff man, I presume, would be a supporter. Mintoff was a charismatic and some would say quixotic leader. One day you'd be his friend, the next his bitter enemy. After the War, Mintoff originally wanted Malta to integrate with Great Britain, to have representation in the House of Commons and so on. He held a referendum of sorts on the subject, and the majority of Maltese voted in favor of integration, but the British were cool to the idea. Mintoff went off the British and started pushing the cause of independence. Malta achieved nationhood in 1964, I believe. One thing you'll find out if you get into a political discussion, which frankly I wouldn't advise, is that politics is a very heated subject in Malta. People are avid—perhaps rabid is a better word—supporters of a particular political party. They hold their political loyalties for their whole lives.''

"That would explain why the Hedgehog—don't ask, Alex!—thought Giovanni was a traitor for changing political parties!''

"I have no idea who Giovanni is, nor do I believe I have ever heard a hedgehog speak, but the substance of what you are saying is true. Politics in Malta has divided whole communities and has resulted in violence from time to time. But I've talked your ear off, and should get off the line.''

"Not so fast, Alex. What's the Gut?''

"The Gut is a backstreet in Valletta. It was originally the only place the Knights were allowed to fight duels. Did you notice several of the steep streets in Valletta are made up of tiny steps? That's the only way Knights in full armor could navigate a steep hill, by swinging their legs out to the side and up. The steps are just the right height for a Knight in armor. Later the street became the place to find sleazy bars. Notorious place. You could get yourself into a lot of trouble. I imagine it's been cleaned up since I was there,'' he replied.

"Alex! This is a whole new side to you I'd never have guessed.'' I laughed.

"You lead a sheltered life, my dear. Be careful, please," he said and rang off.

I told Rob about my conversation with Alex, particularly the part about politics. Rob was very quiet while I spoke, perhaps because the conversation about his injuries had depressed him in some way. I took his silence to be my advantage, and started plotting our next moves.

"This makes me think we should go and have a chat with this Giovanni fellow, the childhood chum of Martin Galea. Maybe the killing was politically motivated. Surely it can't be difficult to locate a Cabinet Minister. Maybe he was to be one of the mystery guests at the social event here. It makes sense, with the two of them having been friends in childhood. And I know Galea was not above using his connections. Maybe he asked Galizia to set it up."

"I doubt Galizia has anything to do with it, and I imagine that it may be easy to locate a Cabinet Minister, but not so easy to get in to see him," Rob replied. I detected, or perhaps imagined—in retrospect I'm not sure—something patronizing in his reply, and it irritated me. I resolved to do a little investigating of my own, without him,

Perhaps as he'd mentioned, I don't have the face for deception, because he said, in a supercilious tone, "You'd do well to remember the words of George Bernard Shaw: 'Hell is full of amateurs.' *Man and Superman*, I think. Actually he said musical amateurs, but you get the general idea."

My, my, I thought, a literate cop. First Umberto Eco, and now George Bernard Shaw. It might actually be possible to have a civilized conversation with this man. But not tonight. "And you might do well to remember," I shot back, "the Chinese proverb that says something to the effect that a man should take care not to anger a woman, because he has to sleep sometime, with his eyes closed."

"Sleep? You who sleeps in a huge bed with a down duvet! You think I sleep on that nasty cot? It's . . . it's—what do you call those temples you're always going on about?—Neolithic, that's what it is. No, way older than that. Pre-Neolithic,'' he sputtered.

"Paleolithic?" I smiled sweetly. "Tough!" I went up to my room and shut the door—I like to think I didn't slam it, just closed it firmly—and resolutely thought about Lucas. Kind, sweet, and hardly ever argumentative Lucas. Not that Lucas was perfect or anything. He had his faults, like everybody. He was still, after a relationship of two years, a bit of a cipher to me, a part of him always held back. There were so many things about him I still didn't know. Like his politics, for example, since that had been a topic of conversation that evening. I knew Lucas had ties of some kind with a radical underground group that fought for the rights of the native peoples of Mexico, but how radical and how involved, I didn't know. I didn't ask either, because I knew he wouldn't tell me. But compared to someone like the Mountie, Lucas was a prince.

That night I dreamed the Mountie and I were taking part in a round dance. We were in a large group of people, several of whom I knew: Marilyn Galea, Anna Stanhope and her Victor, Sophia and the Farrugias, Vincent Tabone. Even the Hedgehog was there. We were dancing in a large circle in front of Mnajdra. It was night, but we were lit by a spotlight.

From time to time the steps of the dance would fling Rob and me into the middle of the circle, where we'd smile and whirl, the picture of friendship. But then the music would change, the pattern would move on, and we'd be separated by the circle once more.

As bright and noisy as the dance was, I knew there was menace there, a terrible darkness oozing around the stones, swirling about the feet of the dancers, insinuating itself in our souls. In the dream I knew it to be Ahriman, ancient Persian god of the underworld, the embodiment of pure evil.

I could not stop the dance.

❧ ELEVEN

HAVE YOU FORGOTTEN WHAT IT is to be a Knight? What has become of the vows you took, the sacrifices you promised, the valor you espoused? Look at you, bickering, brawling, whoring, duelling, drinking, your minds and bodies bloated with dishonor. You disgust Me! Soon, displaced and discredited, you will be driven from My islands, as you so richly deserve.

THE STORAGE SHED AT MNAJDRA was broken into during the night. Anna Stanhope, Victor, and I were called to the site the next morning. Mario Camilleri and his assistant Esther met us there, along with a rather officious policeman who did not appear to have Tabone's sensitivity or sense of humor.

The shed, one of those temporary aluminum structures, a somewhat larger than usual version of a garden shed, had been spray painted in swirls of a rather nasty green. There was also some hastily scrawled text. ''Rude expressions,'' the policeman replied to my query. There was no translation forthcoming.

More seriously, the padlock had been forced and broken. We gingerly stepped inside to find the place in disarray. Clothes were scattered everywhere, and the boxes containing the light and sound equipment had been upset. ''Perverts!'' Anna muttered under her breath.

We got down to work. Anna and I started gathering up the

costumes, inspecting them and putting them on hangers and back on the rack where I'd left them. Most were just dusty, a couple required washing, and one, roughly handled, had caught on the hook of a metal hanger and was torn. I noticed with genuine regret that it was Sophia's. The tear didn't look too serious to me, although no one has ever complimented me on my sewing. Marissa, who'd mentioned that she'd sold her lacework, seemed the logical candidate for the job, not the least because of what I saw as genuine affection for her son's girlfriend. I figured she could probably also use a bit of a diversion too. I told Anna I'd see to it that the costume was taken care of in lots of time for the performance.

Victor fussed around his boxes with Mario's help, but they had not been opened, the locks still intact and functioning. He reported two spotlight bulbs smashed and said he'd get them replaced right away.

"Sheer vandalism!" Anna said. "If they'd wanted anything of value, they would have broken into the boxes and taken the sound equipment. If they can get in the door, those little locks would have given them no trouble. Whoever it was just wanted to stop the performance. Perverts!" she repeated.

It certainly looked that way, although I must say I had the impression that, for a very small island, a lot of very strange things were going on. We all worked at tidying up the place, even the rather retiring Esther.

"Esther, I'm not sure we've been officially introduced," I said when we were outside together straightening out the costumes and inspecting them in the sunlight for dirt and damage.

"Esther Aquilina." She smiled. "I hope you are enjoying your stay in Malta," she said, then looked dubious. "Except for this, I mean," she gestured toward the shed, "and of course, the murders." She bit her lip.

"I am, actually, despite these things. Malta is an exceptionally beautiful place."

She brightened. "You must have a very interesting job, Esther," I said, "working in the Prime Minister's office."

She nodded. "It's Mario who works for the Prime Minister," she said. "I work in the Protocol office, the External Relations Ministry. I work on visits of foreign dignitaries, that sort of thing. It's actually lots of detail work, not very exciting sometimes, until they get here, and then it gets way too exciting. Worrying everything will go okay and all," she explained.

"You must know the Minister, then," I said, in what I hoped was a casual tone. "What's his name again?"

"Giovanni Galizia," she replied obligingly. "Yes, I work for him. But of course someone of my level in the organization doesn't get to deal with the Minister very much. He's very nice, very charming, though. Except, of course, when something goes wrong," she sighed. "I'm hoping he won't hear about this," she said glumly.

"But you must get to meet some very interesting people, and attend some lovely events," I said, trying to sound suitably awed by all this. In fact, I'd had the dubious pleasure of meeting a couple of Cabinet Ministers who'd been patrons of the shop. Neither had particularly impressed me, burdened as they were by unbridled ambition untempered, in my opinion, jaded though that may be, by an equal passion for public service. It sounded, come to think of it, a little like the person the Hedgehog had described, and would not have been out of keeping with a close friend of Martin Galea. Perhaps public service is not the high calling it once was.

"I'm still pretty new to the job," she replied. "So I haven't really met that many people. The Minister, though, is the Prime Minister's closest advisor," she said proudly. "His office is very close to the Prime Minister's."

That might be true about the location; as to the rest of it, not from what I'd heard. "And where is that?" I asked.

"The Palazzo Parisio, around the corner on Merchant Street. Napoleon stayed there; he slept right in the alcove in the Minister's office. In what is now the Minister's office, I mean. He, Napoleon that is, was on his way to Egypt, and he captured Malta first because of its strategic importance."

She went on a bit more about various other aspects of Malta's history, and what she had to say was very interesting. Until I'd arrived here, and particularly until I'd become involved with Anna Stanhope's historical drama, I'd had no idea that Malta had played such an important role in Mediterranean history, and once again wished Galea had given me more than twenty-four hours notice about this trip. But there was something in the way that Esther was talking about it. She sounded as if she'd memorized it all, somehow, as if a button had been pushed and now the speech was to unfold in its entirety. Characteristic of a recent protocol school graduate, I thought, or someone determined to please. I was glad when the speech was over. I had what I wanted: an address for the man I wanted to see. I had learned something else too. Esther made much of the fact that her minister lived in Mdina, among the rich and famous, I could tell.

Soon Victor, Mario, and Anna joined us outside, and we all surveyed the damage.

"We must get this painted," Victor said, eyeing the shed severely. "I have a friend, a cousin actually, who will help us with this." And with a bow in our general direction, he started up the causeway to the exit.

"We'll get some of the boys to help," Anna called after him. "Maybe Sophia's young man . . . Anthony, I think his name is." She turned to me. I nodded.

"Isn't he a lovely man?" she said to the retreating back of Victor Deva.

"Lovely," I agreed.

"I haven't had much experience with men," she said in a low voice. "I'm not the type men go for, you know. Never got to the prom, so to speak. Too big, too loud . . ."

"Too smart?" I added. She smiled at me.

"Thank you. I like that better. I'm such a novice. At my age! I'm just kind of trying to find my way with Victor, taking it one day at a time. I feel totally inadequate but also totally exhilarated!'' She paused for a moment, then said, ''I know what you're thinking. That I'm an old fool.''

''Not at all,'' I said. ''I think he's perfectly charming, and he obviously has a crush on you. I think that's just great.''

She beamed. ''Thank you again,'' she said, squeezing my hand. ''Now we must get back to work. Lots to do before the rehearsal tonight. Do you think you can get these costumes in shape?''

''Sure. Esther is giving them all a good going-over. Most of them just need to be brushed off. There's only one that really needs work, and I will get Marissa, Anthony's mother, to work on it if she's willing. I'll be off now. See you about six.''

She stopped me for a moment as I left. ''I should tell you that the girls are quite chuffed at how well the play is looking with Victor's lights and music and the improvements you've made in the costumes and the way things flow,'' she said rather shyly. ''There's no question that between the two of you, you've moved the production up a notch, professionally speaking. I want you to know I appreciate it as much as the girls do.'' I was grateful for her kind words. With so many bad things happening, any thoughtful gesture almost brought me to tears, and so I waved my thanks and got on my way before I embarrassed myself.

I was in a hurry to get back to the house. It was, with all the fussing about at Mnajdra, getting well into the afternoon, and I was expecting Alex to call. I'd left a message on the answering machine at the shop, knowing that Alex always checked that from home very early, and it had been the middle of the night Toronto time when I'd been able to extract details on the Great White Hunter out of the Mountie. I'd learned, after considerable dancing around the subject, a great deal of pretending that our tiff of the evening before had never taken place, and on top of it all, having to cook him breakfast, that the corpse in the safari suit was an American by the name of Ellis Graham. His home address was Los Angeles; his occupation was listed as film producer. Rob had obviously had a call from Tabone the previous evening. I'd heard the phone ring but was too busy sulking to ask about it at the time, and too proud to ask directly the next morning.

Alex, a man of many talents, had worked very briefly as an actor when he retired and was trying to find a way to supplement his pension. He'd gone to one of those cattle call auditions and actually got to play the grandfather in a commercial for a burger chain. As a result, flushed with success he told me, he'd joined Actors Equity. It was his first and last part, but I figured his union connections might assist us in getting information on Ellis Graham, film producer.

While I waited for his call, however, I had to deal with a sad Marissa and a very agitated Anthony. He arrived just as I was explaining to Marissa what had happened at Mnajdra and was showing her Sophia's torn costume.

"Mum!" he shouted, coming through the door at breakneck speed. "Where are you? They've taken Dad away. The police. They've taken him to Floriana for questioning. What will we do?"

Marissa looked sad and uncomfortable. "Anthony," I said, "relax. They're interviewing all of us. I was there a couple of days ago and so was your mother."

"But Dad wasn't even here when Mr. Galea arrived, I mean, when his body got here. I don't understand this!" he exclaimed, his lower lip trembling.

"I'm sure they are talking to everyone who knew Mr. Galea, to help them with their investigation," I said in my most soothing tone, the one usually reserved for irate customers. "I'm sure your father will be glad to help the police with their investigation." Anthony looked somewhat mollified, but I felt awful.

"Anthony," I said, "how'd you like to help out with a real problem? The storage shed at Mnajdra was broken into last night, and the outside was damaged. It needs to be painted, and with the performance only two nights away, it's a bit of an emergency. Victor Deva, a friend of Dr. Stanhope, is getting paint and some help from a cousin of his, but I'm not sure they can get it done in time. It's a big job. Do you think you could help? I'm sure Sophia would really be pleased.''

Anthony looked slightly dubious.

"You could take the car. That is, if your mother thinks it's okay," I added. Anthony capitulated totally. Soon he was off, engine revving, to help out at Mnajdra.

"Thank you," Marissa said, taking Sophia's costume out of my hands and smoothing it carefully. "I'll take very good care of this dress," she said. Then, as she turned to leave, she asked, "Do you have children?"

"No," I replied.

"Perhaps you should have," she said. "You handle Anthony better than I do."

"You know that's not true. It's always easier for a stranger in these circumstances," I said in an offhand way, but the truth was I didn't much want to think about what she had said. It was a conversation I'd had with myself often enough to know I didn't like the conclusion I reached. Mercifully, the phone rang, and there was Alex.

"Make yourself comfortable, Lara. This will take a while, long-distance call or no. The good news is that Sarah has been assured by the executors of Martin Galea's estate that, unless one of us is found to have murdered Galea, there will be no problem with payment of our account, I'm pleased to say. Dave Thomson has been told the same thing, by the way. Much relief all round. The wolf was nearing the door.

"Now let me get to your question, the possible link between Graham and the Knights of Malta. I'm going to cut to the chase, here. I think Ellis Graham was a treasure hunter, and I even have an idea of what he was looking for. On the surface, Graham was exactly what he said he was: a film producer. He was actually a documentary filmmaker, and he specialized in documentaries on lost treasure: Aztec gold, shipwrecks, that sort of thing. Most recently he did a piece for the BBC on, you guessed it, the Knights of Malta, and on a great treasure belonging to the Knights, which he believed had been missing for a very long time. I actually watched the documentary on television some months ago, but I didn't know who the producer was until I researched this for you this morning.

"The point Graham made quite vividly, as I recall, was that the Knights were fabulously wealthy. To get into the Order, you had to come from only the best—by which was meant aristocratic—background, with an impeccable family history, which is to say, no hint of illegitimacy on either side of the family back for several generations. Technically, anyway. It seems some Popes were able to get offspring into the Order. One can only imagine the contortions they would have put their family history through for that." He laughed. "It reminds me a bit of some exclusive schools and colleges: Parents had to register their sons at birth, and the admission fees were hefty to say the least. So the Knights began life as wealthy people, and they became even wealthier.

"Having been driven from Jerusalem, Acre, and Rhodes, the Knights settled on Malta, and after surviving the Great Siege by the Turks, stayed there for 268 years, growing ever richer. They might have stayed forever, I suppose, except that they had a date with destiny in the person of Napoleon, who took Malta in 1798 on his way to Alexandria and his confrontation with Nelson at the Battle of the Nile.

"Napoleon didn't stay long, but he was there long enough to order the Knights to leave—which they did with barely a struggle, because by this time they had grown lazy and corrupt and were in no position or condition to fight—and he was also there long enough to loot and pillage. For example, it is believed he had the silver platters that the Knights used to serve their patients melted down to pay his soldiers for the Egyptian campaign. Various works of art were loaded onto ships and taken away from Malta, the British in hot pursuit. One ship, the *Orient*, was sunk with its treasure aboard.

"Anyway you get the idea. The point is because of the

Knights', shall we say, ambulatory and event-filled history, there's no way of being certain what they had nor what might be missing. Who's to say what got left behind in Jerusalem, or Acre, or Rhodes, or what got hidden away on Malta before they left thinking perhaps they would return, or for that matter, melted down or carted away by the French? You can almost understand the rumors, considering the history.

"Nonetheless, Ellis focused most particularly, if I recall, on a specific religious relic, a special silver cross the Knights had carried with them all the way from Jerusalem, that he felt might still be in Malta. He left the impression, and I don't have any idea whether or not this is correct, that a lot of the treasures are still on the island, hidden away in wealthy people's homes.

"My recollection is that Graham thought the cross could be found hidden either in Valletta, or in another city, Mdina, I think it was, where wealthy families are rumored to have stored away many treasures of the Order: silver, paintings, (there are rumored to be Caravaggios hanging in back rooms of the old houses) porcelain, stunning jewels. With the chaos that would have taken place when the Knights were expelled, that might have been easy enough to do. I wonder if he thought the Knights would have left clues to the location of these treasures. I have a mind he was searching for clues when you kept running into him. Maybe he thought there was a secret code in the carvings in the crypt or something like that.

"There you have it. I'll get a copy of the documentary as soon as I can and have another look at it, since I'm going on memory here. But it seems Ellis Graham must have been on the track of the treasure of the Knights, perhaps even this silver cross. More money in treasure than documentaries perhaps? That would explain the metal detector and perhaps even why he spoke to you the way he did in the crypt. He thought you were looking for it too—you were looking in all the same places—and so he tried to make a deal."

"Let's assume that's true for a moment," I said slowly.

"Then what did he mean when he said, 'Then it isn't you!' or something like that?"

"I don't know, of course, but perhaps there actually was someone else looking for the treasure. He thought it was you, because he kept running into you, but he was wrong. Dead wrong, as the saying goes. Perhaps this other person killed him to get to the treasure first.

"Actually now that I say that, I don't like it one bit. I want you to stick with that policeman fellow, the Mountie, like glue. This is getting nasty."

"I will, Alex. Really," I said. "And thanks for your usual brilliant research. What you say makes a lot of sense."

I thought for a long time about what he had said and about all I had learned that day. I had the feeling there was something about Ellis Graham that I'd forgotten, but whatever it was, it continued to elude me. I hadn't seen Rob since breakfast. He was off on business of his own, which he wasn't discussing with me. I wasn't sure whether I wanted to discuss this with him either. I felt I was at a crossroads and had to make some choices. I could look for the treasure—that had worked out well enough for me once, if you didn't count almost getting myself killed in the process; or I could pursue Giovanni Galizia, Minister for External Relations and erstwhile friend of Martin Galea.

I thought about it all evening, as I admired the storage shed all shiny and fresh-looking, complimenting Anthony, who was basking in Sophia's praise, as well as Victor and his cousin, a rather taciturn fellow by the name of Francesco Falzon. And again as I watched the rehearsal unfold. You couldn't call it a dress rehearsal exactly, with several costumes out for cleaning and repair, but it went well enough. My mind, however, was elsewhere.

I decided in the end, I have no idea why, that Galizia was the way to go. Maybe, after all, I thought, the two paths will cross. There was treasure in Mdina, that of the Knights, and, according to Esther, Mdina was also the home of the Foreign Minister. Stranger things have happened.

❤ TWELVE

I HAD HIGH HOPES FOR you, the Corsican. Little man with big ambitions. Liberté, égalité, fraternité. You sent them packing, those Knights, grown fat and rich, their vows forgotten. But you are as bad as any other, stealing from My people to finance your campaigns. Be gone. Your destiny awaits you. Trafalgar. Waterloo.

I SUPPOSE I SHOULD HAVE known, when Tabone's car pulled up shortly after I left the Honorable Giovanni Galizia's office, that someone was keeping pretty close tabs on me. At the time, however, I took it to be a coincidence, and a reasonably pleasant one. "Hop in," he said, smiling at me. "I'm glad I spotted you. Do you have time for a coffee?"

We went to the Caffe Cordina on Republic Square, the late morning haunt of businessmen who stand around the bar drinking espresso and eating pastries under painted ceilings that depict the various nations and empires that have over the centuries considered Malta part of their domain. I'd had other plans, but the truth was, this diversion had the advantage of sparing me any ruminations on the ethics of my activities in the Minister's office.

I'd made it into the External Relations Ministry, the Palazzo Parisio, with surprisingly little difficulty. It was exactly where Esther had said it was—I passed the Prime Minister's office to get there. Before I did, however, I paid a visit to the offices of the *Times*, Malta's English language newspaper, to check out what they had on the Honorable Giovanni Galizia. I was treated to a large, bulging file which contained clippings dating back about seven or eight years: a triumphant Galizia on his first election victory, a photo of his swearing-in as Minister, and numerous recent photos of him meeting with various foreign dignitaries, several of them easily recognizable, and many of Galizia opening schools, kissing babies, the usual stuff for a politician. Someone on his staff was working very hard to see that there were many so-called photo ops for the media. He was shown on several occasions with his wife, who I gathered was British and had brought to the marriage at the very least a pedigree, and the impression of pots of money.

There was only one article of any real substance, a rather lengthy but not particularly revealing interview. There was a fair amount of name-dropping of the "as I was saying the other day to Tony Blair" variety, and the usual self-serving pap about championing the little man, the downtrodden, the poor, the abused. But then he was quoted as saying, "I bring to public life the lessons of my early life in Mellieha. I know what it is to be poor. My parents died when I was very young, and I have known betrayal at the hands of someone I looked up to, someone in a position of trust."

The reporter appears to have pressed for details, but Galizia was not to be pinned down. "I'm reluctant to talk about it," he said. "I tell you this only because it is fundamental to my aspirations for Malta. I am committed to building a better life for all Maltese, but particularly the children. Some of my closest childhood friends left Malta," he went on, and I thought of Martin Galea, "as so many of us do. There are as many Maltese living abroad as there are currently living here. That is not as it should be. I think we should have a standard of living here that allows us to prosper here, and I will work very hard as a Cabinet Minister to see that the alliances we need to sustain such an economy are strengthened." A clearly impressed reporter went on to say wonderful things about Galizia's dedication and determination, and hinted he was destined for higher office, by which I understood to mean Prime Minister.

As positive as the article might be, there were tantalizing hints that all was not entirely rosy for Galizia, hints, once again, of a rift, not yet out in the open between him and the Prime Minister. There was nothing really overt about it, just elliptical references to something amiss: the fact, for example, that previous External Relations Ministers had also been Deputy Prime Ministers, an honor which had originally been bestowed upon Galizia, but then for some unspecified reason had been taken away. A demotion, I thought, and a setback for the poor boy from Mellieha. The reporter, obviously a fan of Galizia's, hinted darkly at shortcomings of some sort on the part of the Prime Minister. There was much to chew on here. I decided to pay the great man himself a visit.

The Palazzo Parisio, home of the External Relations Ministry, abuts the Prime Minister's residence on Merchant Street. The main entrance is an imposing one, a large door that opens on to a central courtyard. The door the public gets to enter, however, is on a side street, a plain little door that leads down a couple of steps into the lower level of the building. I expected to find a guard, but I was in luck. If there was one, he was off somewhere, and I made my way to the second floor where, according to the newspaper article I'd just read, the External Relations Minister's office was located. I did not see anyone as I worked my way carefully to the Minister's office.

Here my luck ran out. Galizia's office was guarded by the most formidable secretary, an Englishwoman, left over perhaps from the British regime, who reminded me of the films of Joan Crawford and Bette Davis in their declining years, or perhaps Norma Desmond of *Sunset Boulevard* fame: makeup applied with a trowel, thinning and overdone hair, and a generally cranky disposition. Behind her on the wall were three photos: The center one was the *de rigueur* portrait of the titular head of state, the President; to his right was the Prime Minister, Charles Abela, whom I recognized from newspaper pictures; and to his left Minister Galizia. While protocol had been observed, I could not help but notice that Galizia's picture dwarfed that of the Prime Minister. It was a better photo than those in the newspaper clippings, and a good sight better than the mere glimpse of him I'd had that day at the University, so I tried to memorize his features, should I have the pleasure of meeting him in person.

I summed up the secretary and decided that the imperious approach was my only chance. It was, I confess, singularly unsuccessful, but I'm not sure there was an approach that would have worked. A bribe was clearly out of the question, even had I been able to afford one.

"I would like to have a few minutes with the Minister, please," I said.

"Do you have an appointment?" she asked sharply.

"No, but I would be happy to make one," I replied, appearing to retreat slightly. "How about ten-thirty this morning?" I said, glancing at my watch. It was 10:27.

She was not amused. "What is the nature of your business?"

"I'm a journalist from Canada doing a story on Martin Galea, the famous Maltese-born architect. I am aware the Minister was a childhood friend, and I would like to interview him about it."

"You may speak to public relations, second floor."

"I'm sure the people in public relations have not met Mr. Galea, and their comments would not, therefore, be helpful," I said. "When is the Minister available?"

I thought she would say something like "For you, never," but she didn't. Instead she turned to the telephone, which was awkwardly placed on the credenza behind her, perhaps her way of treating visitors with contempt. She dialed an extension and with her back to me spoke rapidly in Maltese. I couldn't tell from her tone whether this was a positive call or not, but I was not optimistic.

As she spoke, I glanced down at her desk and saw a pile of invitations, a luscious cream paper embossed in gold, very swank. It appeared the Minister requested the pleasure of someone's company at a reception at Palazzo Galizia that very evening, if I were reading correctly upside down. I assumed they were surplus invitations: There was a guest list under them which I couldn't read.

The dragon still had her back to me and was whispering conspiratorially into the telephone, when much to my own surprise and horror, I found myself reaching quickly across the desk and plucking the top invitation off the pile. By the time she'd hung up and turned around, I'd pressed it between my handbag and my hip to conceal it, and the rationalization process had already begun: something along the lines of desperate times requiring desperate measures.

She gave me a triumphant smile and said, "Security is on its way. I suggest you leave before they get here."

"Sure," I said. "I'll send you a copy of my article. I hope you'll be pleased with the way you're portrayed. By the way," I tossed back at her as I opened the door to the stairwell, "you have lipstick on your teeth." I had the satisfaction of seeing her reach for her compact as I beat an ignominious retreat. Childish, I know. Some people just bring out the worst in me!

I was about a half a block from the building when Tabone caught up with me and issued his invitation for a coffee. There were crowds of people on Republic Street when we got there, and it was closed to vehicular traffic at that hour, but one thing about traveling with a policeman: Small details like parking and closed streets are not a problem. Tabone pulled the police car up onto the sidewalk right by the Caffe Cordina and we went in. I wasn't sure why he'd invited me there. It apparently wasn't to discuss his investigations, because he wasn't very forthcoming on that subject, nor did he make any reference to my being in the Palazzo Parisio, if indeed he had seen me come out of the building. I did learn, however, that Joseph would be brought back in for questioning again today.

"I don't want to do it, frankly," Tabone said. "But with that autopsy report on the books, there's not much I can do about it. And he's being such a stubborn old fool. Won't tell anybody what he was doing in Rome. He took the first flight out one morning and came back the next day on the same flight as the deceased, except that Galea was traveling baggage class, of course."

"So when do you expect to get another autopsy report?"

"Today, if we're lucky. Caruana went to Rome to talk to the forensic lab technicians, and he'll be back late today. I still think it was Mrs. . . . Marilyn Galea. Rob's colleagues have looked into Galea. It seems he's given her lots of reasons to kill him. Quite a bit younger than she is. Fifteen years, I think. Known to stray, shall we say. And he probably married her for her money, which maybe he didn't need anymore."

"Yes, but why now? He's been like that for years. What would set her off now, particularly?"

"I don't know. Maybe he was going to leave her for a twenty-year-old. Not unheard of, you know," he said, smiling at me. Obviously he and I were going to have to agree to disagree on the subject of Marilyn Galea.

"And Ellis Graham?"

"We think that was a robbery, actually. All his money was gone, along with his ID."

I'd assiduously avoided thinking much about Graham's demise. It was so grotesque, a dead man held up by the sword on an empty suit of armor. But the unwanted picture now came into my mind as we talked: the body embracing the Knight, the bullet hole in the head, the sword straight through him, the rumpled clothes and hair.

In that instant I knew what I'd failed to notice at the time.

"Did you find Graham's hat, by any chance?" I asked Tabone.

"Hat?" he said vaguely.

"His hat. Big brim, Australian outback style with one side turned up, tied under the chin. Leopard skin band too."

Tabone didn't say anything, but I could see the hat was news to him. I tried to get him to talk, but he clammed up and was being rather closemouthed about everything. Which was fair enough, since I'd had another thought that I couldn't bring myself to share with him or anyone else. If I was so convinced that Graham's and Galea's deaths were linked in some way, who, other than myself, was related to both? The Farrugia family, Joseph, Marissa, and Anthony, that's who. All of my Maltese friends had been in the marketplace when Graham was killed, but only the Farrugias had a relationship of any sort with Galea. It was a tenuous link, to be sure, and I was convinced of their innocence, but I was afraid that mentioning that I had seen them from the window of the museum while I was chasing Graham would not improve their chances with the police, and Tabone had said Joseph would be brought in again soon.

Tabone had brought a newspaper, the *Times of Malta*, and our conversation turned to the arrival of the foreign dignitaries in Malta to discuss the country's entry into the European Union, among other things. The cover photo showed the British Foreign Minister being greeted at the airport by Galizia.

"Are you expecting any trouble?" I asked, gesturing toward the photo.

"Hope not. We have all kinds of security in place, of course. Almost as much as when President Bush and Gorbachev were meeting out in the Grand Harbour."

"I was wondering about the school performance at Mnajdra," I said. "Strange things happening at the site."

"You mean that incident with the storage shed? Probably irate parents, you know."

"But don't you think it's a bit strange that all these things are happening when world leaders are arriving here? I mean, two people murdered, nasty things going on at the site of a performance for these very important people?"

"Hard to see the connection. But we have someone in there."

"In there? At Mnajdra? Do you mean undercover?"

He didn't answer, so I assumed that was a yes. "Who is it?" I asked.

"If I told you that, and if we did have someone undercover there, which I'm not saying we do, then the person wouldn't exactly be undercover, now would they?" It was clear he wasn't going to say. We parted company, and I headed back to the house.

I wasn't sure I'd actually go through with the plan to crash the party at Palazzo Galizia, which was indeed for that same evening at an address on Villegaignon Street in Mdina. This would take more nerve, to say nothing of lack of social graces, than I would normally be capable of. It was Rob Luczka who decided it for me in a rather backhanded way. I told him about my visit to Galizia's office and showed him the invitation. I was thinking that if I could persuade Rob to go with me, I might just risk it. But when I showed him the invitation, his response was, I suppose, predictable.

"How'd you manage that?" he asked.

"I was at his office and told him I was a friend of Martin Galea's and . . ." My voice trailed off. For some reason, although I'd lied my way through the hallowed halls of the External Relations Ministry, I couldn't bring myself to lie to Rob. My face, as usual apparently, did me in.

"You've got to be kidding!" he exploded. "You nicked it, didn't you?" I nodded.

"I'm a policeman. I don't crash parties, and I don't mix with people who steal things either!" He stomped off in a huff.

I, equally annoyed, developed a fallback position. When Marissa brought Sophia's costume back, beautifully mended, washed, and wrapped in tissue, I asked her if she would do me an immense favor and allow her son to be my chauffeur for the evening. I told her I'd been invited to a party in Mdina but didn't want to drive myself, and it would be too late for the bus. She agreed. We arranged for Anthony to meet me at

the house and drive me to Mnajdra for the dress rehearsal—
he'd planned to be there for the rehearsal anyway—and then
to drive me on from there.

There was no indication on the invitation of how to dress.
I expect that's because old families, or those who aspire to
look that way, know the code. I'd brought one good outfit,
just in case Galea had wanted me to help him with his party,
either to help host, or even just to pass the canapés. It con-
sisted of long silk pants that flared out at the bottom—I believe
they may be called palazzo pants, which seemed appropriate
enough for a party at the Palazzo Galizia—and a black silk
embroidered top I'd picked up in my travels. The invitation
said nine p.m., but I did not plan to arrive before ten when
with any luck the party would be in full swing. When one is
crashing a party, it seemed to me, it would not be a good idea
to be the first guest. That would also allow enough time to get
through the dress rehearsal, and for Anthony to drive Sophia
home before going on to Mdina.

Rob was nowhere to be seen when Anthony picked me up
and we headed off for Mnajdra, which suited me just fine. My
face, no doubt, would have given me away.

The rehearsal was a fiasco. The best one could say about it
was that if the old adage about a poor rehearsal meaning a
great performance was true, then the next night would be a
stupendous success. The girls seemed nervous, perhaps because the phalanx of police and army had doubled since the
previous evening, and it was all a bit overwhelming for them.
They forgot their lines, I got the costumes jumbled up, the
music didn't sound quite right, some of the lights didn't work,
and Victor Deva clucked and fussed all evening in a rather
irritating way. The girls were quite down by the end of it all.

Anna Stanhope called them all together just before they
went home. She repeated the adage about poor rehearsals and
good performances, which brought little smiles to the girls'
faces, and then she said, ''You are all citizens of a very tiny
republic with an immense and sweeping history, and you are

heirs to this heritage. The story you will tell to these world leaders tomorrow night is one of which you can be very proud. It tells of people who, although they have been conquered many times, have never been truly defeated, and have never lost their distinctive character despite attempts by many nations to stamp that out.

"You and your ancestors have endured times as dark as any nation could, whether that was the Great Siege of Malta by the Turks, or the second Great Siege so recently, when your parents and grandparents held on against tremendous odds, bombed day and night, food supplies dwindling, while the world watched and despaired for you. Many thought you would not survive it, but survive it·you did. Many thought you were too small for nationhood, but you have proven them wrong. These are the stories you will tell tomorrow, and you will make your parents and your country proud."

A hush had fallen over the site. Even the police and soldiers were paying rapt attention. She put her hand up in what seemed to be a gesture of blessing. "May the power of the Great Goddess be with you tomorrow, the wisdom of Inanna of Sumer in whose temple writing was invented; the power of Isis, whose name means 'the throne' and who provided the foundation for kingship in Egypt; and the strength of Anath who wading through blood, confronted and defeated Mot, the God of Death. But most of all we ask the blessing of the Great Goddess of Malta, who inspired your ancestors to build these temples right here where we stand, as a reflection of her strength and power."

She lowered her hand and said simply, "See you tomorrow." The girls left, standing taller perhaps, than they ever had before.

"You are a wonderful teacher," I told her, wanting to voice my admiration but not being sure how.

"It is something I love to do," she said simply. "Now let's get to work," she said, resuming her normal tone.

Sophia and Anthony helped me sort out the costumes, Victor and his cousin Francesco packed up what equipment they could and covered the rest, Alonso as usual did the heavy work, lifting the boxes and stacking them in the storage shed. Mario and Esther saw to it that a guard was posted on the shed all night. I changed into my party duds in the shed, and then we headed for Mdina.

Technically I knew that Anthony was supposed to drive Sophia home first, but I said nothing. I expect they didn't have much time alone together, what with Sophia's father's coolness toward Anthony. It was fine with me. I could be trusted to keep my mouth shut.

I showed them the invitation and they were clearly impressed. "Minister Galizia is a very important person," Anthony said, quite unnecessarily. "And rich. I'll take you to the Main Gate of Mdina," he went on. "Only residents with permits are allowed to drive in the city. It's not really designed for cars, as you'll see. But you'll have no trouble finding the house. Villegaignon Street is the main street. Lots of beautiful old houses. It's where the oldest Maltese families live. It runs off the square inside the Main Gate, and it's not too far to walk. Then I'll drive Sophia home . . . slowly." He grinned. "What time would you like me to pick you up?"

"What time would be good for you?" I smiled back. I was happy to see him cheerful again. He'd been a very subdued young man after Galea's death, and was obviously very worried about his father, or the man he knew as his father, I should say. Being with his Sophia was obviously good for him. Sophia, I recalled, meant wisdom, and somehow she provided Anthony with the calm center he needed.

"I'll be back here by eleven-thirty. I don't think we'd get away with much more than that, do you, Soph? I'll wait until you get here."

"Eleven-thirty it is." They pointed out Mdina in the distance. It was beautiful, high on a hilltop, the rooftops and domes lit up against the night. Soon we arrived at the Gate, a baroque archway, and Anthony dropped me off with very explicit instructions as to where he would be, and equally precise directions to the Palazzo Galizia.

I crossed through the Main Gate and found myself in the town. It was quite extraordinary really, a perfect little medieval city, glowing in yellow stone. While the rooftops were lit, at street level, once you moved away from the plaza, the light was dim. The ground floors of the houses were quite austere, except for very elaborate doorways, complete with coats of arms, beautifully carved. Some of the buildings had no doorways or windows on the main street. I could only assume the doors were on a tiny side street. It was also surprisingly quiet.

I could see why cars were restricted. All of the streets were narrow, some very much so. I could stand in the middle of some of them and almost touch both sides with my outstretched arms. There were few sidewalks. The streets were also angled quite sharply: no straight grid pattern here. The houses seemed to hang, or perhaps hover, over the streets, sometimes literally. Several had windows on second and third floors, ornately carved, that overhung the narrow street below, like Romeo and Juliet balconies.

I was left with an impression of hidden secrets, a certain brooding quality, a watchfulness almost. But perhaps it was just the normal reticence of those with money and power who wish to protect it.

The Palazzo Galizia was impressive, although the house did not yield up its secrets easily. The entrance was not particularly imposing certainly, dark green double doors which in my opinion could have used a lick of paint, topped by a semicircular transom window. There were two bronze door knockers shaped like dolphins, one on each door, but before I could knock the door was opened by a staff person in full regalia. I found myself in a rather austere foyer with what appeared to be a small chapel off to one side. The chapel, complete with burning votive candles, spoke to a piety that for some reason I'd assumed would be lacking in a politician, although this may say more about my opinion of politicians than of Galizia's religious convictions.

I presented my invitation. The doorman looked mildly puzzled, for reasons that would soon be apparent to me, but he tried to hide it, well trained as he obviously was, and he excused himself to consult with another man stationed at the foot of a marble staircase directly opposite the door. I stood there attempting to look nonchalent as he did so, debating whether, should entry be refused, I would try righteous indignation or simply slink away quietly. I was leaning toward the latter when, apparently satisfied, he beckoned me toward the stairs.

It was not until I was on the landing of the staircase that I began to see the palazzo for the sumptuous abode that it was. The dominant feature of the staircase, which could be seen only if one were permitted to ascend, was an amazing three-tiered chandelier, clear glass shot with pink, Murano I assumed. Through a window on the landing, I could see that the house was built in a square around a central courtyard. We turned right at the top of the stairs, then right again, down a long hallway dominated by a series of portraits. The first of these looked very old, maybe late seventeenth or early eighteenth century, I thought, although paintings are not my area of specialty. The oldest, darkened with age, portrayed elaborately dressed men in aristocratic poses. Two of these men were posed in front of landscapes that did not look Maltese, which meant, if I remembered my fine arts courses of many years ago, that these men owned lands in foreign countries. Portraits of women and children, all looking very properous as well, rounded out the collection.

As we walked along the hallway, the portraits became progressively more modern, culminating in an oil painting of Galizia and another of a woman with the kind of horsey look I've come to associate with some branches of the English aristocracy. I assumed this was Mrs. Galizia, the British wife. I had the impression that Galizia, subconsciously or otherwise, was trying to imply a distinguished family history very much at odds with the upbringing I'd glimpsed in my visit to Mellieha, and his little speech in the newspaper article about knowing what it was to grow up poor.

The deeper one penetrated into the palazzo, the more elaborate it became. At the far end of the hallway we turned right again and entered the library, a real library, I might add. None of that awful wallpaper that is supposed to fool you into thinking there are rows of books for our friend Giovanni Galizia. Walls of books, most of them leather bound, dominated the room. And lest anyone think that Galizia had bought his books by the yard, never to crack a spine, in one corner was a charming little scene, a worn and comfortable-looking leather chair with a reading lamp, still on, behind it, and a book open on a side table, reading glasses resting on the open page, as if the owner had reluctantly torn himself away from his reading to greet his guests. It was all so studied that I began to wonder if Galizia had hired himself an image consultant.

Two large archways led out of the library. Through the first I could see, as we passed by, the dining room, the table elaborately set for a late supper. Here any notion of decorative restraint had been tossed aside. The ceiling was painted a dark blue with silver stars, the walls mustard-yellow, stenciled with feathered patterns in gold with streaks of blue. There seemed to be more gilt almost than St. John's Co-Cathedral, and the wall opposite the archway featured a *trompe l'oeil* fresco that gave the impression of a view through a window to a garden that would have done Versailles proud.

There were high back chairs, the velvet fabric worn sufficiently to erase any traces of new money, lots of gleaming crystal and silver and decorative pieces, elaborate candlesticks and the like. I tried not to gawk; people invited to parties in a palazzo, after all, should be more sophisticated than that. But my acquisitive shopkeeper's heart was aflutter at several things I saw. I caught myself eyeing these treasures wondering which, if any, had belonged to the Knights.

Martin Galea, the master of the clean line, an airiness of

space, and the deceptively simple detail, would choke if he saw this decor, almost claustrophic in its sumptuousness, I thought, and perhaps he had been there. I wondered if the master of Palazzo Galizia had seen Martin's new house with its restrained Mediterranean elegance. Comparing their homes, it was hard to imagine the two of them as friends.

The second archway led to an antechamber off the dining room where my arrival was announced. It did not take me long to realize why the doorman had seemed perplexed. There wasn't another woman in the room.

The air was filled with cigar smoke, and about twenty men were drinking either sherry, expensive no doubt, or champagne, a celebration of some kind. I got the impression, I have no idea why, that a deal of some kind had been concluded. I recognized Galizia and one other person, a member of the opposition party whose photo I had also seen in the newspaper. It was quite the group. Several of those talking to the minister were military types, high ranking, obviously, with so much braid and so many medals I was surprised they could stand. All turned to stare at me, and they did not appear glad to see me.

"Did I come on the wrong night?" I said brightly, with a bravado I did not feel. In fact, I think I would have made a run for it, had my feet not felt rooted to the floor and my exit not been blocked by the staff person who'd led me there.

Galizia came forward. He was not a large man, but he was built like a fighter, barrel-chested and light on his feet. He was not particularly good-looking, but he radiated assurance, a kind of oily smoothness that I could not help but feel masked other less attractive qualities, like cunning, and, if the Hedgehog's story was true, ambition and opportunism. What I noticed most about him were his eyes, expressionless, almost opaque. If eyes are indeed the windows of the soul, then either Galizia didn't have one, or he'd crafted for himself an extraordinarily effective mask. He did not extend his hand, nor did he offer me a drink.

"I believe you were at my office today. A journalist of some kind," he said. His voice was virtually without inflection too, the counterpart of his eyes. It was difficult to tell from his tone his true feelings, although I assumed a contempt for journalists. "My secretary told me you wanted to interview me about someone called Martin Galea. I can assure you I don't know this person."

"How about Marcus Galea?" I asked. For some reason my terror, for terrified I was, was translating into a sort of stubborn aggressiveness that surprised even me. I was here now, I remember thinking, and before they throw me out I might as well find out whatever I can.

"Not him either," he replied. "And now I believe you have overstayed your welcome." The words were not said in a threatening tone, but the threat, I knew, was there. He pulled a tassled cord in the doorway, and two very large men appeared. I was hustled out of the room and into a back staircase, then down what seemed to be a couple of floors. For a moment or two I had the irrational feeling that they were going to lock me in a horrible dungeon in the basement—it was that kind of house—but instead I was pushed rather roughly out onto the street. Not out the front door either, but onto a narrow, ill-lit alleyway. I wanted to say something soigné like "I've been thrown out of better places than this," but they were very large men, and the truth is, I was really quite frightened.

I was also completely turned around. I wasn't sure which way would take me back to Villegaignon Street and thence to the Main Gate where I had determined I would stay in a well-lit area waiting for Anthony's return. I knew he'd wait for me, and it really was a small town, so I decided it didn't much matter which way I went. Eventually, I was reasonably sure, I'd get my bearings and find my way back.

I picked a direction and started to walk. I had a sense of being followed, and I picked up the pace. When I was a block or two from the Palazzo, I heard a car skid, and headlights flashed against a wall at the end of the street. I remember thinking, and this was the last rational thought I had for some time, that Maltese drivers really were the worst. Then I heard the car accelerate, turning down the street at top speed, and I realized that this was something much more sinister than bad driving. I froze, like an animal paralyzed by headlights, as the car came straight at me. Behind me I heard footsteps coming fast, but still I couldn't move. Just as I was about to be hit, someone grabbed me from behind and hurled me against the wall. I heard a thump, someone said, "Run!" I heard someone gasp and fall, and I looked over my shoulder to see a man lying motionless on the street.

It was Rob. He just lay there, on his back, eyes closed. Unconscious, or even, I feared, dead. I was having a great deal of trouble thinking clearly. I kept trying to tell myself this wasn't happening, that events like this only happened in bad dreams or worse movies. Finally, however, a sound penetrated the fog in my brain. It was the car, the same one, I could tell, and it was turning somewhere. It was coming back, and even though in these narrow streets it might take a while to turn, I had very little time to escape.

There were three doors on the street. I tried the first. It was locked. I tried a second across the little street, then ran a few yards to another, a strange little door that was down a couple of steps from the street. Miraculously it opened. But Rob was still lying unconscious on the street, and if they came back, he would almost certainly be killed.

As I watched a tiny pulse beat in his temple, I knew that I was not going to let anyone hurt him anymore. I put my arms under his armpits and dragged him the few yards to the door, pulled him down the steps and across the threshold, closed the door, and tried unsuccessfully to latch it. He was unbelievably heavy, and I've wondered since how I managed it, but I guess you do what you have to do. It was dark inside, and I had no idea where I was.

The dim streetlight shining through a grated window above the door was not too helpful, but eventually my eyes adjusted

to the light, enough to see that I was in what I took to be a
small chapel. I had heard the car sweep by, then stop near the
end of the street and two doors slam. They were coming back
to look for us. They began banging on the doors on the street
and trying to open them. Ours, I knew, would open.

I dragged Rob again, this time for cover behind a large stone
structure with a marble figure, arms across the chest in the
position of death, laid out on top of it, and a skull and cross-
bones carved elaborately on each side. This was not really a
chapel, I realized, but a crypt, the stone structure the tomb of
some important personage. But now was not the time to get
squeamish, I knew, so I gave Rob once last heave and pulled
him behind it. He had the longest legs, and I had real difficulty
getting us both wedged in where we wouldn't be seen.

I knew that even a cursory tour of the place would lead to
our discovery—it was just one room—but it seemed to be the
only chance we had. I sat on the floor with Rob leaning back
against my chest, my arms around him to keep him from falling over. I could hear them approaching the door. Rob, still
unconscious, started to murmur. I put my hand lightly over
his mouth, and held my breath. The door began to open.

Just then I heard the most beautiful sound, the wail of a
siren. Someone stopped crossing the threshold in mid step, and
then turned and ran. I heard the car pull away quickly. Moments later, I could see a blue light flashing through the upper
window.

Rob's hand reached up and pulled mine away from his
mouth.

"Where are we exactly?" he asked.

"In a crypt of some kind, behind a tomb," I replied.

"Wonderful!" he said in a decidedly irritable tone. "What
is it about you and crypts?"

"Would you accept an unfortunate coincidence?" I said,
trying to keep my tone light. In truth I could have wept with
relief. Not only were the men who were trying to kill us gone,
but I felt anyone this grumpy was bound to recover.

"I'm not sure," he replied. Then, "I'm starting to take this mess personally."

"Me too," I said fervently. "Me too."

"I'm also thinking I'm getting too old for all this action."

"I'd have to say the same for me," I agreed.

"Call Tabone, okay?"

"Sure," I said.

"There's something I can't figure out."

"What's that?"

"Who was on the plane? Ask him that, will you?" And then he passed out again.

♀ THIRTEEN

WHY ARE YOU HERE? A new flag run up on the battle-ments. Another occupying power. Rule Britannia. The sun will never set, you believe? You bring your poets, your statesmen, your laws, and your ways. But you also bring your enemies to My shores.

"IT'S A BOTHERSOME QUESTION, NO doubt about it," Tabone said in a whisper, gesturing in the general direction of Rob, dozing gently in the big bed at the house. Tabone and I had taken Rob to the hospital where they'd diagnosed multiple bruises and a mild concussion. He'd insisted on coming back to the house, even though the doctors hadn't wanted him to, but he had to be wakened every couple of hours and his eyes peered at for symptoms of worse concussion. I'd insisted he have the bed, and promised Tabone I'd be diligent in my nursing duties. It was the least I could do, after all. He'd saved my life. Tabone offered to take the first shift, but I couldn't sleep, so we sat chatting quietly at the end of the bed.

"You'll have to explain the question to me," I said.

"Then Rob hasn't told you about the autopsy report," Tabone said.

"Been busy. Haven't had time," a sleepy voice from the bed said. Rob kept drifting in and out of sleep and our conversation in a disconcerting way.

"Galea died approximately twelve hours before you found

him, according to Dr. Caruana. I say approximately because of the time lapse between the first and second autopsies. There were indications of freezing in the extremities just as Rob predicted. So he was, we're almost certain, killed in Canada. The good news is that this should let old Joseph Farrugia off the hook, although I'd still like to know why he went to Rome, just to reassure myself there's absolutely no connection.

"The bad news . . . well, you know what it is. They also found two different blood samples on the chest. One, of course, is Galea's. The second is B positive. Marilyn Galea's blood is, or was, B positive. It's not a particularly common blood type for white North Americans, either. We can't compare it directly to hers, because we can't find her. But I think we can safely assume it's hers. Either she cut herself in the act of murdering her husband, or, she was herself injured, or perhaps," he said carefully, "killed at the same time as he was. I'm not sure which way I'm leaning on that one. The blow that killed him was, according to Caruana, masterful. A quick slice up and between the ribs, puncturing the lung and left ventricle of the heart. Either the work of a professional, or a very lucky, if I may use that term in this regard, blow for an amateur.

"But the fact remains, someone used the ticket, got on the plane, and presumably used Galea's travel documents to get into Italy. Who and why, I have no idea.

"However, to get back to the problem of the hour. Go back over, one more time, what happened tonight in the Silent City. That's what they call Mdina, by the way, and it's what saved you. They don't call it that for nothing. The fancy residents of Mdina don't like their peace disturbed. Called the police right away. You and your pursuer, or pursuers as the case may be, were making quite a ruckus, I gather, banging on doors and revving engines and all. We were told there were hooligans loose in the city."

I went back over the evening's events. Tabone's eyebrows raised very slightly and there was the slightest hint of a smile when I told him about stealing the invitation, but other than that, his reaction was low-key, with none of the stomping about that Rob had done. He interrupted my narrative with questions from time to time.

"Did you see a license plate?" Answer: no.

"How many people were in the car?" Answer: two, or at least I thought I'd seen two.

"Are you absolutely certain they were deliberately trying to hit you? You know how we drive here. Perhaps they came back to make sure you were all right."

"To apologize, you mean?" I asked incredulously.

"It's possible," Tabone said in a somewhat defensive tone.

"Noooo," came a muffled reply from the bed.

"All right, then," Tabone said. "I'll check up on Galizia's party, although there doesn't seem to be anything unusual about it. Except for your arrival, of course."

We sat quietly for a few minutes.

"Alex!" the voice from the bed said. "He called. I forgot to tell you. He wants you to call as soon as you get in. Sorry!"

It was still relatively early back home, and I knew Alex was a nighthawk, so I returned his call while Tabone watched over Rob. I apologized for calling him back so late, explaining only that I'd been to a party.

"I got a copy of the Ellis Graham documentary and had a look. It's a quite sensationalized account of the history of the Knights of St. John, but a rather good television show, I must say. He mentions a lot of objects that have gone missing, and talks about the old families of Malta who may be hoarding them, but the one object I think he'd be looking for now is the cross I told you about, a silver and gilt cross supposedly carried from Rhodes to Malta by Philippe Villiers de L'Isle-Adam, Grand Master at the time of the Knights' defeat by Sulieman the Magnificent and their consequent wanderings about the Mediterranean looking for a home."

"So you think producing the program gave him an idea of

where the cross might be, and he came on a treasure hunt of sorts," I said.

"That was certainly my assumption when I'd finished watching the documentary, and I've had my hunch confirmed. I talked to an old friend of mine in L.A. Turns out he worked out of the same studio as Graham, and he says that after doing the documentary, Graham became absolutely obsessed with the idea of finding that cross. He talked about it and the Knights incessantly, to the point where people thought he was a bit daft. He was convinced that the Knights would have left a secret message of some kind, telling where they'd hidden it before Napoleon threw them off the island. That would explain why you saw him peering at tombstones and the like. Anyway, I was convinced we were on the right track here, but then I learned something new. I don't know whether this is good news or bad, but the cross has been located."

"You're kidding!"

"I'm not. I joined a little chat group on the Internet, a bunch of museologists who get together regularly. I thought I might get some information from them. Anyway, I was following along the conversation when one of them said that a museum in one of the former satellite states of the old USSR had just released a catalogue of their collection, and we should all have a look at it because so many of these things had been hidden from us during the Soviet era. I'm sure you've guessed the rest. A silver and gilt cross said to have belonged to the Knights of St. John and supposed to have been carried from Jerusalem to Rhodes to Malta, then passed from hand to hand, or should I say Grand Master to Grand Master, after the Knights left Malta, eventually worked its way into this museum. I can't believe it, but I also can't imagine there are two. The catalogue even mentions de L'Isle-Adam."

"But presumably Graham didn't know that, if the news is as current as you say."

"Exactly. He may have been looking for it, but he couldn't have been killed for it, because it wasn't there to find. He could have been looking for something else, of course, but it doesn't sound like it from what my showbiz friend has told me.''

"This is getting rather bizarre," was all I could think to say. I thanked Alex for his detective work, and then went back to watch over Rob. Tabone left shortly thereafter, and I sat watching Rob and doing a mental catalogue of my own of where this whole mess stood.

Galea was killed in Canada. Marilyn was either guilty of his murder, or was herself a victim. It looked as if he'd been killed in his own home, since there seemed to be no other opportunity to do it. But someone drove his car to the airport, parked it, used the airline ticket, and got into Italy using Galea's travel documents.

A second murder victim, Ellis Graham, was looking for something, of that I was reasonably certain, what with the connection to his documentary and his metal detector, and all the places I'd spotted him. But the most likely object of his search wasn't here; it was in a museum somewhere, something it was unlikely he could have known.

Joseph Farrugia had gone to Rome for some reason he would not reveal, had been in the vicinity at the time of Graham's murder, and Tabone was still a little suspicious because of his reticence.

Rob and I had just had what he would describe as a close encounter of the automotive kind, right after I'd been thrown out of the Palazzo Galizia by the Minister himself, a man with sumptuous tastes and blank, soulless eyes. He was also, according to someone called the Hedgehog, a boyhood friend of Martin Galea, a fact he had denied to my face.

All sorts of important people were in town, foreign ministers of various European countries and lots of military types, and Galizia, in his role as External Relations Minister, was associated with them all. Several of these people were to attend a performance at Mnajdra the following evening, a place which had had its share of strange events and controversy.

It was an interesting catalogue, but it didn't seem to be leading anywhere in particular, and soon I fell asleep curled up in a blanket across the end of the bed. It seemed the easiest thing to do. I just rolled over from time to time, woke Rob up, shone a flashlight in his eyes, then we both went back to sleep.

MARISSA ARRIVED THE NEXT MORNING, and made both of us breakfast. She and I then had a brief discussion about looking after Rob, which she agreed to, because I knew there were a couple of things I had to do before I went to the performance that evening. The first was that Marissa and I had to have a serious talk.

"Marissa," I began, "I'm sure you're very happy to have Joseph back home, but you need to know that Detective Tabone still has some reservations about him, primarily because of his refusal to say why he went to Rome."

"I know," she sighed. "He can be a very stubborn man. I'll tell you why he went, but only if you promise me not to tell anyone else, and also to give me advice as to what I should do about it." I agreed to her terms.

"Anthony, as you know, wants very badly to be an architect and we want the best for our son. But now with Galea dead, it will simply not be possible, I think. We cannot afford it," she said sadly.

"But before all this happened, we were waiting for Anthony to hear from the University of Toronto and the school in Rome. Joseph and I—we shouldn't have, we know that— opened the letters before Anthony got home from school. The first to come was an acceptance from Canada. You know how we felt about our son going to be with Marcus. We hid the letter, hoping for a similar reply from Rome. But when it came, it was a rejection letter. Anthony was not accepted. It was, in a way, our worst fear. Only one acceptance, and from so far away, where Marcus could continue to influence our boy.

"We didn't say anything to Anthony—he continued to watch for the letters, but it kept gnawing away at Joseph. He couldn't sleep, he fretted all the time. Finally he decided to go to Rome and plead, beg, the people at the school to let Anthony in. We had difficulty putting together the money for the ticket, and we couldn't afford a hotel. Joseph spent the night sitting up in a cafe. He had trouble finding the place, and the right person to talk to, but finally he did.

"They were horrible to him, polite, of course, but horrible. He knew they were laughing at him behind his back, his workingman clothes, even though he wore his best, his only, suit. They sneered at his poor Italian and his working-class manners. He looked out of place, and he knew it, but they made it clear to him even if he hadn't known.

"They refused to change their decision, of course. I knew it was hopeless, but Joseph wouldn't admit it to himself. He thought if he just explained it to them, they would understand and change their minds. He is a proud man in his own way, and the whole experience was profoundly humiliating for him. He forbade me to speak of it; he could hardly tell even me when he got back that night. Not that I was particularly helpful, what with Martin's body and everything.

"I know he should have told the police, but I think he really felt, naively, that because he was innocent, everything would be all right, and he wouldn't have to tell anyone about his humiliation in Rome.

"The thing is, we haven't said anything to Anthony yet. Even though Marcus is gone, and he knows there is no chance he'll be able to go now, he checks the mail every day, perhaps just for the satisfaction of being accepted somewhere, or else the closure of knowing he couldn't get in to either place anyway, so the money doesn't really matter anymore. I'm torn really. I don't know what to do. What do you think?"

"I think Anthony will be able to go to the University of Toronto if he wishes to. You obviously haven't heard yet, but Martin left Anthony a rather large sum of money. It will definitely see him through school. You'll be hearing from the executors of Galea's estate soon, I'm sure, and as long as you are all cleared of any wrongdoing in Galea's death, Anthony will get the money. It's $100,000.''

She looked stunned. "That is so much money," she gasped.

"It is and it isn't," I replied. "I'd consider it a small payment in light of what he owes you. That's my opinion, of course. But you will have to tell Anthony eventually, and you'll probably have to tell him everything. For all we know, the wording in the will may even reference the fact that Anthony is Martin's son.''

"I understand what you're saying. But I'm afraid it will kill Joseph. He has a strong heart, the heart of a workingman, but not perhaps strong enough for this," she said with tears in her eyes.

"You don't have to do anything immediately, so give Joseph time to deal with it in his own mind, and in his own way," I advised her. We talked a while longer, and she calmed down a little.

Then I headed out to answer my second question of the day. First I checked the refrigerator and was pleased to see a six-pack of beer there, chilled and ready. I packed it into the car and roared off across the island, heading once again for Mellieha and another conversation with the Hedgehog.

I found him in exactly the same chair and the same location, but he was looking, if anything, even scruffier than he had the first time we'd met, and there was a certain air of vagueness, or perhaps puzzlement, about him. He was pleased to see the beer, however, and told me to sit down.

"I was here a few days ago with a friend of mine," I said. "From Canada."

"Were you?" he said vaguely.

"I asked you about Marcus Galea," I said, remembering to pronounce it the way the Hedgehog liked to.

"Did you?" he replied. I was getting a sinking feeling that this expedition was a hopeless one, but I soldiered on.

"I've been thinking that perhaps I asked the wrong questions," I said.

"Perhaps you did," he agreed.

"I think I should have asked you about Giovanni Galizia."

"I expect so, yes," he said.

"Do you remember Galizia?" I asked tentatively.

"Of course I do," he said irritably. "It's you, a few days ago, that I don't remember. The past I remember vividly. It's both a blessing and a curse."

"And in the case of Galizia?"

"A curse. I would have to say a curse," he sighed. "Is that beer for me?" I handed him a bottle. "Have one!" he ordered. "I hate to drink alone." He took a long swig from the bottle, then watched as I took a smaller swig from mine.

"You're not one of those social worker types, are you?" he asked me. I shook my head, and he looked at me very carefully. Then, apparently satisfied with what he saw, he began. "Things happen to people around Giovanni Galizia. Bad things. I should know." He paused. I waited. I knew, somehow, that this conversation would have to play its way out at the Hedgehog's own pace.

"I was a teacher at the local church school. High school. I was a good Catholic, I might add, although what good that has done me, I don't know. Giovanni Galizia was one of my students. Not my best student. Marcus Galea was my best student. Giovanni was, if anything, one of the worst. But somehow, things always worked out for him. Not always the way you would expect, perhaps. But work out they did, just the same.

"I remember when he was trying to get on the football team—they call it soccer, I think, where you come from. The coaches were down to the last pick, and it was between two boys, Giovanni Galizia, and Pawla Bonnici. I think Pawla was the better player, actually, but then he had an accident. Fell off some scaffolding on the school. One of the walls was being repaired. The boys were drunk, of course; they seemed to be most of the time at that age. Pawla claimed he'd been pushed, but he couldn't say who'd pushed him, and, of course, no one believed him. I didn't at the time. Later, I would come to understand. Giovanni made the team.

"Another time there was an oratorical contest at the school. Giovanni and another boy were generally considered to be in a dead heat for first place. Giovanni might not have been a good student, but like the politician he was to become, he was a good talker. His speeches, while empassioned, were a little derivative—is that the word?—in my opinion, which is a polite way of saying that I suspected someone else had written them for him. Nonetheless he made it to the finals. Then the other finalist got sick, really deathly ill from food poisoning. The boys had all gone out the night before to celebrate the last day of classes, and, of course, the final of the oratorical contest. Only the one boy got sick, and Giovanni won the contest, but you probably figured that out already.

"Then there were the exams to get into a foreign University. They were a very big deal. You need to understand that it was very difficult to get into University in Malta in those days. You had to know the right people, and people like Giovanni and Marcus did not have those sorts of connections. The only hope they had was to get into University somewhere else, and in both cases, coming as they did from very poor circumstances, needed to win scholarships. Giovanni did very well, much better than I had expected, but then I found irrefutable evidence that he had cheated on his exam. I confronted him with it—it was a Friday, I remember, and I gave him the weekend to think about what he would do. I told him that if he did the right thing and told the principal what he had done, I would stand by him, and see there were no further repercussions, that is that he'd be allowed to write the exams again a few months later. If not, however, I told him I would report him myself. It was the biggest mistake I ever made, giving him time to think about it, that is.

"I went away for the weekend. I remember I took the ferry

to Gozo and enjoyed the weekend there with friends. When I returned Monday morning, the story was all over the school. I was summoned to the principal's office, and summarily dismissed right on the spot. After an impeccable career spanning twenty years! I was so shocked I could barely manage to ask why I had been sacked. The principal said I knew perfectly well, that I should have known that something so disgusting would have to come out, but I didn't have any idea what he was talking about. I was utterly baffled. I left the principal's office and went looking for some of my colleagues and friends, but they wouldn't speak to me.

"Eventually, of course, I heard the rumors. One of the students, unnamed of course, had reported an incident of abuse involving me. You know what I mean by abuse, don't you? I don't have to spell it out for you, do I?"

I told him I knew what he meant.

"I was never given an opportunity to defend myself. I couldn't charge anyone. They wouldn't say who the student was. It was dreadful, and I was totally ruined.

"It got worse, partly of my own doing. I entered into a rather hasty marriage to a widow with a young daughter, to try to prove I was normal, that I wasn't the kind of person they thought I was. Totally loveless marriage, I might add. I endured years of harangues from that sharp-tongued woman. In the end I had a nervous breakdown. I'm said to have never fully recovered, but I'm not as daft as they think. My wife is gone, thank God for that. Her daughter looks after me, not because she loves me—she's like her mother in that—but because she likes to be seen as a martyr. And I sit here and follow the career of the Honorable Giovanni Galizia with a sort of all-consuming interest."

Suddenly he leaned toward me and grabbed my wrist. "Have you seen his eyes?" he asked, his fingers, surprisingly strong, digging into my arm.

"I have," I replied.

"And what did you see?"

"Nothing. Absolutely nothing."

"Exactly. No heart, no soul."

His stepdaughter must have been keeping a wary eye out for her father, because when he grabbed my arm, she came outside. "Is my father bothering you?" she asked. She was a brittle-looking woman who probably looked much older than her years.

"Not at all," I replied. "Your father is telling me some of the really interesting history of Malta." The Hedgehog looked away.

"None of your conspiracy theories now, Father," she said. "None of that nonsense about Giovanni Galizia!" The Hedgehog made a face at her retreating back.

"They all think I'm cuckoo," he said, tapping his forehead with his fingers when she had gone back inside, "but if you've seen him, you know."

"So what happened after that?"

"His meteoric rise to fame continued. His family had been Labour, supporters of Dom Mintoff originally. Galizia was going to run for Labour, but then it became clear the Republic Party would win the next election, so Galizia switched sides. There was no clear candidate in this area for the Republic Party, and the only one who stood a chance of winning had to withdraw. No one would say why, but there were lots of rumors. Does this sound like a pattern to you?" he asked rhetorically.

"Where was Marcus Galea in all this?"

"Marcus and Giovanni were best friends in school, although Giovanni was a year or two older. Both had had a rough start in life, both were highly ambitious. But there I like to think the resemblance ends. Marcus was genuinely talented, genuinely charming. He did well to get into the University with a scholarship, and I saw no indication that he cheated to do it. I would think well of him were it not for what happened to the little Cassar girl—I could tell you about that, if you wish."

"You already have. The last time I was here, a few days ago," I reminded him.

"Did I?" he replied. "Wasn't long enough ago for me to remember, I guess." He grinned ruefully. "The real difference betwen the two boys was, I think, that Marcus was not so much consumed by ambition as delighted in the pleasures that success brought. Giovanni could not enjoy it, because, whatever it was, it was never enough. This may not seem like much of a difference, but I believe it is a profound one."

"I went to a party at Galizia's house last night," I confessed. "Actually I crashed a party at his house, the Palazzo Galizia. I stole an invitation. I got caught, though. I was the only woman there." The Hedgehog rocked back and forth on his chair with silent laughter.

"There were a lot of high-ranking military people there. Very high up, I'd say, although I'm not an expert in these things. And I thought I recognized one other person, but he was a member of one of the other political parties. Would Galizia be thinking of changing sides again, do you think? Maybe he disagrees with the Prime Minister's stand on the European Union?"

"You are making assumptions, dearie," he said, wiping tears of laughter from his eyes. "You are assuming that Galizia changes political parties because he changes his mind about which political platform he supports. This is not about politics. It is not about beliefs, political or otherwise. It is not about values. He doesn't have any. The only thing he believes in is himself. He will do whatever it takes to get ahead."

"I did some reading about Galizia, you know. People seem to think highly of him, at least the journalist did. He sounds intelligent and charming when you read about him."

"Oh, he's smart enough, and he is not without charm. That is, perhaps, what makes him most dangerous."

"But the kind of person you are describing, someone with no values or beliefs, and no compunction of any sort. That person is . . ."

"A psychopath?" the Hedgehog replied. "Is that the word you're looking for? Call it whatever you will, the point is, whenever someone is in Galizia's way, something bad happens to them. They get hurt, they get sick, they are disgraced. I should know."

"Who do you think is in his way now?"

"I have no idea. But there will always be someone. Make sure that someone isn't you, dearie."

❦ FOURTEEN

*O*H, I AM BURNING, THE *evil Axis ranged against Me. My
people starve, My history is in ruins. Will help never
reach Me? Endure, I will. Survive, I will. My time will come
again.*

LET THE PERFORMANCE BEGIN.

The champagne is chilling nicely, little pots of caviar and
oysters on the half shell glistening in their bed of crushed ice,
the linens crisp, the silver and crystal gleaming, flowers art-
fully arranged. Mario Camilleri, right in his element, is strut-
ting his stuff, walkie-talkie at the ready. Esther, his shy
assistant from protocol, nervously straightens rows of champagne flutes and lines up napkins with obsessive precision.

I survey the scene with a mixture of amusement and anxiety.
Anna Stanhope is rather formally dressed, blue chiffon and
pearls. She seems her usual well-in-control self, except for two
round pink spots on her cheeks, and very bright eyes that
betray her excitement. I am back in my palazzo pants ensem-
ble, these being the only clothes I have with me that befit the
occasion. I hang back in the shadow of the temple, sincerely
hoping not to be recognized by the Honorable Giovanni Galizia.

The students' emotions run the gamut, one or two feigning
total indifference, Sophia her usual placid self, a couple of
girls threatening to either throw up or faint dead away. They

are all set in the costumes for their first appearances, their
usual well-scrubbed faces now covered in powder, blusher,
and eyeliner. Several of them keep peeking around the edge
of the temple entrance to see what's happening, reporting back
eagerly to those too nervous to even look. My own hands
shake just a little as I apply troglodyte makeup to Marija's
sweet little face, as I give a tug to Napoleon's white vest
bulging over Gemma's pillowed stomach, and straighten the
Roman centurion's helmet on Natalie's bobbing head. I think
how much I want the performance to go well for them.

As I watch over the final preparations, I idly look at all the
faces of the adult helpers, wondering which, if any of them,
is Tabone's undercover officer. Is it Alonso, the big, somewhat
loutish older brother who's been general dogsbody and mus-
cle? The girls have complained he spies on them. Maybe that's
his job.

Perhaps it is Victor Deva, now putting the finishing touches
on the lights and fussing over the final placement of the sound
speakers. Presumably it isn't his cousin Francesco, who is
missing the performance due to what Victor describes as
"tummy trouble." As a result of Francesco's ailment, I am
now Victor's designated assistant, and have followed him
around the set making note of what I am to do. It is an easy
enough task. Instead of being inside the temple helping the
girls with their costumes, I am given responsibility for a spotlight high on a metal pole to one side of the temple. I am to
switch it on and off—an electrical cord runs down the pole
and the switch is within easy reach—at points marked on Victor's copy of the script, which he gives to me saying he has
his role memorized. He will be nearby, he assures me, on the
other side of the temple entrance with the lights he has placed
there. The girls will be on their own for costume changes, now
that I have these additional responsibilities, and with Anna
Stanhope out in front to give direction from there. But the
girls seem comfortable enough with that and I know that So-

phia will keep everyone calm and see that what needs to get done is well taken care of.

Mario Camilleri undercover? Unlikely, I think. He is, like most PR types, a good talker, but not one, I decide, for action. That leaves me, Anna Stanhope and Esther as the only other adults around, unless one counts the myriad soldiers and policemen who, all in uniform, could hardly be called undercover.

It is the latter part of dusk, just before dark, the time when our eyes make the transformation from day vision to night, when colors fade for a while to a crepuscular silver. It is a beautiful evening, we were fortunate in that, clear, no rain on the horizon, and as warm as it has been since I arrived.

Mnajdra sits right on the coast, protected by the sea on one side, and nestled into the side of an incline on the other, the temple of Hagar Qim on higher ground some distance away. Between the two temples, running parallel to the sea, there is a long stone wall. To protect the notables, the authorities have positioned soldiers along the length of the wall only a few yards apart, well within sight of each other, and with a clear line of sight in all directions. Others patrol an area on either side of Mnajdra's temples, between the wall and the sea. It should be an easy enough job. In this part of Malta there are no trees to block their view. Anyone trying to get to the site will have to cross one of these lines, and to do it without detection would be a difficult, if not impossible, task.

In addition to the foreign dignitaries who have their own special seating arrangement and hospitality, thanks to Mario Camilleri and the Maltese government, the parents and families of the students have received invitations. These contain instructions on where to present themselves and when. In addition there is to be limited seating and some standing room for the general public. Not terribly comfortable, I think, but it is considered, I am told, a hot ticket.

Guests for the performance have to funnel through a single entranceway set up in a break in the wall. Here everyone, including the students and accompanying adults like me, are all carefully searched for weapons before they are allowed through. We watch from inside the temple entrance as the parents and families are escorted to chairs on either side of the VIP tent, and along the edge of the hill. I am happy to see Tabone and Rob, moving slowly I note, take their places not far from the tent. The general public get to sit on blankets and cushions further up the hill.

While we wait for the official party, I wander to the edge of the site overlooking the water. Way down below and off-shore are two or three police boats ready lest some intrepid swimmer and climber decides to crash the party from that direction. From a security perspective, the only way to get at the VIP contingent, it seems, is from the air, and I am assured by Mario that the control tower at Luqa is ever watchful. Interceptor aircraft are standing by to respond at a moment's notice.

While I'd thought the selection of Mnajdra as a backdrop for the performance an inspired choice, I worry now that the logistics at the site may be a nightmare. Between Hagar Qim at the high point of the site, and Mnajdra nestled in its hollow near the sea, lies a stone sidewalk of sorts, a causeway a little more than a quarter of a mile long by my reckoning. It is a place, I'd been told, where prior to the arrival of the security forces several days ago, locals liked to ride their motorcycles back and forth. It is by this causeway that the honored guests will arrive. Although it isn't that far to walk, I cannot imagine world leaders and their spouses, decked out for a formal state dinner afterwards, walking that distance. The pathway is not wide enough for a car, nor for a *karrozin*, the Maltese horse-drawn carriage.

But I have underestimated Mario Camilleri's ingenuity, and the Maltese love of a parade. "Show time!" he shouts suddenly, and I hear applause from the assembled guests further up the hill. The honor guard, members of the armed forces in dress uniforms, inky black in the darkness except for a red stripe on the trousers, a wide white belt, and lots of brass buttons, steps forward briskly to take their place flanking either side of the lower end of the pathway. I look up the pathway and first hear then see a brass band, followed by a row of little golf carts, spanking new and brightly painted, each decorated with colored lights, flying the flags of the country of the occupants. It looks very festive, and is, I have to admit, ingenious.

In the first cart, leading the group of dignitaries is the Prime Minister, Charles Abela, followed by the British Foreign Secretary, Sir Edmond Neville, followed in turn by the foreign ministers of Greece, Italy, and France. I am interested to see the Prime Minister. Until now he has been a bit of a cipher, a man I have never seen, someone I have come to know only as the man who does not like Giovanni Galizia. It is not good, I remember, to stand in Galizia's way. Bringing up the rear is Galizia himself, who, when his cart reaches the assembled guests on the hill, urges his driver to stop and gets out to walk the rest of the way, shaking hands, pointing to people he knows, pausing briefly to have his photo taken with children, and generally pressing the flesh. His wife, the British-born aristocrat, whom I recognize from her portrait but have not had the pleasure of meeting at her lovely home due to the male-only restriction at the palazzo party, goes on ahead in the cart.

The guests help themselves to champagne, caviar, and oysters, then take their places. In the front row are Charles Abela and the foreign ministers, in the second their wives and Galizia. In the third row sit a few people that I can only assume are security staff and other hangers-on. It is galling, no doubt, for Galizia to be considered second tier, and I notice that rather than take his seat in the row, he stands a little to the side, in line with the first row and well in view of the crowd.

At a sign from Camilleri, the lights go down, and we find ourselves in darkness for a few seconds. Victor has arranged to bring the lights back up very gradually, so that for a moment or two, the temple ruins seem bathed in an eerie glow. A hush falls over the crowd. The setting is truly magnificent. Impressive as these ancient stones may be in daylight, in the dimly lit darkness, they have a primordial power that reaches deep into the psyche.

It is as if, for a short time, the ghosts of ages past inhabit the site, and for a few moments are almost visible. It is possible to imagine in those few seconds how those early people would have felt in the presence of their Great Goddess, omnipotent, omniscient, a Goddess to be loved, adored, and feared. I feel a frisson, a sense of impending disaster, and suddenly I very badly want the performance to be over, and everyone to be safe. But then the lights come up, I turn the spotlight on the sacred entranceway to the temple, and the performance begins.

Sophia stands there, in a long white dress, her voice strong and sweeping across the night air.

''I am at the beginning, as I am at the end. I am the sacred circle, spinner of the web of space and time. I am the Cosmic 'And': life and death, order and chaos, eternal and finite. I am Earth and all things of it.

''For periods of time you call millennia, we lived in harmony, you and I. I gave you the bounty of the lands and seas to nourish you, and taught you to use them. I gave you artistic expression so that through your sculpture, painting, and weaving, you might honor me, and through me, yourselves. And I taught you writing that you might remember me.''

The audience sits in rapt attention. Even the politicians, cynical and bored though they must usually be by many of the official activities planned for them, are drawn into the spell of the place. All except for Galizia it seems, because he steps away from the tent and lights a cigarette.

As Sophia speaks, I realize I am once again the apex of a perfect triangle. This time it is not the sun, but the rising moon that is low to my horizon. With my left hand I can point to

Anna Stanhope, with my right to the man, Victor Deva, standing with his back to the sea.

As I look from one to the other, a breeze wafts up from the sea. It catches his hair and blows it forward across his face. For a second or two it sits there, hugging his skull, emanating from a tiny bald spot on the top of his head, perched like a polar ice cap on some small planet, like a bowl on top of his head.

"Neglected, devalued, insulted, and profaned I may be, but I remain," Sophia says. "I wait in my sacred places. I live in your dreams. Nammu, Isis, Aphrodite. Inanna, Astarte, Anath. Call me whichever of my manifestations you will. I am the Great Goddess."

Finally the mental match is made, and I know now what Ellis Graham was trying to tell me was wrong. I remember when I first saw Victor Deva. It was only in profile, but I recognize him nonetheless. He was a priest, on an airplane, the seatmate of Graham.

But now he is not dressed as a priest. My mind, slowly, as if mired in some sticky substance, works its way through the permutations and combinations. If he is a priest, he is toying with Anna Stanhope's affections. And if he is not, then what, and why? There is danger, Ellis Graham had said. As I ponder this, I sense, rather than actually see, Galizia move further away from the tent. Somehow I know something terrible is about to happen.

And then I see the gun.

Victor Deva steps out of the shadow of the giant stones and takes aim at the VIP tent. I hear a collective gasp, but everyone is frozen, captives of space and time. Except Anna Stanhope, who sees, and in a single instant understands. Her emotions dance across her face, first disbelief, then comprehension, then a mask of pain I know even in that moment I will never be able to forget. She races forward and intersects the line of fire as the gun goes off.

She stumbles, her body jerks twice, then falls, collapsing

like a large rag doll in a party dress of blue chiffon, blood all over her. Somewhere the Great Goddess weeps.

The gunman, undeterred, raises the gun again.

I am standing by the light standard. I push the tall pole as hard as I can. We stand, Victor Deva and I, mesmerized by the arc of light as it sweeps across the night sky. It catches him by the shoulder, he stumbles and drops the gun.

Now there is screaming everywhere. In the tent there is chaos, security personnel pushing their charges to the ground, chairs crashing, glass breaking. Over that there is the roar of an engine. A helicopter with police markings races toward the site, low to the ground. I think help is coming, but then, for reasons I cannot understand, Victor Deva runs in a direction that will have him intersect with its path, vaulting over a low stone wall that surrounds the temple to do so. I see Tabone and Rob, limping badly, and Esther, gun out, running behind him. To my amazement, Tabone fires, several times, at the helicopter, as does a soldier. It veers and weaves out of control across the temple site, and as it passes one of the lights, I see Francesco, his face contorted in terror, at the controls. The aircraft screams over the edge of the cliff and out to sea where it crashes in a huge orange ball of flame.

Victor Deva, his escape route gone, cornered, changes direction. Tabone and Esther race to intercept him, but I know I am now closest. Propelled by a fury so intense it absolutely consumes me, I run after him. Both of us stumble on the rocky ground, but both of us keep going. There is a roaring in my ears, I can hardly see, and I want to hurt him very, very badly. I am only a few yards behind him when he reaches the edge of the cliff. With nowhere to go, he turns, looks right at me, and then steps—or stumbles?—backwards off the cliff. I am howling with rage, and I believe I am prepared to follow him into the very jaws of Hell to exact my revenge, but strong arms pull me back and a voice says, "You can stop now, Lara. It's over." I lean on Rob's shoulder and cry.

We leave Esther and Tabone looking over the edge of the

cliff to the broken body I know must be on the rocks far below, and we go back to the place where Anna Stanhope lies. A doctor from the crowd attends to her, and I hear the comforting wail of a siren nearby. For a minute her eyes open and she sees me. She reaches for me, and with surprising strength pulls me down to her. Then she laughs a little, coughs, and grasping my hand very firmly whispers, ''There is no fool like an old fool.''

❦ FIFTEEN

*M*Y GORGE RISES. WHEN WILL *this end? My people have been enslaved, betrayed, converted, deserted, patronized, anglicized. They've fought other people's battles, died for other people's causes. Leave them be. Let them choose their own future. Those who worshipped Me best.*

"SO WHAT HAVE WE GOT?" Rob asked. It was the day after the disastrous event, and we were sitting once again in Vincent Tabone's office.

"We've got a real mess, that's what we've got," Tabone replied morosely. He sighed. "But perhaps you were hoping for more detail than that."

"Indeed," Rob said. "Like who, what, where, why, and how, for starters. Something a little more concrete than mess, or Lara's contention that it was Galizia in a fit of ambition."

"Well, we've got one of the who, at least," Tabone replied. He slapped a photograph on the desk in front of us. It was fuzzy but recognizable. "Marek Sidjian, alias Victor Deva, along with a long list of other aliases. Not Italian, but a master of disguise, and someone who seems to have acquired many convincing accents along the way, to say nothing of passports. We believe he learned his craft with the Russians in Afghanistan. He is a suspect in other similar plots, some unfortunately more successful than this one. Do you recall the shooting of an Italian businessman, a banker, in broad daylight on a crowded street in Milano just a few months ago?''

We both nodded.

"He's a suspect in that, and others like it. I've been working with Interpol, and Rob with U.S. and Canadian authorities, all night, and we've learned a good deal about how Sidjian operated. He was not only the killer, but quite the businessman, the one who dealt with the clients, and who used his charm to insinuate himself into a position to carry out the deed. He actually studied acting, wouldn't you know? Perhaps he should have stayed with it. On the face of it, at least, he would have been good at it. Usually he had an accomplice, an assistant, which brings us to cousin Francesco, whoever he is. I'll have some photos coming in soon I'd like you to look at for me, Lara. Essentially Sidjian was a hired gun. I do not believe that he selected targets himself, nor do I think he had any particular political agenda. He was not burdened by any philosophical or religious convictions that I can see. He was just a thug. He did what he did solely for the money.

"We know, thanks to Lara, that Marek got into Malta from France, disguised as a priest. . . .''

"I keep kicking myself that I didn't remember him sooner," I interjected. "If I'd realized he arrived in disguise, I'd have known there was something wrong, even if I didn't know exactly what it was."

"Don't do this, Lara!" Rob said sharply. "You said yourself you only saw him in profile, and you saw him when you'd been up all night on the flight over. In fact you'd been up for almost twenty-four hours straight!"

But I couldn't let it go. "My friend Alex said we should have known, in a way, about Victor, because of the name he chose for himself. In the ancient Roman and Persian cult of Mithra, a Deva is a creature of darkness, vice, and suffering. I wonder if Victor knew that, or if it was just a coincidence."

"He may well have known," Tabone said. "He is apparently a well-educated man. Choosing a name like that would suit his style. In addition to being intelligent, well-educated, and gifted with a sense of irony, he was also supremely nasty. He prided himself on thinking up innovative ways to kill people.

"As to your other questions," he said, turning to Rob, "we definitely have the where and how down. Where? The play at Mnajdra. How? We're told that Sidjian was noted for planning his hits down to the last detail. He would be out scouting for possible locations. He meets Anna Stanhope at the site and he gets an idea. One of the students remembers Dr. Stanhope telling Victor or Marek about the play, about all the notables who would be attending, and even about Mifsud, the caretaker who was supposed to be helping with the production. Mifsud gets taken out of action—a neat fall down a flight of stairs— and miraculously, Victor Deva appears to save the day. Old Mifsud still can't remember anything much about the accident, but he does recall seeing Sidjian around the school the day he fell—we showed him a photograph this morning. Mifsud's a drinker, of course, but he seems pretty definite about this one, and if it was early enough in the day, he might still have had his wits about him."

"The play and his role in it—those large boxes of sound and lighting equipment—gave Marek the opportunity to hide the weapon," I said. "He couldn't carry the gun in directly; all the boxes were searched. But he, and possibly Francesco too, simply come back at night before there's the full contingent of soldiers and police on twenty-four-hour guard duty. They have to break into the storage shed, because they don't have the key, but they don't need to break into their own boxes. That's why their boxes looked untouched, but it is undoubtedly where the weapon was stashed. Then, to cover their tracks, they make it look like vandalism, the work of angry parents.

"It also gives Marek a chance to show Francesco the site in daylight," I added. "He brought him along to help paint the shed. So he could look around for somewhere to land the helicopter," I added.

"Don't remind me!" Tabone said sharply. "There'll be hell to pay for that, I expect. They stole a police helicopter right from under our noses. If it hadn't been for the fact they radioed me about the chopper right away, those two might have got away."

"I'm surprised they would think they could get away with it, in such a public place," Rob said.

"Sidjian prided himself on his rather spectacular killings. I mentioned that murder of the Italian banker. Do you recall it was carried out right in front of one of those huge and expensive shopping complexes in Milano, at the height of Christmas shopping season?" We nodded. "I think he banked on the fact that there is so much chaos after one of these shootings he had time to slip away.

"Another characteristic of this fellow is that he is truly ruthless about anyone who gets in his way. Which brings us, I think, to Ellis Graham."

Tabone reached into the bottom drawer of his desk. He extracted a large plastic bag in which rested a hat. Not just any hat. A broad-brimmed safari-style hat, one side turned up, with a leopard skin band. "I remembered that conversation we had over coffee, and lo and behold, the missing hat, I think, is found. Look familiar to you, Lara?" I nodded. It was Ellis Graham's hat. It seemed unlikely there would be two like it on this tiny island, and I said so.

"I helped search Francesco's room last night," Tabone went on. "Francesco was staying in a sleazy little place near the Gut, incidentally, and Sidjian got to stay in a nice hotel in Sliema. Proof that Sidjian was in charge. Both rooms were stripped bare, of course—they had no plans to return—except for this hat. Nasty touch, wouldn't you say? Note the bullet hole in it. I wouldn't want to be the person to place this hat on the head of the corpse, but we'll get someone to do it, and I'm sure we'll find the bullet holes in the hat and the head match up. I think we must assume either Sidjian or Francesco killed Graham and left the hat to taunt us. I guess the question remains why they killed him."

"Ellis Graham was a snoop and a nuisance," I said. "I'm convinced he was looking for the lost treasure of the Knights of Malta—we have a documentary he did that would certainly point in that direction—and he was also keeping an eye on me because, I think, he thought I was after the treasure too. Once he got that feeling, he was much more than a nuisance. He was scary. He tried to run me off the road! He would have seen me with Victor, and having been unfortunate enough to sit beside Sidjian, dressed as a priest, on the flight from Paris to Malta, he probably recognized him and realized something was wrong. He even went so far as to say there was danger, so he may have known even more than that. He could have said something to Marek as well. Maybe he thought for a time that Marek was looking for treasure too. He certainly leapt to that conclusion with me, and that was on the strength of a few chance encounters.

"Marek was definitely in the market the day Graham was killed, and could easily have seen, and possibly even heard, Graham try to warn me. I think that was what led to his death. From what you've told me, Sidjian does not strike me as someone who would leave anything to chance."

"I suspect we'll never be able to prove why, but with that hat as evidence, we can be almost certain either Sidjian or Francesco killed Graham. My money is on Francesco only because the hat was in his room, but it doesn't really matter because they're both dead," Rob said. "What is more important is the question of who was Sidjian's client and who was the intended victim. Frankly the intended victim could be anyone in the front row of the VIP tent, including the foreign ministers of three European countries, but Lara, I know, thinks it was Prime Minister Abela who was the target, and Giovanni Galizia the culprit, and it's as good a place as any to start, I suppose. Did you check Abela's schedule, Vince?"

"I did. We're working with European authorities on the

subject of the possible target, but if the Prime Minister was the intended victim, there were not too many opportunities to do it, because Abela's been ill. He hasn't been doing much in the way of public appearances since his surgery; just the play and state dinner were in his official schedule. What's interesting, however, is that it seems Galizia was the one who prevailed upon Abela to come to the play. The Prime Minister's secretary told me that because he was convalescing, he was only planning to attend the state dinner, but he was persuaded by Galizia to do both. The Prime Minister's attendance was critical to the success of the negotiations, Galizia apparently said."

"But what's the motive here?" Rob asked.

"Abela was in his way, metaphorically speaking. Minister of External Relations wasn't good enough," I interjected. "Galizia wanted the top job. Pathologically ambitious, I'd say."

"Hasn't that man heard about nice democratic processes like elections?" Rob grumped. "Anyway, this is all speculation, isn't it?"

"On the strength of a hunch, to say nothing of the persistence, of a Canadian shopkeeper whose main tourism experience in Malta would appear to be the finding of dead bodies," Tabone said, "I have begun an investigation of the Honorable Giovanni Galizia. I sincerely hope this shopkeeper's hunch is correct," he added, looking at me, "because otherwise, this investigation will undoubtedly put my illustrious career in policing at risk."

Rob raised his eyebrows. "So what have you got? I hope it's more than getting the PM to come to the play."

"Not much, so far. I have moved very quickly to get phone taps on Galizia and to get Galizia's bank accounts—it's amazing what police powers you acquire after something as messy as an assassination attempt—and I already have a forensic accountant following the money. He's told me there are some interesting large bank transfers, done through rather convoluted means, but he is already convinced they will lead to a numbered Swiss bank account. We'll see where that takes us. You don't suppose the accounts would actually be in the name of Sidjian, do you?''

We both shook our heads.

"Too bad. We haven't much," he sighed. "With Sidjian and Francesco dead, it's going to be hard to prove Galizia was involved. In fact, he's already positioning himself as the hero of the events of last night, although what he did that would earn him that title eludes me for the moment. I don't know how we'll get him.''

"What about that nasty little incident in the backstreets of Mdina?" Rob asked. "Are you still insisting they were coming back to say they were sorry, Vince, or do you think there might be something there we could hang on Galizia?''

"Maybe. If Galizia is the guilty party, then I think our friend Lara would have been getting to him," Tabone replied. "If he really was working with Sidjian, then he'd know who she was. He'd know that she'd found the body of Martin Galea, that she was staying at the house, that she was involved with the performance at Mnajdra. She turns up at his office with some story about being a journalist and asks about his friendship with Martin Galea, then is really foolhardy, stealing an invitation and crashing the party. Now, whether it was Sidjian and Francesco in the car or just a couple of goons who are employed by Galizia, I don't know yet, but I fully intend to find out, I can assure you. We're going door to door right now to see if anyone heard or saw anything that might help.''

"Still, pretty sketchy evidence," Rob said.

We all sat for a while, brooding over that one.

"What bothers me about this is, Rob's right. Short of a miracle, Galizia will get away with this," Tabone said. "He'll get to be PM someday, not as fast as he'd like, maybe, but he'll get there. And then what? If that isn't good enough for him, what will he aim for next? Head of the European Union?

Director General of the United Nations. Head of NATO? It boggles the mind!''

''It seems to me you're doing everything you can,'' Rob said soothingly. ''And I'm happy to help as long as I'm here. But I was sent over here to help out with the investigation of the murder of a Canadian citizen, Martin Galea, and now that the autopsy has determined he was murdered in Canada, there won't be much more I can do here. I don't suppose anyone can think of any link between Galea's death and these other incidents? I can't believe I said that, actually. I sincerely hope Lara's harebrained ideas aren't contagious.''

I glared at him. ''I think there is a link. Galea's house. I know it's a long shot, but I think we should at least talk about it. You said yourself, Vince, that there were very few opportunities to get the Prime Minister these days. What about the party at Galea's house? What if Sidjian had a plan A and a plan B? You've said he planned every detail; surely a fallback would be included. Maybe plan A was the party at Galea's. According to Marilyn Galea, her husband renewed acquaintances with an old boyhood friend. Galizia, perhaps? Do we know if either Galizia or the Prime Minister were included in the guest list? That should be easy enough to find out. It was supposed to be important people. Surely they would qualify.''

Tabone shrugged and with some reluctance, I could tell, picked up the phone. After waiting for a few moments, Tabone spoke to someone in Maltese, and then, with a look of some surprise, jotted something on his notepad.

''Well, well,'' he said as he hung up. ''That was Abela's secretary. She told me she was holding an evening a few nights ago for a private party. It didn't show up on the official schedule because the Prime Minister apparently considered it personal, and because it was just penciled in as tentative. It was a small get-together, just five or six guests, at the home of Martin Galea. It was to be confirmed by Galea when he arrived, and of course, when he turned up dead, it was simply deleted from the diary.

"And guess who issued the invitation on behalf of Galea? Our friend Giovanni Galizia, of course."

"Forgive me, but so what?" Rob said. "We have nothing linking the house with Sidjian."

"Oh, I think we may," I said slowly. "The first night I was here, I thought I saw someone, a man wearing a hood over his head, at the back of the yard. I was pretty frightened at the time, and I never saw him there again. But there was something about him, his stance, perhaps, and although I can't prove it, I think it was Sidjian. When he was standing for that second or two on the edge of the cliff last night, before he went over . . . I don't know . . . something just clicked.

"And there was the incident with the dead cat and the car. Strange, these kinds of incidents only happened after I arrived. The Farrugias have told me they'd never known anything like this."

"It does sound as if someone wanted you to leave the house," Tabone agreed. "But you, being exceedingly stubborn, didn't budge."

"I didn't. I think that right from the start, the idea of using the house as the site of the assassination just didn't work out. They would need to have access to the house at some point, to move the weapon in and look the place over, but the workmen were there all day, and I was there at night. So they tried to scare me off, but that didn't work. That's when Sidjian started to develop plan B, the play at Mnajdra."

"And Galea? Are you saying they killed him so they could use his house? Rather drastic, wouldn't you say? And surely that wouldn't work. The party wouldn't go on if he didn't show up."

"You're right," I agreed. "Unless, of course, they were going to pretend he was there. When I first saw Sidjian, at Mnajdra that first day, I thought to myself that he looked a little like Galea. Do you think he might have been planning to impersonate him?"

"Could do, I suppose," Tabone said. "It does sound a little

far-fetched, though, you have to admit. In any event, Sidjian was already here. He arrived at the same time you did, so he couldn't have been in Toronto killing Galea.''

I shrugged. ''I know. But what about Francesco? Where was he and what was he doing all this time?''

''Good question,'' Tabone said to me, as a young policeman came to the door with an envelope. As he took it, Tabone said, ''No way to find out until we know who he is, either. Maybe this will help,'' he said, taking two photographs out of the envelope. ''Take at look at these for me, will you?''

The two photos were placed in front of me. I looked carefully at each. They were not very good quality, having been taken with a long lens from a considerable distance, I thought, but they were good enough. I pointed to one.

Tabone grimaced at me. ''Afraid you'd pick that one. Franco Falcone, actually Franco Falzon. Maltese, regrettably. From Xemxija on St. Paul's Bay. Left Malta as a very young man to go to Italy, where clearly he picked up some nasty habits.''

''Franco the troublemaker,'' I said. ''The boy who grew up to be a gangster. That's it! That's what we need!'' I was up and dancing around the room.

''What is she talking about?'' Tabone asked Rob in a puzzled tone. ''Is it shock, do you think?''

''Franco the troublemaker. That rings a bell. Why does that ring a bell?'' Rob asked me.

''Three pals at school. Marcus the young bull, Giovanni the rat, and Franco the troublemaker. Marcus grew up to be an architect, Giovanni became External Relations Minister, but Franco grew up to be a gangster. Ask the Hedgehog.''

''The Hedgehog?'' Tabone groaned. Rob just grinned at me.

''Grizzled old guy who sits on a deck chair beside the grocery store at some steps that lead up the hill in Mellieha. If anyone would know about this, the Hedgehog would,'' Rob said.

''Send Esther,'' I added. ''Tell her to take a six-pack of

Cisk lager. He'll like her. I'd tell her to mention my name, but he wouldn't remember me.'' Tabone threw up his hands. ''Don't worry,'' I said. ''He may not remember me, but he'll remember Giovanni the rat and Franco the troublemaker just fine.''

Rob turned to Tabone, still smiling. ''I'm calling this name in, Vince. See what we can find out about Falcone's and his activities in the last while. Back soon,'' he said as he left the room. While we waited, Tabone got on the phone to Esther and gave her instructions on how to find the Hedgehog. ''Get on this, Esther. It may be the break we need in this mess.''

About fifteen minutes later, Rob returned with a rather bemused expression on his face. ''I'm a bit reluctant to tell you this, because I can already see what you'll want to do with this bit of information,'' Rob said slowly, ''but I guess I have to. I've just been talking to a friend of mine in the CIA. I'd called him with Lara's ID of Falcone and asked him what information he had on the man. I mean, we know how Sidjian got here, but where did Falcone come from? As it turns out, the Americans have been wondering where Franco went to. The CIA caught a glimpse of him in a random check of airport video footage a week or so ago—he's a known criminal wanted all over the place—but he'd vanished without a trace. The photograph you saw, Lara, was taken off the videotape, which is why it was rather grainy. On a hunch, I asked them to check where he was videotaped and when—the tape will give them that—and then to check them against flight schedules and departure gates at that time. It seems our friend was just a few yards from a gate where a flight bound for guess where was about to take off.''

''Rome,'' Tabone said.

''Malta,'' I chipped in.

''Both wrong. Toronto!'' the Mountie said. ''About twenty-four hours before Galea died.''

''So are you saying Lara might be right about Galea being killed because of the assassination plans? Do you think it was

Franco who killed Galea and then used his ticket and travel documents?" Tabone exclaimed.

"It's a long shot, but I suppose it's possible. On the strength of this bit of information, let's throw caution to the winds here, and see if we can pull it all together."

"Sidjian does the deal with Galizia and checks on the PM's schedule," Tabone hypothesized. "Not too many opportunities here, because as we know Abela's been ill. But there is the soiree at Galea's house and they decide to do it there. Sidjian makes his way from France, planning to set up operations in the house. Franco kills Galea in Toronto to get him out of the way, then travels to Rome using Galea's documents. I suppose Sidjian could have planned to impersonate Galea. I mean, Galizia knew what Galea looked like, they grew up together, but the Prime Minister might not, nor might the others. Galea left here a long time ago, and he's an architect, not a movie star, after all. Galea was not exactly a household name around here, at least not until he died. And if Galizia were the perpetrator of all this, then he wouldn't say anything. Marissa and Joseph might be a problem, but, not, I would think, an insurmountable one. They could be avoided. I'm not sure he'd have to, however. With Galea out of the way, he could just wait in the house until the victim showed up.

"But the house, when he gets there, is now occupied," Tabone said.

"Exactly!" I said. "I show up at the house and spoil that part of it. So they try to scare me away with the dead cat, and maybe even try to kill me with that business with the brakes, but neither works and the house would remain off limits to them."

"If this is true, then where the plan to use Galea's house really ran into a glitch," Rob said, "is when Galea turned up here dead, a fact that must surely have put a crimp in their plans. It's ironic when you think about it. Sidjian plans this down to the last detail. But Franco stuffs Galea into a large chest to buy himself some time, not knowing that the furniture is destined to arrive here the next day.''

''But what about the yellow sticker? It was the wrong piece of furniture,'' I asked, then answered my own question. ''It's probably as simple as Galea changing his mind about which piece of furniture he wanted to send. He changed the sticker himself probably, or Marilyn did.''

''We'll probably never know the answer to that one, with Martin dead and Marilyn nowhere to be found,'' Rob replied. ''But given that this is what happened, which I still really can't buy, your explanation is as good as any.''

Tabone said excitedly, ''Sidjian, who is already here and has seen Lara in the house, begins working on alternate plan B, the fallback position as Lara calls it. He isn't in contact with Franco yet, and anyway, he has no way of knowing how long Lara will be here. She might well leave before Franco arrives, and they can go back to the original plan. But then Galea turns up in the furniture, and that means plan A is as dead as Galea is. What a terrible waste, if it's true.''

We all sat and thought about it for a while. Finally Rob spoke up, ''I don't suppose that I have to point out that if the evidence linking Galizia to the assassination plot is rather thin, the evidence linking him to Galea is virtually non-existent. It wouldn't even qualify as circumstantial, interesting though all this may be. We'll have to continue the investigation into Galea's death in Canada. I'm not the officer in charge of the investigation, but I'll tell him about Falcone and our theories about the link. It'll be up to him and our superiors as to whether they think this does it or not.

''One thing, though, Lara. You may have to come to terms with the idea that Marilyn Galea is dead. If our theory is true, then Marilyn was probably killed by Falcone too. He just did a better job of dealing with her body. Maybe he killed her, hid the body, and waited for Galea to come home. It was the maid's day off, you'll recall. In any event, her credit cards have not been used, no checks have been cashed, since the day Galea died. It doesn't look good.''

"I know," I said. "I'd already thought of that. As much as I don't want her to be the killer, I don't want her to be dead even more."

"I think," Rob said gently, "that we would be better off concentrating on how to prove that Galizia is guilty."

LATER THAT DAY, ROB AND I went over to the Farrugia house in Siggiewi. Marissa had called to tell me that she and Joseph had decided to tell Anthony everything—about his acceptance at the University of Toronto, his inheritance, and about his father. She said they'd very much appreciate having me there, and Rob too, if he'd come, as neutral parties, and in case their courage failed them.

We joined them in their tiny living room for a cup of tea. All three Farrugias were there as was Sophia. There was lots of idle chitchat for some time, but eventually, Marissa got around to the subject at hand. Joseph sat quietly, almost numb with anxiety, in a chair in a dark corner of the room.

"Anthony," Marissa said quietly, "we have some news for you. About University, and about other things. Your father and I have done something we aren't proud of, and we owe you an apology. Our only excuse, I guess, is that we love you and we have been afraid of losing you, so afraid that our judgment has been clouded."

Anthony looked surprised and slightly baffled by this turn in the conversation.

"You've been accepted at the University of Toronto," his mother told him, "but not, regrettably, in Rome. We opened your letters and we shouldn't have done that. I'm sorry. We both are. The letters are here," she said, handing them to him.

Anthony looked at them carefully, and then said, "I know there's no way we can afford for me to go," he said to his parents. "I'm just happy to know I was accepted."

"But it is possible you will be able to study," Marissa went on. ''Mr. Galea has left you some money in his will. It may be a while before you get it, but Lara has talked to Mr. Galea's lawyers, and we think you can get a student loan until Mr. Galea's money comes to you.''

Anthony looked absolutely stunned, then jubilant. He got up and hugged his mother, then Sophia, and then went over to Joseph. Joseph, looking close to tears, patted his son on the shoulder, but said nothing.

''That's nice of Mr. Galea, isn't it, Mum?'' Anthony said. ''Why would he do that, I wonder?''

''He did it because . . . I knew him before, a long time ago. But he went away. I thought he'd come back, but he didn't, until last year. He didn't know, then, I mean, but when he came back, he knew. He did it because he knew, because he was . . .''

Anthony looked at her, trying in vain, I could tell, to comprehend what she was saying. Joseph slumped in his chair and covered his eyes. Marissa looked at me, and then Rob, pleading with her eyes. She tried to speak, but couldn't. I opened my mouth to speak, but my throat felt dry, and I couldn't get any words out either.

''What your mother is trying to tell you, Anthony,'' Rob said gently, ''is that Martin Galea was your dad.''

Anthony's eyes searched all our faces, looking intently at each of us for a few seconds. Marissa had tears running down her face, I still couldn't speak, Joseph slumped even lower in his chair and would not look at his son.

''No!'' Anthony exclaimed suddenly. ''Dads help you with your schoolwork. They go and speak to the school principal so he won't expel you when you've done something bad. Dads teach you to play football and tell you everything about girls. And most of all,'' he said, his face flushed, ''dads are nice to your mum!

''Mr. Galea may have been my father, but this,'' he said, pointing to Joseph, ''this is my dad!''

We all cried. Marissa and I held on to each other and sort

of sobbed quietly, and even Rob looked a little misty-eyed.
Joseph was completely overcome. Only Sophia remained dry-
eyed, and she looked at Anthony as if seeing him in an entirely
new light. And perhaps we all did. Anthony had the easy
charm and rather quixotic moods of his natural father, but he
obviously had something Martin Galea had lacked: a generosity of spirit and a very solid grounding in what was important in life. I had the feeling I'd watched a little boy grow up
in an instant, and he went on to prove that.

"I have something more I'd like to say," he went on when
we'd all recovered slightly. "I really want to be an architect,"
he said. "I know it won't be easy, but I think I can do it. So
if there really is some money, I'm going to go to Canada to
study. I'll come back when my studies are done."

He turned to Sophia and smiled at her. "I won't forget you,
Soph, I promise."

"Of course you won't," she said firmly. "I'm coming with
you."

Perhaps, I thought, history does not always repeat itself.
How pleased Anna Stanhope would be.

"Don't worry, Marissa," I promised, as we left a little later.
"I'll keep an eye on them for you."

"Me too," Rob said and hugged her.

LATE IN THE AFTERNOON THE day before I went home, I returned to Mnajdra. The area was still cordoned off, but a policeman, one of Tabone's men, recognized me and let me in.

The VIP tent, one of its tent poles broken, slumped sadly,
canvas drooping like a ghostly sailing ship becalmed. The light
standard lay where it had fallen, its lamp shattered, jagged
pieces of glass fragments caught by the late afternoon sun. I
could see where Anna Stanhope had fallen, and the memory
of that night flooded back very painfully, the horror and sense-
lessness of it almost choking me.

I thought about Anna as I had seen her that morning, lying
in her hospital bed, pale, ill, and with her emotional pain per-

haps worse than her injuries. A nurse let me into the room, whispering that Anna was to be flown back to England by air ambulance the next day, to complete her recovery there.

I had thought she was sleeping, she lay so still, her eyes closed, but she began to speak after a few moments, without looking at me.

"I should have known, shouldn't I," she said softly. It was a statement, not a question. "I should have known that a man like him would never be attracted to a woman like me. The signs were all there, of course, had I not been so busy behaving like a silly schoolgirl."

"I don't know how you could know," I said, "I didn't guess."

"When I make a mistake, I make a big one," she said and laughed a little. "Never been one to do anything by halves." She paused for a moment.

"Do you know what the topper is, though?" she asked, opening her eyes and turning to look at me. "Biggest blunder of my life, and can you believe this? Look at this!" she demanded, waving a piece of paper in front of me. "They're giving me a medal for it!" I looked at the paper. It was, indeed, a letter from Prime Minister Abela telling her he was recommending her for a medal of some kind.

"I suppose it will have a heart on it," Anna went on. "Do you have to be dead to get a Purple Heart?"

"I don't know," I said.

"Oh well, either that or some other medal with a heart on it, I'll wager. Appropriate enough."

"Of course it's appropriate," I said, taking the conversational high road. "You saved those people's lives, you know. They'd be dead if it weren't for you."

She was silent for a few minutes. "Time to retire," she said. "Get myself a nice little cottage in the country. Devon, Cornwall, something like that. Nice long walks by the sea, a pint at the local pub, long evenings with a good book. I expect they'll let me retire a little early, don't you? Being a hero and all.'' She smiled slightly.

"I don't think you should make a decision like that right now," I said. "Wait until you're feeling better." She nodded. The nurse came and signaled it was time for me to go.

As I reached the door, I heard her voice, very soft, behind me. "Dead, is he? They haven't told me."

"Yes," I said. She closed her eyes and I left her there. I thought about how Sidjian had flattered and charmed his way into her heart, and despised him, not her, for all of it.

I came to Mnajdra just before I left, I think, to try to get my emotional bearings once again. I sat on the ground, leaning against one of the ancient stones of the Great Goddess's temple, and thought of the friends, old and new, that I'd lost: Martin Galea, for all his faults, a remarkable man. He had always shunned the banal and striven for, and given us, the beautiful, a creative flame, intense and passionate, snuffed out too soon. Anna Stanhope, in whom, if she chose to retire as she said she would, the world had lost what it could ill afford: a wonderful, inspiring teacher. And Marilyn Galea, a woman who might well have died without ever having really lived. I wanted to avenge them all.

But revenge in whatever form, justice or retaliation, does not bring the victims back. Tabone had said, "*Min na jgarrabx il-hazin ma jafx it-tajjeb*—he who has had no experience of evil cannot know the worth of what is good," and I tried to concentrate on that. As the sun went down and turned the walls of Mnajdra to gold, I thought about the builders of these ancient temple walls, now forgotten as individuals, but with a legacy that had extended through centuries and spoke for them still. I felt better thinking this, and I thought that perhaps Martin Galea's buildings spoke for him, just as Anna Stanhope's students, inspired by her teachings, would continue to speak for her.

I did not know what, or who, would speak for Marilyn Galea.

ANATH

❧ SIXTEEN

GONE. ALL OF THEM, GONE. Free at last.

IT WAS A FEW DAYS before Rob and I were able to head for home. Tabone drove us to the airport to say good-bye, and as we left, handed us each a copy of the *Times of Malta*.

"CABINET MINISTER QUESTIONED IN ASSASSINATION SCARE," the immensely satisfying headline trumpeted. Even if the link to Galea's murder could not be made, and something told me it wouldn't be, at least the man I thought might be responsible would pay. Perhaps too, I thought, the Hedgehog would yet have his day in court.

Rob's girlfriend Barbara and his daughter Jennifer met our flight from Paris. Jennifer was an attractive girl but with a rather sullen expression that I thought might be in danger of becoming permanent. Barbara, on the other hand, was bright and perky, young, of course, and presumably athletic, dressed as she was in a white tracksuit and shoes, her blond hair pulled back into a ponytail. They offered to drive me home, and although I thought them quite sincere in wanting to do it, I insisted on taking a taxi, happy to sit in silence in the darkness of the backseat as the familiar sights sped by.

I was so glad to turn the key on my little Victorian cottage that I almost wept. I could see the lights on at Alex's house next door, but decided to take some time for myself. I knew he'd be watching out for me and would be over in the morning to see how I was doing, but in the meantime I needed some time to think.

There was a huge pile of mail on the kitchen counter, sorted by Alex into little piles—''Junk,'' one said; ''Read at Leisure,'' another said; ''Bills'' was the terse message on the largest; and finally ''Read Now.'' Life was coming back to normal.

There were really only two items in the ''Read Now'' pile, one postmarked Belize, the second a postmark and stamp I hadn't seen before.

I poured myself a glass of wine, threw a log or two on the fire, and sat down to read. First, I turned to the letter from Lucas. It had occurred to me that isolated as he was at the archaeological site in Belize, he might know nothing of my adventures, and I looked forward to a letter devoid of any sad references to the last few weeks. But if I thought the letter would put the world right for me, it was not to be.

Dear Lara,

This is a very difficult letter for me to write, and it may be equally difficult for you to read.

I have spent a lot of time thinking about the future, about what I need to do, and about us. You have always respected my wish not to discuss my ties with one of the underground groups agitating for change in my country, but I think you have always known how important these ties are, how critical I consider the cause.

I have been persuaded that now is the time to move forward to the public stage, to begin a political push for change, rather than a clandestine one. In a way it is because of you that I make this decision. Your optimism and faith that justice will always prevail have made me dare to hope that I can change the inequities that exist in Mexican society, that if other people truly understand the situation, they too will support change.

This is, I believe, a very positive decision, except for

one thing, and that is that I do not believe I can continue our relationship and do what must be done. I cannot see these two aspects of my life—my relationship with you, and my aspirations for my country—as compatible, in part because our lives, our cultures are so very different, but also because I do not, as you know, believe in doing anything by halves. To attempt to do both would deny both of us the relationship we need and deserve, neither would it serve my cause and my people well. Given that I must choose, I believe I must take the path that benefits my society, rather than the one I might personally prefer.

I think you will not be happy with what I have to say, but perhaps I presume too much. If you take anything from this letter, indeed from our time together, I hope it is that I love you. This may be the hardest thing I have ever done.

Please forgive me and try to understand. Love, Lucas.

I reread the letter many times that night, the pain so great I could not even cry. In the end, I set the letter aside. No, Lucas, you do not presume too much, I thought. This hurts me more than I will ever let you know. I promise only to try to understand. I do not know if I can forgive you.

Finally, I opened the mysterious letter.

Dear Lara,

I trust I may call you that? I hope more than I can tell you that this letter finds you safe and well. You have been through a terrible ordeal, if the newspaper reports are anywhere close to accurate, for which I feel in some way responsible, although I think my actions did not directly cause it.

But perhaps I rationalize. Perhaps what happened precipitated a chain of events that have caused you considerable pain, and this grieves me, more, I must tell you, than the original deed itself.

I did not plan for this. There is a Swiss bank account, set up by my father for emergencies—and surely this qualifies—so I am not penniless, though far from the financial status I once enjoyed. But I am rambling, wishing to delay telling you what I must.

Perhaps I should start at the beginning as they say, at least where life seemed to begin for me, when I first met Martin Galea. Before that I was a gawky, homely, painfully shy woman, afraid of life and living. When I met Martin, I was a librarian at the University of Toronto—not a real librarian, you understand. The McLean women do not seek employment, real work being, in the opinion of my father, beneath the dignity of the "ladies" in his family. I was a volunteer, such charitable activities considered the proper role for a woman of means.

My mother died when I was very young. I have only vague memories of her, but I have her picture. It is one of only two things of this kind I thought to bring with me. She was lovely. I, unfortunately, take after my father in looks, and was, in this and almost everything else, a disappointment to him. My upbringing was therefore given over to a housekeeper, a rather stern woman of limited imagination, and then a series of tutors of whom I have no fond memories. All of them, while uninterested in me as a person, had very definite ideas about what I should do and what I should think.

Despite his disappointment in me, my father saw to it that I was well educated, schooled in the great masters, taken as a child to the great centers of culture on my vacations. In my early twenties, I was sent to what was rather quaintly called finishing school in Europe. It was then and there that I discovered Italy. More specifically, I discovered architecture.

One of my fine arts professors used to say that the world could be divided into two kinds of people—those who love Venice, and those who love Florence. I think I can understand that. To me, Venice, while stunning, has a reckless quality to it, a sense of impending darkness, a certain dangerous wetness, like damp sheets after an afternoon of illicit lovemaking.

But Florence—ah, Florence. To me this is a city where reason and order prevail, not in a static way, but in a way that attains the sublime. Those porticoes with sunlight streaming in perfect patterns between the perfectly proportioned columns were the most beautiful urban spaces I had ever seen. I roamed the streets, captivated by the grandeur, the soaring domes of Brunelleschi, the spacious piazzas—my favorite, Santissima Annunziata, completely soothing in its proportions, the most beautiful square, I think, anywhere in the world.

But I digress again. After Florence, I desperately wanted to be an architect, but my father would not permit it. You may think that in this day and age women should be free to do as they please. This is not, after all, Victorian England. But I have never been one who had the strength, the courage, to defy those around me, most particularly, I must say, my father. In a way though, he was right, if for the wrong reasons. I lack the unshakeable confidence in one's own abilities, the certitude that one's decisions and choices are invariably correct, that being an architect seems to require.

Since I was not permitted to be an architect, I became, I suppose, what is rather unflatteringly called a groupie. I worked as a volunteer at the library at the School of Architecture, hung out at the back of the lecture halls to hear the guest speakers, sat in the cafeteria listening to the students talk about their work.

One day as I was tidying up, I found, sound asleep in one of the study carrels, the most beautiful man I had ever seen. His features were perfect, dark eyelashes flecked with gold, a perfectly shaped nose, cheekbones chiseled in marble, a Greek god in the living flesh. His head was cradled in his arms, resting on a set of architectural drawings I assumed he'd been working on.

I sat looking at him for several minutes, just watching him breathe, until he awoke with a start, embarrassed to find me there. To ease his discomfort, I asked him what he was working on, and he showed me the drawings on which he had been resting his head.

They were magnificent, as he was, and his enthusiasm for his work apparent. He looked very tired, and in a gesture so uncharacteristic of me that it surprises me to this day, I asked him if he would like to go for a coffee. At first he declined, then he laughed apologetically and confessed he didn't have the money to pay for it. I told him money was not an issue for me, which of course it wasn't.

We went to a little coffee shop nearby—the Cake Master Cafe in Yorkville, do you know it? He was effortlessly charming, in a way I could never be. He told me about his passion for his studies, how he wanted to be the world's greatest architect, and thought he could be. However, he said, he might have to drop out of school before he qualified, because his scholarship had run out, and he couldn't come up with the next installment of his fees.

At some point in that conversation over coffee, I knew my aimless days had come to an end. I had found my métier, my calling, and that was to support—to nurture— what I believed, and still believe, to be a prodigious talent. I paid his tuition, not just that year, but for several years of graduate study to follow. I cooked, although I dislike cooking intensely; I shopped; I bought his clothes, seeing to it that he looked and acted the part of the successful architect.

A couple of years after we met we were married, against the wishes of my father, who threatened to disinherit me. In the end he didn't, he couldn't, because of a promise he had made to my mother. I was much older than Martin, a good fifteen years. In fact, I was thirty-seven—the age he was the last day of his life—while he was only twenty-two. He said he didn't care about age, that what counted was that I was his muse, his patron, his very own de Medici.

And I was. I introduced him to my friends, my father's friends. I made sure he walked the halls of the wealthy and the powerful. I saw that his life was a comfort, his work unhampered by the demands of the sordid realities of having to pay the bills. In turn, our life together shielded me from the loneliness and fear I had come to dread before I met him. I did not have to face the world alone. He was charming enough for both of us. We were invited everywhere, at first because of my social status, but later because of his.

And he met, no, exceeded, my wildest expectations. He is—was—a genius, my own Brunelleschi. I think that history will judge him as one of the greatest architects of our age. How history will judge me to a large extent remains in your hands.

How can I describe to you what happened that day? That one bright flame of passion in an essentially passionless life. To a certain extent, I viewed my life with him as a job as much as a relationship, and I thought myself fairly sanguine about it.

I knew his faults, every last one of them. I knew he was arrogant, but I thought he was entitled to be. I knew there were other women. That part of our lives together—the physical—had never been a big part of the relationship. Perhaps at first it was my fear of pregnancy, being so much older than he. And how could I have a child by someone I essentially regarded as a child himself?

Nonetheless, he stayed with me—I comforted myself with that—long after his success made my fortune unnecessary. All I asked was that I be permitted, as his wife,

to share in his successes, bask in his reflected glory. And
that he never lie to me nor humiliate me.

Strangely though, as his social skills increased, mine
seemed to decline even more. I was so long in his
shadow, as I had been in my father's, that I became almost invisible. At some point, I think, I ceased to have
a separate identity at all. I went almost nowhere alone,
and an old dread of social situations I had known as a
child came back with a vengeance.

Except at my club.

I think I described a little of my life to you that day
you visited the house. I'm not sure if I was able to convey
to you how much I enjoyed the few hours every day I
spent at my club, cocooned in a soft pink haze against
the world.

I'd go for lunch, almost every day. I knew the staff
and many of the other members by sight, if not inti-
mately, the menu from memory, although it didn't matter,
since I had the same meal, the house salad, every time.
After lunch, I'd swim in the pool, relax in the sauna, and
then, anonymous in a pale rose bathrobe, I'd curl up in
the lower lounge pretending to read a book, but in actual
fact, listening, eavesdropping, I suppose, on the casual
conversations of the women around me. I listened to them
talk about their children, their husbands, their hairdress-
ers, their various medical conditions. It didn't matter to
me what they talked about, only that I could experience
their lives, banal though they might be, in this vicarious
and comfortingly safe way.

But then that day, the last I was there. One of the
women in the club I like least, detest actually, is a woman
by the name of Rose Devere. She calls herself a journalist, but she is really a gossip columnist. She insinuates
her way into people's lives—hinting, falsely I'm sure, of
some exotic personal background—and then reports in a
petty and occasionally malicious way about the people

she seeks to befriend. It was a wonder to me that she is able to move in the circles she does. She is, in my opinion, and I hope I do not sound too much of a snob, simply common.

In the lower lounge of the club there is a telephone for use of the members. Rose got all kinds of calls, of course, and I really tried not to listen to her conversations because they invariably disturbed the tranquility of my day.

That day, that fateful day, she was called to the telephone as usual. I tried not to listen, also as usual. But one word caught my attention.

"Malta!" she exclaimed. "You expect me to drop everything and fly off with you to some tiny little island I've barely even heard of? Why would I do that?"

I could not, of course, hear the reply. "Help you entertain important people? Like who?"

Another pause while the person on the other end of the telephone apparently pleaded with her to come.

"All right, but I'll need new clothes," she said at last, putting the phone down. "Gotta run, girls. Things to do, people to see, dresses to buy," she said to no one in particular as she hurried from the room, taking with her all the pleasure, the comfort, the security, I had ever felt in that place.

I actually didn't feel anything. Not then. I calmly changed back into my street clothes, called the valet for my car, and drove home. I listened to the phone messages, one about a party a week or so later, the other a message from your shipper saying he would be by for the furniture before eight. I packed Martin's suitcase for his trip as I always did. And then because he had asked for a light meal before his flight and it was Coralee's day off, I set his place at the counter in the kitchen with my characteristic care—Martin liked everything to be just so—and sat in the darkening room, waiting for him to come home.

When he did, for a time I did nothing. If he thought it strange that I had been sitting in the kitchen in the dark, he didn't say anything. I made him bacon and eggs and toast as I always do on Coralee's day off. I am not a good cook, and this is really the only thing I can make that Martin likes . . . liked. While he ate, he talked a bit about the project he was working on in Rome where he was going to spend a couple of days, about the flight that evening, complaining there was no first or business class, then he started talking about Malta.

"So sorry you can't come with me this time. But it's business. Lots of boring entertaining. The Prime Minister and a couple of Cabinet Ministers. Men only. Just as well. It's not your cup of tea, I know. You find these social events difficult. But when I get back, we'll go to the house in the Caribbean, just the two of us, for a rest. A little romantic interlude, okay?"

I tried to respond to him, but I couldn't. I felt as if all the air had been sucked from the room, my lungs, then my veins and arteries, collapsing in the vacuum until a film, a kind of reddish haze, covered my eyes.

What was I feeling? Fear? Anger? Rage?

The knife was just lying there. I have asked myself over and over, what would have happened if it hadn't been there, if it had not been Coralee's day off? But it was. Perhaps the question I should ask myself is, why? After all this time? Knowing him as I did?

With a strength I didn't know I had, I stabbed him. He did not die immediately. Instead, for a few moments we were both locked in suspended animation, he with a surprised, almost sad, expression on his face. Then he just fell.

There was surprisingly little blood, not nearly as much as I would have expected, just a few spots brilliant red against the white marble. The strength that had driven the knife into him with such ferocity stayed with me as I lifted him into the oak chest, pulled the knife out, cutting myself in the process, and closed the lid.

With a strangely methodical quality, I cleaned up the blood with a paper towel, which I then flushed away, and then I removed your yellow marker from the sideboard in the hallway, and put it on his—coffin. I owe you an apology for that. I wasn't thinking very clearly and it pains me to think I had inadvertently ensured you would be the one to find the body.

I changed my clothes and packed a few of my own clothes, only the barest of necessities, in his suitcase, took his billfold with the airline ticket, money, and passport, and drove his car, wearing his driving gloves, to the airport. I knew your shipper would be calling for the furniture shortly, but I also knew Coralee, predictable as always, would be home by the time he arrived. Indeed, as I got to the end of the street, I saw Coralee descending from the bus, but I don't believe she saw the car. On my way to the airport, I dropped the knife and my blouse with Martin's blood on it into a large garbage bin in an industrial park far from the house.

At the airline counter I presented his ticket and my own passport. Have you noticed how they never really look at you? No one noticed that the M. Galea on the ticket was a Mr. rather than a Mrs., and I boarded the plane, which was full. There was a mix-up with the seats of some kind. I did not get the one allocated to me, but it didn't really matter. Nothing did.

In Rome, I encountered no difficulties. Here too they barely look at you. I'd worried all the way over about filling in a tourist card, but none was required. I showed my passport to the customs official, but he was talking to one of his colleagues in the next booth and never directly looked at me at all when he stamped my passport. And then I just disappeared.

I will not tell you where I went from there, nor how I

did it. There were people who helped me out of sheer kindness, and I would not wish their generosity blunted by learning they helped a murderer. All I will say is that it is surprisingly easy, and requires very modest sums of money, to effectively vanish.

As I think I told you earlier, I have a little money, not much, but enough to live relatively well in a place where poverty is the norm, and where relatively small amounts of money have the potential to greatly ease the misery of those around me. I have pledged myself to do that, at least, to make up in some small way for what I have done.

It will be a novel experience for me, living without the perpetual advice and counsel of either my father or my husband, but I believe I will grow a little more confident every day. The Worryman you gave me that day in the shop is with me still, and I think of you when I rub my troubles on his back.

You will be surprised, no doubt, when I say that while I do not regret that last fateful act of my relationship with Martin, would even do it again, if the circumstances were the same, that I miss him so very much. I dream about him vividly, and wake with a feeling of his presence so real that I reach out to touch him. If I could bring him back, if I had godlike powers to make that happen, I think perhaps I would. But we, the two of us, would have to work out a new relationship, one where my newfound independence could be accommodated, where my opinions were held to be of some consequence.

I gather from the newspapers that the authorities believe that I may be dead, killed by whoever killed my husband. I would wish to remain so, yet I feel compelled to write to you. You were very kind to me on those few occasions we met. You seemed interested in what I had to say and respected my feelings. Now my fate rests with you. If you choose to tell the authorities of this letter— this confession—then so be it. I do not know if they can find me, but I know they will surely try. That decision I leave, perhaps unfairly, to you.

With best regards—and love, Marilyn Galea.

I sat for a very long time that evening, very still, watching the flames in the fireplace flicker in front of me, thinking about what I had read. I thought about all the truly dreadful things that had happened in the past weeks, the ache of the loss of friends, the anger that still was in me. Where was the Goddess now?

I AM AT THE BEGINNING as I am at the end. I am the sacred circle, spinner of the web of space and time. I am the cosmic "And": life and death, order and chaos, eternal and finite.

How is it that you wrenched apart that which is inseparable? Why did you create the Either/Or? Because when you did, when you replaced Me with your despotic sky gods who rule from Without, you made Me something to be mastered, something to be conquered . . .

Neglected, devalued, insulted, and profaned I may be, but I remain. I wait in my sacred places, I live in your dreams. Nammu, Isis, Aphrodite. Inanna, Astarte, Anath. Call me whichever of my manifestations you will. I am the Great Goddess, and I will be avenged.

I TOOK THE LETTERS, BOTH of them, and page by page, consigned them to the flames.